Lobster
Trap

LOBSTER TRAP
By C.W. Wells

Published by Creative Texts Publishers, LLC
PO Box 50
Barto, PA 19504
www.creativetexts.com
ISBN: 978-1-64738-133-2

Lobster Trap

by
C.W. Wells

In Memory of Dave McKown

"A lobster in the pot is worth two in the sea."

- Anonymous proverb

Table of Contents

Chapter One—Lobster Verrine

Spencer Tate stood her up . . . *again.*

Pixie McGee was no shrinking violet. Real estate empress, sports agent, and former dancer, she'd had enough. Tate could kiss her derriere, which was, if she said so herself, a fanny far too lovely for the likes of Tate's cheating lips. Tate, with his aristocratic nose, old-world elegance, and Brahmin blood, was the Commissioner of the most powerful league in professional sports. *And a dirty, stinking, two-timing rat.*

Pixie sat with her hands folded in her lap, seething, as Marcel, who with his pencil-thin mustache, resembled an oily Gomez from the *Addams Family*, stood to the side in the softly lit private dining room, a starched linen napkin draped over his forearm, waiting as if for the grand entrance of a king. Except Pixie knew the king was a no-show. She'd suspected all along that Spencer, who had professed his love and devotion when he had presented her with a rare Cartier diamond engagement ring that glittered on her finger like a small mountain, was shacked up in a hotel with the South American cutie he'd cozied up to at a reception for the Brazilian Ambassador a few nights earlier. In a post-coital haze of Chanel Coco Mademoiselle and sex, he'd no doubt forgotten – or didn't care – that he had a dinner date at Ferrar with his fiancée.

Pixie pursed her lips and turned to Marcel, who looked at her with sad, knowing eyes, which Pixie interpreted as, *"Why do you put up with this, Madam?"*

She wanted to smash the empty Waterford crystal goblets resting on the table next to the gleaming Robbe & Berking art deco flatware as her anger boiled red like a lobster in a pot of salted water. She could hear her mother, that beautiful and crude Port Arthur trailer queen with a Camel hanging from her lips and bourbon on her breath, warning her about rotten, no-good men. Pixie took a deep breath, trying to tamp down her fury, and felt a sudden calm when she remembered the old but timeless truism: *Don't get mad, get even.*

"May I see that fancy-dancy wine list, Marcel?" she asked sweetly.

"Yes, Madam." He, with the creepy mustache and slicked-back hair, handed her one of the most celebrated wine lists in the world. "Will you be ordering for the Commissioner?" he asked.

Pixie broke into a devious smile. "What a dandy idea, Marcel. Surely Mr. Tate wouldn't keep a lady waiting much longer, would he?"

Marcel briefly cocked his head but maintained his deferential pose.

For a few moments, Pixie fell into silence as she scanned the celebrated grape selection. Soon, with Marcel hovering over her expectantly, her eyes settled upon a $10,000 bottle of Chateau D'Yquem, from that splendid year of war and plague, 1918. She pointed. An almost imperceptible smile formed on the waiter's lips.

"Excellent selection, Madam. Shall I bring this superb vintage to you now, or when the Commissioner arrives?" Marcel asked. Pixie had seen his tight-assed countenance enough to realize that this was probably the same tone he would use if informed that he'd won the lottery.

"Now."

"Would you like anything else?"

"The Almas, Marcel. The Commissioner will adore it."

Almas, the world's most expensive caviar, was listed on Ferrar's gilded menu for the ridiculous price of $35,000. "Ah, a wonderful choice. But with a vintage champagne, Madam? That is how Almas is usually served."

Pixie shook her head. "No bubbly for me. I want the caviar with that fancy wine. And I'd like the menu now, Marcel. I think I may just order his highness's meal too."

"Without delay, Madam." Marcel nearly tripped as he dashed through the service entrance.

A few minutes later, after Marcel had laid the menu in front of Pixie and meticulously uncorked and poured the Chateau D'Yquem with all the precise grace of a master sommelier, Pixie took a whiff and a measured sip, pursed her full red lips on the glass, exhaled with a beautifully mischievous frown, and waved her hand. "Take it back, Marcel."

"Excuse me?" Marcel's face fell, dumbfounded, as if he'd watched his pet poodle scamper under a train.

"It tastes like cat pee. This bottle's spoiled. Bring another."

"Of the Château D'Yquem?" he asked, aghast.

"Of course."

"But–"

"I know what you're thinking, Marcel. Charge that bottle to the Commissioner. Maybe someone in the kitchen will be brave enough to drink it."

Marcel's eyes widened as he began to grasp the game being played. "Yes, Madam. I'm sorry you were disappointed."

"Bring another bottle, Marcel. Chop, chop! Don't stand there like a West Texas mule deer."

"Yes, Madam."

"And Marcel."

"Yes, Madam?"

"I've changed my itty-bitty mind. I'm feeling especially peckish. How about two orders of the Almas?"

Marcel's jaw dropped. "Two?"

Pixie flashed a grin. "One for me and one for the Commissioner. I'm a growing girl, so bring the caviar out now."

"Both orders?"

Pixie nodded. "Oh, Mr. Tate will be here soon. I know it. Bless his overworked heart."

Without a word, Marcel turned and made for the service door, but this time with the gait of a man whose greed was now accompanied by a tinge of trepidation.

Pixie picked up the heavy menu with gold leaf script. The cuisine had been touted by food critics as perhaps the most exquisite in the world. Pixie sighed. Spencer loved Ferrar, but she knew it wasn't about the food or the wine. He was a narcissist, pure and simple. He liked to be seen. He would saunter through Ferrar with his noble chin held high, gleefully relishing the moment as heads turned to catch a glimpse of the most powerful man in sport. At first, Pixie enjoyed the attention and excused Spencer's superficial ways. Now she had to wonder why she accepted a rock as big as Mont Blanc and the promise of happily ever after with a man no one trusted, or worse, liked. Yes, he was sophisticated, educated, fabulously wealthy, and lived in the most rarefied air. She had felt drawn to him in the hope that entering his world would give her respectability, and she even dreamed he would be able to give her what she coveted most: love. In the end, he was like all the others.

A selfish, lyin', cheatin' tomcat. In moments of reflection, Pixie acknowledged that there was only one man she'd really loved. Delvin Davis. But he was a dumbass, so she'd chased him off.

Pixie scanned the ridiculously priced menu with entrees she couldn't pronounce and portions the size of a thimble. Spencer always ordered at Ferrar. He'd learned his French in prep school and childhood trips to France, and he took pride in pronouncing such delicacies as *A La Girondine* or *Consommé De Canard*, always to Marcel's feigned delight.

Pixie longed for real food. She was tired of the trendy places where they ate fanciful concoctions by "world-class" chefs, who'd kill their firstborn to be on the cover of *Saveur*, went by first names like Adele or Bono, and where you'd need a nuclear microscope to find the food on your plate. *Oh look, a radish!*

Her eyes drifted down the menu until she came to "Maine Lobster Verrine." She loved lobster with all her heart. She adored it broiled, baked stuffed, bisqued, Newburged, and especially on a toasted roll slathered in hot butter with a sprinkle of paprika. But Ferrar's Maine Lobster Verrine, where she'd be lucky to get half a claw's worth of meat and a garnish resembling a blade of wilted fescue? It would be like eating brisket on the steps of a Hindu temple.

She set the menu down as Marcel brought the second bottle of Chateau D'Yquem and went through the ritual of uncorking the century-old vintage. After a sniff and a sip, Pixie grimaced and shook her head.

Marcel's jaw dropped.

"To your satisfaction, Madam?" he asked with a quaver.

"I'm afraid not, Marcel."

"Oh, Madam. Perhaps a different vintage then? It seems the D'Yquem is not to Madam's taste."

Pixie broke into a sly smile. "No, keep that D'Yquem coming, Marcel."

"But don't you think the Commissioner will be upset, Madam?" Marcel asked with growing alarm.

"Will he?"

"I would imagine. Three bottles of Chateau D'Yquem?"

"Don't you mind him." She held up her hand and pointed to the ring. "Pixie's got him wrapped around her finger. Another bottle. Chop, chop!"

Marcel stumbled away now more like a man sentenced to die than one who had just hit the Mega Millions.

Pixie's azure eyes turned again to the menu and they fell once more to the Lobster Verrine. She'd bought a cottage in Maine to save Delvin's hide and hadn't been back since that snowy November. When Pixie bought Millbridge Island, she'd envisioned selling the cottage to Delvin. But Spencer Tate had swept her up in a whirlwind, and soon after, Delvin moved to Phoenix, thanks to Pixie's subtle and, if she did say so herself, miraculous efforts to help him secure a coveted Arizona coaching position. So, the island, one of the most breathtaking, desolate places she'd ever laid eyes on, remained hers.

Marcel returned, trailed by another waiter – pinched face, hair combed in thin strands over his scalp – who carried the Almas caviar as if it were the Crown Jewels. He set it down delicately, before giving a slight bow like a performer concluding an intricate act. In front of Pixie sat the Almas, nestled in a ceramic dish atop crushed ice, with toast wedges arranged elegantly on a René Ozorio bone-white serving plate and a mother-of-pearl spoon beside it. Pixie despised caviar. It wobbled like gelatin, had the texture of Cream of Wheat, and tasted like ocean brine mixed with festering tilapia.

"Bravo," Pixie told the pinched-face waiter, fighting the urge to wrinkle her nose. She turned to Marcel, who had summoned a third bottle and was reluctantly beginning the process of uncorking it, and asked, "So, this bottle won't taste like turpentine?"

"Madam," Marcel replied, sounding wounded, "we are serving you one of the finest wines in the world. A masterpiece."

"Alright, let's get to it."

Marcel uncorked the third bottle of Chateau d'Yquem and poured a small measure into a fresh glass. Pixie swirled it, brought the glass to her nose, inhaled with the elegance of someone born to do so, and sipped, her lips parted just so.

Marcel and the pinched-face waiter held their breath, eyes fixed on her as she swallowed and set down the glass.

"How many bottles left?" Pixie asked, a glint of mischief in her eye.

"Madam, perhaps one or two remain, but we must consider our other patrons. Soon, there will be none."

She sighed. She counted silently to ten, enjoying keeping the two obsequious men on tenterhooks, and finally murmured, "I guess this one will do."

"Will do?" Marcel's face twisted in disbelief, and the other waiter muttered, "A Chateau d'Yquem will do?"

"Guess so," she said with exaggerated reluctance. "Now don't get your knickers in a twist, Marcel. I'll drink every drop."

Marcel exhaled, visibly relieved.

Pixie looked up. "Do you have catsup?"

Marcel stiffened. "Catsup, Madam?" A wave of shock crossed his face. "Do you mean . . . ketchup?"

"Call it what you will. What's that saying? A rose is a rose . . ."

"May I ask, Madam, why one would request 'catsup' at Ferrar?"

"Why, for the caviar, of course."

Marcel and the waiter nearly collapsed.

"Madam, no one puts ketchup on caviar," Marcel managed, struggling to regain his composure.

Pixie smiled sweetly. "Bless your heart. I do."

"I am terribly sorry, but that I cannot do, Madam," Marcel said firmly.

Pixie propped her elbow on the table, resting her chin in her hand. "Why not?"

"It is a crime against humanity."

The other waiter nodded vigorously, his pinched face mumbling, "A blasphemy, a tragedy of the worst order."

"Well," she said, deadpan, "if you won't serve me catsup, how about hot sauce?"

"Hot sauce, Madam?" Marcel's mouth twitched.

"That's right, honey. Hot sauce. You got any Texas Pete?"

"Texas Pete?"

"Clear the earwax, Marcel."

Beads of perspiration formed on Marcel's forehead. He raised his nose in the air. "I'll need to consult with Ferrar."

"Consult? This ain't brain surgery – it's a condiment."

"This is a most unusual request. He will need to be informed."

Pixie waved a delicate hand. "Oh, don't bother. I don't want to talk with Ferrar. Matter of fact, I don't feel much like talking to anyone." She sighed, glancing at the empty seat across from her. "Do me a little favor, though."

"What, Madam?"

"If the Commissioner drags his sorry ass in here, tell him I said 'bon appétit'." She rose from her chair.

"But the Château d'Yquem? The Almas?"

"Enjoy."

Marcel whispered distastefully, "The check?"

"Put it on the Commissioner's tab. And give yourself and your amigo a forty percent tip."

Marcel's face lit up. The horror of hot sauce on the world's most expensive caviar seemed forgotten. "Madam is most generous. This is highly unusual and most appreciated."

"And Marcel, if he doesn't like it, tell his highness Spencer Tate, he can shove it where the sun don't shine."

Marcel gave an almost imperceptible smile. "I will be sure to convey your sentiments, Madam."

The June evening was warm and windless as fading light played over the Manhattan skyline. Pixie walked in the shadows past closed storefronts, trying to make sense of her life. She'd followed Spencer to New York and now felt a familiar tug of self-pity trying to drag her back to that girl in Port Arthur that had nothing and no one. So, she reminded herself she was no ordinary woman, no doormat to be stepped on and sullied. Spencer could have put a ring on any woman's finger, but he chose to put the Cartier on Pixie's. She often wondered why. Maybe because he understood that despite the Dolly Parton twang, her impoverished upbringing, and her stint as an exotic dancer, she was a challenge – sharp as a whip, stubborn as a mule, crazily successful, not to mention her looks. But it still hurt. She'd fallen once again for a sumbitch. Standing on East 65th and Park Avenue, she knew from the lump in her throat and her racing heart she couldn't stay in New York. This was Spencer's town, his seat of power. Dallas? She imagined the heat rolling in, 100-degree days and burning pavement. She shook her head.

Then it struck her. Lobster Verrine.

She'd paid two million dollars for an island in Maine she'd only seen once. She'd been struck by its stark beauty but quickly returned to Texas to tend to her real estate business, which was growing faster than a field of bluebonnets. She may have been unlucky in love, but

D Magazine had called her the most successful businesswoman in the Lone Star State. She'd fought all her life to make something of herself, had all the money she needed, and at forty, was a beautiful woman with soft blonde hair and a figure that still drew stares. But when it came to relationships, she tended to fall for dogs like Spencer because of how eagerly they sniffed around her.

As she made her way through the crowds enjoying an early summer evening, the thought of lobster stuck in her mind. With sudden resolve, she yanked off her glittering engagement ring, stuffed it in her purse, pulled out her phone, and called Billy Grisom, Tate's personal pilot.

"Ms. McGee?" Grisom answered, surprised.

"Grab your scarf and goggles, Billy," Pixie said.

"Scarf and goggles? Where to?"

"Maine."

"When?"

"Now."

"Will the Commissioner be joining you?"

"Not tonight."

"But Ms. McGee, this flight isn't on the schedule. Is it League business or personal?"

"Definitely League business, Billy."

"Where in Maine?" Grisom asked, growing even more confused.

"Bangor."

"May I ask why?"

"Don't you worry, Billy. I got the blessing of His Highness, Spencer. I got a hankering for a big ole lobster. Plain and simple. And where better to get one than Spring Harbor, Maine."

Chapter Two—Fish Bloke

Dirk Peters spotted his landlord, and worse, a Los Angeles County sheriff from his condo window and immediately hid behind the dusty curtains. Goldberry stood in the driveway with the officer staring at Peters' apartment with an envelope in his hand. Most likely an eviction notice, Peters guessed. For weeks Peters had done all he could to avoid Goldberry. He was four months behind in rent, but so far had managed to dodge his weaselly landlord, who pounded on his door weekly, threatening to evict him.

Peters sneaked a peek around the curtain and saw that Goldberry and the sheriff looked determined. Peters began to panic. He'd been about to leave for a meeting with a guy named Marley that he hoped would yield some work, and if he didn't get there, he was in trouble. Other than that one call, it had been crickets for what seemed an eternity. Peters could see Goldberry eye Peters' Jag, shake his bald head, and start up the walkway with the sheriff in short, fussy steps. Peters fell to his knees and skittered on his stomach and elbows on the thin-napped carpet like a crab toward the Jaguars' fob resting on a milk crate he used for a table. In a feeble attempt to stay ahead of his creditors, Peters had pawned most of his collectible mid-century furniture he'd purchased after binge watching *Madmen,* as well as a prized vintage Rolex, supposedly owned by Steve McQueen. But he was damned if he was going to part with the Jag. He grabbed the fob just as he heard Goldberry begin to pound on the door.

"I know you're in there, Peters," Goldberry yelled with his squeaky voice. "I've got the sheriff and an eviction notice, mister."

There was no way out. A few nights before, in a drunken stupor, Peters had tried to sling open the patio glass sliders and had jammed the doors so they wouldn't budge. He was bloody trapped.

"You're a bad man, Peters," Goldberry shouted, pounding on the door. "A liar and a cheat. Open up."

Peters' mind whirled. He gulped and started crawling to the bathroom. When he reached the loo, he shut the door and caught his breath before eyeing the transom window above the toilet. He precariously stepped on the commode and began to yank open the small rectangular window. He could hear keys rattling and knew he only had a few moments before Goldberry and the sheriff pounced.

After a few seconds of tugging, Peters finally slung open the window, unhooked the screen, and began wedging himself through the space. He could feel his shoulders scraping the sides of the window frame, and his stomach rubbing against the narrow aluminum sill as he wiggled desperately to escape. With a sudden push he fell face-first into a hedge that bordered the building. Seconds later, after bolting in his Jag, Peters noticed a slight tear at the shoulder of his Armani suit, the one he had once rakishly worn to the Academy Awards, and a scratch running across his cheek.

An hour later, Peters found himself sitting by the washroom entrance at the Wilshire next to a water-starved fern impatiently waiting for the guy Marley who called himself a "fish bloke," whatever the hell that meant. Only a couple of years before, the idea of being seated next to the loo would have been unthinkable. But since his only source of income was pitching ERECTO LIFE drops on late-night TV to shriveled old men too cheap to buy Cialis, Peters' fall from stardom had brought new lows and a desperation for money to support a Hollywood lifestyle that was bleeding him dry. Peters desperately wanted a martini, but the cocktail cost $25. He cursed under his breath and ordered a beer.

The call had come a week earlier. The man had said he admired Peters' work and wanted to talk about "a once in a lifetime" opportunity. Even though he was looking at one hundred seventy grand in credit card debt, rent on a ridiculously expensive condo in Malibu, and insane lease payments on his Jaguar, Peters was skeptical. The last time he'd agreed to a meeting like this, a Ron Swanson look-alike wearing tight jeans and a garish rayon shirt had met him in a shoddy Mexican restaurant, where after ordering the macho meat burrito, he offered Peters the starring role in a porn sci-fi detective thriller entitled *Dicks from Another Planet*.

Peters' fall had been meteoric. After the movie *Bango and Dash* struck Hollywood by storm, Peters found himself the toast of Tinseltown. He could waltz into the Tower Bar, the Polo Lounge, Nobu, Spago, or anywhere else he desired and be wined, dined, and pampered as if he were the second coming of Laurence Olivier. The paparazzi followed him like a pack of jackals and the women swooned. Dirk Peters, with his posh British accent, designer shades, gorgeous blonde hair, and granite jaw found himself in the jet stream of fame. He loved it, craved it – and blew it.

Peters made the worst career decision in film history. Despite the pleadings of his agent, he turned down a chance to be the next James Bond. He thought himself too artistic, too talented, and of course, too important. He sniffed at the cool $8.5 million offered to play 007. Instead, he made an artistic decision to recreate the role of Captain Vonn Trapp in a dim-witted remake of *The Sound of Music*. Next, he played a West Virginia coal miner with a fake American accent and sounded like Kermit the Frog with a sinus infection. The fact that it had co-starred a drug-addled and paranoid Judy Stromberg, who hid in her trailer between scenes with a bathrobe pulled to her throat popping Adderall and Valium, smoking Virginia Slims, and incessantly texting her therapist, further secured its status as the flop of the year, if not the decade.

Only months after *Appalachia* bombed at the box office, Dirk Peters found himself waiting in line with the unwashed at places like Catch LA and Sur. Soon he was scrambling for roles. And after desultory television cameos in *NCIS: Los Angeles* and *Hawaii Five-O*, where he played the bad guy and uttered forgettable lines such as "He got what he deserved" and "How'd you know I did it?", his fall from stardom was fantastically meteoric. Peters thought he hit rock bottom when his agent desperately tried to book him on the British game show, *Moneybags*. Peters knew he was ruined when the producer didn't return the call. As *The Hollywood Reporter* scathingly wrote, "Dirk Peters had Hollywood by the balls and now Hollywood has him by the throat."

So there Peters sat, waiting for Marley, who had described himself both as an international venture capitalist and a "fish guy," and told Peters to meet him at the Wilshire lounge.

Impatiently, Peters tapped his finger on the table and nervously glanced at his phone. The fish guy was late. Peters wondered if the meeting was a hoax, a set-up by one of the multitudes of jilted, vengeful women he'd tossed aside like cigarette butts on a sidewalk.

Finally, Peters spotted a middle-aged man wearing a light gray worsted wool suit and a white open-collared shirt cutting through the maze of people toward his table. The man had dark hair, and a trimmed beard covered a weak chin.

He stuck out his hand when he reached the table. "Dirk?"

Peters nodded and shook his hand as Marley sat across from him. Marley's accent had a tinge of something. He wasn't an Aussie. South African?

"Lovely table," Marley said, glancing at the bathroom entrance.

Peters felt a wave of embarrassment. If his acting career stayed on the same miserable trajectory, soon maître d's would be seating him next to the dumpster in the parking lot. His fists tightened. He had had it all. Fame. Power. And now he was hawking bogus erectile dysfunction products on late night television and sitting next to the loo in the Wilshire.

Marley flagged down a harried waiter. "I'll have a martini, shaken but not stirred." He gave Peters a wry, knowing smile and frowned at Peters' beer. "I imagine you're wondering why I wanted to meet with you, Dirk?"

Peters nodded.

"I have a proposition."

"A film?" Peters asked hopefully.

"I'm not in the entertainment industry."

Peters leaned back in his plush red velvet seat and tried to suppress a wave of disappointment.

"I'm in the seafood industry."

Peters squinted. "Seafood?"

"That's right. And you're wondering why a person in the seafood industry wants to talk with Dirk Peters." Marley put his elbows on the table and clasped his hands. "I need an activist."

"You mean an actor?"

"An actor activist. A rabble rouser. Someone who believes in protecting the environment and goes to extraordinary lengths to protect all of God's creatures. A tree hugger."

Peters snorted.

"Are you familiar with Greenhaven?"

"Crazy bastards."

"Maybe. But useful. Very useful, Dirk."

"I thought you said you were in the seafood industry?"

"Yes. But a very specialized niche." The waiter placed Marley's martini on the table. Peters stared at it for an instant, longingly. "Have you heard of 3D bioprinting?"

12

Peters shrugged. He barely finished secondary school. Once upon a time, Dirk Peters had been Archie Roach, an East End lout with a petty criminal history who had transformed himself into the Hollywood star, Dirk Peters. The only biology he understood was how to suavely convince women to shed their underwear.

"Cellular seafood," Marley continued. "Heard of that?"

Peters scrunched his nose.

Unfazed, Marley pressed on. "My company, Utami, is on the brink of a revolutionary bioengineering breakthrough. It will revolutionize luxury seafood."

"How so?" Peters asked, feeling his eyes beginning to glaze.

"Let me cut to the chase. We grow lobster meat in petri dishes."

"Huh?"

"We're on the verge of mass-marketing cellular crustaceans. Lobster is a $1.5 billion business. 1.5 BILLION, Dirk. It's not as they call it here in America, 'chump change'."

"Sorry, mate. But I don't get it."

Marley's eyes narrowed. "I need you to go to Maine and stir up trouble. Create a reason for Greenhaven and any other crazy environmental group to wreak havoc on the lobster industry."

"I'm confused. You don't want to sell lobsters?"

"We do and lots of them. But not from the sea. From our labs in Burbank."

"Sounds ghastly."

"It's not. It's the future. But to convince consumers to trust bioengineered food, we need to prove to them that not only is the product delicious and safe, but that it's ethically responsible to spare those poor creatures in the North Atlantic from being boiled alive."

The situation was slowly starting to dawn on Dirk. "Is your lobster tasty and safe?"

A cloud passed over Marley's face. "We're working on it. Believe me, Dirk, we are near a breakthrough."

"So, you want Dirk Peters to go to Maine?" Peters loved referring to himself in the third person. It always gave him a shiver of excitement.

"Exactly."

"One thing I don't understand. Why me?"

"Well, Dirk. We've done our homework. A rigorous vetting process was undertaken prior to our even reaching out to you."

Peters perked up. He was beginning to relish the attention.

"Did you not join Friends of the Earth?"

"I was chasing a lovely French girl with big boobs."

"Perfect . . . And didn't you try to save the Quino Checkerspot Butterfly with a swarm of Hollywood celebrities?"

"My agent said it would be brilliant for my career."

"You've got activist credibility, Dirk."

Peters smiled.

"And nothing to lose," Marley added. "We know it's been tough for you, Dirk. No acting offers. Credit card debt. The rented condo. The leased car. The whole Bond thing."

Peters frowned and looked longingly at Marley's martini.

"Imagine what this will do for your career? The hero who saved those poor crustaceans from slaughter. Every producer in Hollywood will be wooing you. You'll be back in demand. Eventually, a star on the Hollywood Walk of Fame. And you won't be sitting at the Wilshire next to the loo."

Peters leaned forward. "What does Dirk have to do?"

"Show the world that harvesting lobsters in the wild is cruel, inhumane barbarism."

Peters tapped his forefinger on the table. "And how much is Dirk going to be paid for destroying an entire bloody fishing industry?"

Marley broke into a grin and sipped his martini. "You're in?"

"How much?"

"Easy now, Dirk. It will be generous. Very, very generous."

Peters' eyes narrowed. "Swampland in Florida?"

A hurt expression washed over Marley's face. "This is real, Dirk. Shares in Utami. A percentage of the company's profits. It could add up to millions."

Peters rubbed his chin. "If Utami succeeds . . . but what is Dirk going to live on in the here and now?"

"There's no 'if'. It's a sure thing. We have the best bioengineering scientists on the planet. We've invested millions. And one of our chief backers is a very prominent man."

"Who?"

Marley gave a coy smile. "Promise you won't tell?"

"Scout's honor."

"Oscar Leonid."

"The crazy billionaire?"

Marley nodded. "The one and only. A brilliant inventor and futurist. He wants nothing more than to see the world's oceans brimming with life again." He paused. "And to top it off, we have a very, very powerful person on our side in Washington. A senator."

Peters looked away for a moment. His mind raced with thoughts of rekindled fame. "Tell me again what Dirk has to do, and how it will benefit him in the here and now?

Marley grinned. "Does this mean you're in? And to answer your question about the here and now, your initial payment will be $50,000."

Peters thought about pushing for more but let the urge pass. He didn't want to blow it. The initial payment would at least allow him to pay his rent and keep creditors away from his car. Besides, pissing on the lobster industry with feigned righteousness sounded more promising than pitching erectile dysfunction products. It would allow him to work on his craft.

"We have a lot to plan, Dirk. This isn't going to be a simple operation. We need disruption on a grand scale . . . chaos . . . We need to make people believe those lobstermen are worse than ISIS. The second coming of Vladimir Putin. But we must have deniability. It must be a covert operation. Are you up to it?"

Peters ran his hand through his lush hair and flashed a smile – a smile that used to captivate Hollywood. "Of course."

"Good. Cause this will be big. It's going to make headlines."

"Where am I going?"

"A small Maine fishing town not far from the Canadian border."

"What's it called?"

"Spring Harbor. The town calls itself the lobster capital of the world."

"Not for bloody long," Peters quipped, hiding what he really thought about the bioengineered lobster meat lolling in petri dishes.

"Now we're talking, Dirk," Marley said with glee, tipping his martini at Peters before taking a generous sip. "A match made in heaven. Shall we order dinner? It's on me."

"Of course."

"What will you have?"

Peters smiled deviously. Before he went belly up, the Wilshire's Lobster Verrine had been one of his favorites. He pointed at the menu.

"Marvelous!" Marley exclaimed, slapping the table. "I'll have it, too."

Chapter Three—Spring Harbor

Elrod Tibbetts yawned as he waited for Pixie McGee's arrival. It was past midnight, and the widowed caretaker sat in the Stringer Cottage kitchen with its peeling linoleum floor, faded green wallpaper, and canary yellow dial telephone hanging crookedly on the wall, listening to the ancient steam radiators hiss and pop. Earlier in the evening, after McGee had told him she was coming to Maine, he'd gone to the IGA and stocked the fridge. Outside, it was 57 degrees with a stiff northeasterly blowing and rain beating against the roof. It was a hell of a night to be traveling, Tibbetts thought.

Since Delvin Davis had left, Elrod's life had slid back to a routine that now seemed tedious. He missed Davis and the ruckus he'd brought to Spring Harbor. He'd never met someone like Coach Davis, who had effortlessly captured him in his orbit. Elrod now looked back on that time as one of the happiest and certainly the most action-packed, of his life. Davis nearly turned the town upside down and found the love of his life to boot. Tibbetts missed Hannah, too. She and Davis had run off to Arizona, and now Tibbetts found himself taking care of an empty house perched on the edge of Frenchman's Bay and putting the finishing touches on a restored Cadillac Eldorado Brougham. His dream was to have the gumption to climb in the 1950's classic that he and Davis had worked on and drive to California, a place he'd never been and, sadly, probably would never see.

When McGee bought the island, Tibbetts wondered if he'd still have a caretaking job. For years he'd hauled traps, but he gave up lobstering after his wife died and, in his retirement, had settled into taking care of the Stringer Cottage as well as a few other odd jobs around town. Luckily, McGee had not only kept him on but left him to his own devices. He awaited her with a mix of emotions. You never knew with people from away. They'd bring crazy notions, a truckload of problems, and dump them in your dooryard. Or worse. But nevertheless, Elrod found himself looking forward to her visit. She was certainly a piece of work, not unlike Delvin. He needed some excitement to break the tedium. He closed his eyes and sensed sleep coming on as he sat listening to the hiss of radiators. He was about to nod off when he heard the faint sound of a car pulling onto the property.

Pixie climbed out of the battered minivan and directed Bebe, the driver, to pull her suitcase out. The elation of sticking Spencer Tate with a $100,000 bill at Ferrar and commandeering his private jet had worn off, and the familiar feeling that accompanied the aftermath of another train-wrecked relationship tugged at her heart.

Yet when she stood outside of Bebe's taxi, Pixie was struck – she'd never smelled anything so alluring in her life. While the rain pelted down in chilly drops, instead of racing to the house, she closed her eyes and took in the scent of pine, salt from the cold and vast North Atlantic, and the faint whiff of juniper. Heaven. In the darkness, she could hear the waves pounding against the granite shoreline over the gusts of wind. Pixie took a deep breath and vowed to cleanse her soul on Millbridge Island.

After paying for the cab and tipping Bebe, who'd slogged her bags like a sherpa up the wooded path to the house, she found Elrod Tibbetts in the kitchen, wearing green Dickies standing by the door looking as if he'd just woken up. Pixie smiled at Elrod and slowly began surveying the kitchen. After they exchanged greetings, she shook her head.

"Elrod, we got a lotta work to do," she said as water pooled at her feet.

Elrod raised an eyebrow. "We?"

"That's right. You don't think Pixie McGee is going to live in a house with green wallpaper and a yellow rotary phone?"

"Guess not."

"We're going to have us some fun. I got a whole lotta forgetting to do." After breakups, Pixie would bury herself in a project. After Davis had left, she took cooking lessons from a French Chef who called himself Serge. She found herself a hopeless cook and discovered it was impossible to forget Davis, though she stubbornly considered her methods sound.

"Is that right?"

"We're going to spruce this ole cottage up and bring it into the twenty-first century."

"That will take time and money."

Pixie smiled and winked. "I got both."

"You don't say."

Her eyes swept the kitchen. "We'll need paint, Elrod. Lots of it. New appliances. Flooring. And who knows what else. In the meantime, I'll take stock of the rest of the cottage. I been gone too long."

"No offense, Ms. McGee, I'm a caretaker, not a miracle worker."

"Don't you worry, Elrod. I know how to spiff up a house. I ain't the best realtor in Texas for nothing. And I ain't afraid to get dirty."

"Mr. Davis said you're a force of nature."

"That sweet thing said that?" Pixie asked, a smile forming before it was replaced by a frown as she ran her finger along the dusty, cracked linoleum counter. "What else did he tell you?"

"A few things better not said."

Pixie's eyes narrowed. "Did he kiss and tell, Elrod?"

"Don't know, can't say."

"He did, didn't he?"

"I plead the fifth."

"It must have been a short conversation. The only stiff thing he gave me was a vodka tonic."

A smile pursed Elrod's lip.

"Well, bless Delvin's heart, Elrod, but you ain't seen nothin' yet."

"Is that right?"

"It sure is. Now go home and get some sleep. We got a lotta work to do come morning."

Except morning came and went. Pixie found herself in a deep sleep as noon approached, drugged by the lullaby of the sea and the salty air. When she woke with a start, she realized she hadn't slept this late in years. Running a multi-million-dollar business had left her no time to dawdle. Even before, when she'd put herself through community college by dancing at night, she woke at the crack of dawn. Pixie had big dreams and the brains and work ethic to make it happen. When she'd escaped her dirt-poor life in Port Arthur for the hum of Dallas, she was determined to make something of herself. She may not have known what, but even with the glaring stage lights shining on every inch of her and men stuffing hundred-dollar bills in her G-string, she had big plans.

When she earned her real estate license, she used her gift for gab, a sweet smile, astute financial acumen, and, yes, her looks, to establish a sales trajectory that would have made Warren Buffett proud. Not long after she'd begun selling houses, she found herself one of the top real estate agents in swanky North Dallas. Then she established a sports agency that took off as well, which was how she met Spencer Tate at the League meeting in Palm Beach. While she initially resisted his advances, he had promised wine and roses, proffered love, and eventually put a ring on her finger. In hindsight, her main regret was that he'd convinced her to sell her business so that there'd be no conflict of interest, and they would have more time to spend together. Why she believed he loved her, she didn't know. As savvy a businesswoman as she was, she was a fool for love. And Spencer Tate sure suckered her.

Pixie stretched and reluctantly checked her phone. It was laced with texts and missed calls from Tate. She shook her head, swore, and ghosted him.

A few minutes later, when she stepped out of the empty cottage in her terrycloth bathrobe into an unusually warm and sunny day after the cold and rain of the night before, she was mesmerized by the stunning view. At that moment, Pixie realized why Hannah had burst into tears when Pixie had saved Millbridge Island from a greedy developer.

Pixie gazed out at the ocean, glittering in the light, and to the distant pine-covered islands with their pink granite bluffs. She brightened. She loved pink with a Texas-sized heart. She spotted a couple of lobster boats cutting across the bay. It made her even more determined to have lobster for dinner. She vowed then and there that she and Elrod were going to have a night on the town. She was going to have the biggest lobster she could order and a nice glass of wine. Maybe two. She was going to put Spencer Tate in her rearview mirror and lose herself in the crack of claws, melted butter, and chilled Chardonnay.

Thirty minutes later, after a mug of steaming coffee and wheat toast slathered with peanut butter and a dab of Maine blueberry jam, Pixie had tossed on a fabulous floral Amalfi Amore bikini, dragged a lounge chair in front of the cottage for a view of Frenchman's Bay, put on her earbuds, and closed her eyes to the sounds of her *amiga*, Sammy Swain, who'd become a fast friend after Pixie had sold the country and western superstar a 10,000 square foot Tudor in Highland Park.

Before Pixie drifted off, her mind flashed to the shame of being stood up and cheated on by Tate. Never again, she vowed. *Never, ever, ever again.*

Caleb Gray munched an apple and sat on the gunwale of his 37-foot lobster boat, the *Mary G.* He'd been hauling traps since the early morning when he'd headed out of Spring Harbor after the storm with his LED lights beaming toward Mt. Desert. Now he was finishing his lunch and taking a break from the grind of fishing. The bay was like a millpond, flat and blue, not a puff of wind or a cloud in the sky. June could bring rain, wind, and bone-chilling fog. But the day felt like August. Caleb would take it. He thought about the frigid days he fished in winter and shivered.

Caleb glanced toward Millbridge Island and was surprised to see a cluster of lobster boats. They sat like idle ducks beyond the old Stringer Cottage. It was good lobstering this time of year around the island, but he'd rarely seen that many boats clumped together except for the Lobster Festival, when all the fishermen would bring their rigs into Spring Harbor on the Fourth of July and parade.

Caleb wondered if there was trouble – a lobsterman overboard or another kind of accident. The casual onlooker didn't realize how dangerous fishing could be. A line around an ankle, a rogue wave, and you could be swept overboard before you knew it. The Gulf of Maine sea temperature in June was 52 degrees. Cold as hell.

There were times when Caleb wondered why he'd stayed in Spring Harbor. Lobstering was getting harder. The lobster industry found itself under siege: rising fuel and bait prices, inflation, and state and federal environmental regulations were strangling the ability to make a livelihood. A few months before, a national marine science research institute had declared lobstermen responsible for killing whales. After the announcement, two major upscale grocery chains declared they would stop selling lobsters. In all his years fishing, Caleb had never seen a whale entangled in his gear or any other lobsterman's. Once, after Mary had died, he'd thought seriously about moving away, but he realized that he couldn't run from his wife's death. Despite a mechanical engineering degree, he'd followed his father, grandfather, and great-grandfather's way of life. Even with the hardships, at the age of thirty-nine, he relished the independence and couldn't imagine a life stuck behind a desk staring into the glow of a computer.

Caleb tossed the half-eaten apple overboard, pushed the throttle forward, and swung the *Mary G.'s* wheel toward Millbridge Island. Something was going on, and he needed to check it out.

Elrod Tibbetts walked around the house and squinted. At least a half dozen lobster boats lingered off the Stringer Cottage point. It was an armada, and Elrod wondered what the lobstermen were doing. As he turned the corner, the cause became obvious. Pixie McGee was lying in the sun sleeping on a lounger wearing the skimpiest bikini Elrod had ever seen. The woman revealed more in her swimming trunks than she would have in her birthday suit, Elrod thought. Elrod was no prude, but he forced himself to pull his eyes away. When he saw that Pixie had those ear contraptions on, Elrod realized she had no clue that half the fishing fleet had rendezvoused off Millbridge Island for the view. And it wasn't to gaze at Frenchman's Bay.

Elrod stood with his hands on his hips and shook his head. He was about to walk down to the point and tell them all to go the hell away when Pixie slowly lifted her head off the lounger, pulled off her earbuds, popped on her sunglasses, and gazed at the clump of boats in front of the cottage.

She turned and smiled when she saw Tibbetts and said, "All those pretty boats, Elrod. There must be enough lobsters out there to feed an army."

Pixie waved. A few of the lobstermen waved back with wide grins.

Tibbetts shook his head. "It ain't lobsters they're looking at."

Pixie shot him with a puzzled look. "What are you saying, Elrod?"

"They're sightseeing."

"What are you talking about?"

Tibbetts raised his eyebrows.

Pixie suddenly broke into a knowing smile. "Well, it's not the first time I've been the focus of hungry men's hearts . . . or should I say groins?"

"I bet."

Pixie waved again.

"You think you better put something on? They might be getting pretty stirred up."

"Am I making you itch, Elrod? Haven't you seen a woman before?"

"Not built like you."

"Well, consider this your lucky day."

"You'll be the talk of the town before the day's over."

"You think?"

"I know."

"Well, it ain't the first place I've taken by storm."

"Mission accomplished."

"And Elrod . . . how about fixing me a vodka tonic?"

"It ain't five o'clock."

"It is somewhere. I got a whole lotta forgetting to do and all this attention is making me thirsty."

Elrod pulled his eyes away and looked out at the lobster boats. "I know one thing."

"What's that?" Pixie asked, waving once more to the fleet with her bright pink, lacquered nails sparkling in the sun.

"They ain't going to forget this day."

Pixie put her hands on her hips. "Bless their lobster-fishing hearts."

As the *Mary G.* pulled closer to Millbridge Island, Caleb Gray spotted the woman and knew instantly what the fuss was about. She was spectacular. She was wearing a bikini and waving to the men assembled off the point like a movie star. Yet he had no time, or desire to ogle. There were traps to haul. As he turned the *Mary G.* toward open water, he wondered if he could desire another woman. His sense of loss was still a constant presence.

He took a last look at her majesty the bikini queen perched in front of the Stringer Cottage and slowly turned the *Mary G.* toward open water.

Chapter Four—Utami

Utami Headquarters rested in a nondescript warehouse that had once housed one of the most iconic Hollywood TV studios. Now the building included a series of sterile laboratories lit by bright fluorescent lights where men and women dressed in white coats roamed, tending to an assembly line of putrid smelling slabs of meat vaguely resembling lobster.

Dirk Peters stood next to a foul-smelling tank brimming with a bubbling red concoction as Marley excitedly explained the "miracle" of the 3-D cellular process. As Peters listened, the odor began to overwhelm him. He fought the desire to throw up as the smell was especially toxic to a man with a hangover that would halt a moose in its tracks.

"As you can see, Dirk," Marley said with the sweep of his hand, beaming like a proud father, "the labs are impressive. Cutting edge. A miracle really."

Peters nodded dully and then paid the price.

Marley pointed to a series of large petri trays containing what looked like moldering hunks of roadkill. "We're getting close. Look at that succulent meat."

Peters thought "the meat" resembled the carcass of a skinned hyena. He tasted bile in the back of his throat. "Have you tasted it?" Peters asked, scrunching his nose.

"Soon, Dirk. Soon," Marley said gleefully.

Peters wanted to bolt, but thought with anguish about the rent he owed, his gutted condo, and his staggering credit card debt. He couldn't afford health insurance and hadn't had Botox in nearly two years. The $50,000 upfront payment Marley offered would bring immediate relief, but he'd need a bundle more to lift himself out of financial ruin. As if he could read Peters' thoughts, Marley added, "We're going to pay for your trip to Maine. You'll have an expense account. Transportation. Hotel. Food. And of course, activist expenses."

"Activist expenses?"

"Yes. You'll need resources to be disruptive, to make the world, the whole wide world, Dirk, realize the pain and suffering those poor crustaceans feel when they are tossed cruelly in boiling water. It's terrible, Dirk. Horrible." Marley swept his hand again in a grand gesture and beamed. Tubes, tanks, bioreactors, and tubs filled the lab. "Look at this miracle of the twenty-first century . . . before long, those harvesters of death will be in the unemployment line and everyone will be feasting on Utami lobster."

"When do I start?" Peters asked, realizing he had no options. "And more importantly, when do I get my advance, mate?"

Marley rubbed his hands together. "Soon, Dirk. Soon. This will be like launching the Normandy Invasion. Meticulous planning, logistics, rallying the troops."

Peters raised his eyebrows. "Troops?"

"You don't think you're going into battle alone? We need to assemble an army of do-gooders. Greenhaven is the organization best suited for this operation, assisted no doubt by celebrities like yourself who won't be able to resist the publicity of trying to save the beleaguered and tortured species, Homarus americanus."

"Come again?"

"Lobster, Dirk."

"Bloody hell. Why didn't you just say so?"

"Spring Harbor, Maine won't know what hit it! And you'll be leading the charge."

Peters turned and looked at the bubbling tank of red liquid. "What's in that?

"A special dye. Red 42."

"What do you use it for?"

"Just part of how we're going to make the meat resemble lobster."

"You dye it?"

"It works quite well actually."

"Isn't that dye horribly poisonous?"

"Only to mice, Dirk," Marley said finally, before leading Dirk Peters, fallen star, debtor, and budding activist, determinedly to another part of the lab where they would begin planning for their assault on the small fishing village of Spring Harbor.

Elrod Tibbetts and Pixie McGee pulled in front of Granderson's Hardware and climbed out of Tibbetts' bruised and battered pickup, which still stunk of baitfish from all the years of carrying barrels of bait. Pixie had rolled down the window and daintily pinched her nose as they drove over the rickety wooden bridge connecting Millbridge Island to the peninsula.

After sunbathing, Pixie had thrown on jeans and a white t-shirt, and announced to Elrod that they had work to do and were going to "spruce up" the Stringer Cottage come hell or high water. Elrod figured that hell would come faster, but he was game. Pixie was an excellent cure for boredom, and he had to admit that since Davis had left, life had been dull.

All heads turned when Pixie strode into the hardware store. Alden Granderson greeted them by the paint section and Elrod stepped back as Pixie tugged a list from her cleavage and swept her eyes across the gallon cans of paint like a veteran quarterback sizing up the defense.

She turned to Granderson, her eyes sparkling, "We'll need paint and lots of it, and carpeting, not to mention flooring, counter tops, and appliances." She laughed. "After I get done with the Stringer Cottage, you'll be able to buy that dream home in Florida."

Granderson gave Pixie an appraising look and turned. "You going to supervise, Elrod?"

Pixie rolled her eyes. "Now why is it that men always think that a woman needs supervision, can you tell me that, darlin'?"

Granderson looked at Elrod in alarm.

Tibbetts raised his eyebrows. "She's a nor'easter."

Pixie put her hands on her hips. "You're right about that, Elrod. I'm going to take Millbridge Island by storm. Wait until you see it when I'm through. That cottage is going to pop after we paint it a perty pink."

Elrod shook his head. "Not pink."

"My favorite color in the whole wide world, Elrod. It brings sunshine to my heart, and my heart needs a lotta rays."

"We don't have any pink exterior paint, but I can order it," Granderson said.

"You do that. How about granite countertops and kitchen flooring to replace all that linoleum that's got enough asbestos in it to kill an elephant."

Granderson nodded.

"And the bathrooms! I forgot all about them, Elrod. Can you imagine that? Now, I love the old fixtures and the clawed tub, but we need a new shower stall, vanities, and commodes. I'm not putting my fanny on those seats any longer than I have to. They've seen enough."

"Don't say," Tibbetts said.

"We're going to have a makeover, Elrod."

"How long do you think this project is gonna take?" Tibbetts asked.

"As long as it takes. I've got all the time in the world and nowhere to go."

"Have you hired a contractor?" Granderson asked.

"You're looking at her," Pixie said. "I'm no stranger to getting dirty and Elrod's going to be my assistant."

"Sounds like you're gonna be a busy man, Elrod."

Elrod shrugged.

Pixie softly punched Elrod on the shoulder. "Come on. Brighten up. You look like a steer going to slaughter. You're never going to have so much fun."

"Think so?"

"I know it." Pixie smiled. "You wait, Elrod. It'll be the time of your life."

Caleb Gray visited his wife's grave nearly every day. The cemetery sat on the Old Bangor Road no more than a mile from the harbor. He missed Mary terribly. It had been three years. She'd been his high school sweetheart and the light of his life. They'd been best friends and lovers, and although they never could conceive children, Caleb felt as whole with Mary as a man could be with a woman. One early January morning as she'd slept, he'd kissed her softly on the lips in the darkened bedroom before heading out to fish, and later in the morning, she'd been hit head on by a pickup that had struck a patch of ice and veered into her lane. She'd been driving to the elementary school where she taught second grade.

Since her death, Caleb kept to himself. He'd withdrawn from the world and life's allure had slipped away. He knew friends were worried. They'd tried to match make a few times, but their efforts failed miserably. The last "date" took place in the early spring. She'd been nice enough and had a good job working at the local historical society in Machias. Yet, Caleb spent the evening listening to her grouse about her ex-husband with a piece of lettuce stuck to her front tooth. By the time the check was delivered, he was ready to flee.

27

And while his friends had told him to try dating apps, Caleb had no desire to swipe one way or the other.

After selling his catch, he pulled into the cemetery and slid out of his truck in the late afternoon. Caleb still wore his rubber boots and oilskins and needed a shower and lots of soap after a long day hauling traps. He wondered if there was going to be anything more to his life. His routine was numbing. His parents were gone and he'd been an only child. The world for Caleb was a lonely place.

Caleb stood over Mary's grave in the late afternoon with a sinking heart. On the days he visited the cemetery, he'd tell her how much he missed her. He'd ask her how she could have left him to live in a world he didn't much care for anymore.

Caleb climbed into his truck and pulled out of the graveyard. He turned onto the Old Bangor Road and a few minutes later was about to drive past the narrow dirt road that led to Millbridge Island. On a whim, he soon found himself going over the rickety wooden bridge. He wasn't sure what caused him to make the turn, but the island held special meaning. He'd put a ring on Mary's finger as they looked out to sea and then into one another's eyes. That moment had been so long ago it almost seemed like a dream. Sometimes he went to the spot where he'd proposed to remind himself that she'd been real and that he indeed had the capacity to love.

He was nearing the dirt two-track to the Stringer Cottage when he heard a whomp, whomp, whomp and the high-pitched sound of what sounded like a jet engine. Within seconds, his truck was engulfed in dust as bits of gravel struck his cab and in the wild confusion, a rock kicked up and shattered his windshield. He pulled to a stop and for a few moments, Caleb sat stunned until he realized that a helicopter had landed next to the road in a field of early summer wildflowers. And it wasn't one of those rickety tourist trap helicopters that ferried people to offer a birds' eye view of Acadia. Caleb knew instantly the helicopter was corporate – sleek, black, and powered by twin turboshaft engines. He'd grown familiar with Sikorskys shuttling executives when he worked installing wind turbines his first year out of college in the mountains of Western Maine.

Caleb could feel the back of his neck grow hot as he watched the pilot cut the engine and a tall, middle-aged man wearing chinos and a preppy yellow sweater bound out of the helicopter and find the wooded path to the Stringer Cottage. Here Caleb sat in his 14-year-old pickup with 182,000 miles brushing bits of glass off his lap. He was clearing the cobwebs and realized that either the man didn't know the helicopter had shattered Caleb's windshield or didn't care. The man didn't even come over to Caleb's truck to apologize for scaring the bejesus out of him much less make sure that nothing had happened to his truck.

Caleb swore, shook his head, and reached for the door handle.

Chapter Five—Spencer

When she heard the helicopter, Pixie stepped out of the kitchen with Elrod and knew immediately Spencer Tate had found her. Fifteen minutes before, she and Elrod had returned from Spring Harbor and now she stood on the narrow slate walkway watching Tate stride across the patchy lawn dotted with granite outcroppings and bordered with bursting yellow and orange daylilies. Beyond were a tall stand of pines and the desolate blueberry barrens shadowed in the dying afternoon light.

Tate strode toward the Stringer Cottage with a determined look. As usual, Spencer chose a dramatic entrance. He could have flagged down Bebe at Bangor International, one of the emptiest airports Pixie had seen, and taken the taxi to Spring Harbor. But Spencer Tate was an important man. He had to arrive like a Saudi prince in the type of helicopter Darth Vader would have used. As usual, he was tanned and impeccably dressed. A cashmere sweater, cream-colored knitted polo, pressed chinos, and Gucci loafers. But what really put Pixie off was that look on his face – self-assured, entitled, smug. He was good looking enough in that smooth, pretty boy way, but now his very presence seemed an insult.

Pixie braced herself.

"Three bottles of Chateau D'Yquem?" Spencer fired the first salvo twenty paces from the house. "Two orders of Almus? A 40 percent gratuity? He stopped a few feet away from Pixie and shook his head of perfectly coiffed, sandy hair. "You even commandeered the League jet? Who do you think you are?"

"How was she, Spencer?" Pixie asked, standing her ground, her voice a velvet-covered hammer striking an anvil.

"How was who?"

"That Brazilian sweetie. Did you think I didn't see you punch her number into your phone and rest your philandering hand on her hip."

For an instant, a cloud passed across Tate's face. "She wanted a tour of League Headquarters."

"She got a tour alright," Pixie snapped.

"Honest, Pixie. I simply forgot the dinner."

Pixie looked away before returning her stare. "I thought you cared for me. You put a ring on my finger and told me you loved me and the only thing you love is good ole Spencer Tate."

"Not true."

"Oh, it is, darlin'."

"We're going back to New York."

"Not a chance."

Tate's eyes contemptuously settled on the Stringer Cottage. "You're going to stay in that dump and hang around with him?" He sniffed and pointed at Elrod.

Pixie felt fury rise in her throat. "Elrod's my friend, and I'd rather be here with him than anywhere on the planet with you."

"Let's go," Tate demanded, ignoring her.

"No."

"I didn't cheat."

"I bet."

"I'm not leaving without you."

"Then I guess you'd better find a place to stay. There's a hotel in town, though I'm not sure it will rise to his majesty's standards."

"You're not hearing me." Tate reached out and grabbed her arm.

A strong voice cut through the air. "Leave her alone."

Pixie swung her head. A man stood at the end of the pine needle-covered path to the house dressed in yellow oilskins. He was tall and strong with an intelligent and honest face. He looked rugged and weathered like the shrimpers Pixie knew from her days in Port Arthur.

"What do you want?" Tate sneered.

The man stepped closer. "I'll tell you what I want. I want you to leave the lady alone, and I want you to pay for my windshield."

"Your windshield?"

"Your helicopter kicked up a rock and shattered it."

"Nonsense."

"I've got glass all over my truck to prove it."

Elrod stood by the house watching as Tate ignored the man by turning back to Pixie, still grasping her arm. "Let's go," Tate commanded, as if he were shouting orders to one of his minions.

Pixie shook her arm loose. "Go away. I don't ever want to see you again. Hear me? It's over."

31

Tate narrowed his eyes. "No one walks out of my life without permission."

"Go shove it, Spencer."

"Didn't you hear her?" The man broke in stepping closer. "Go back where you came from."

Tate stared hard at the man and then turned back to Pixie. "Who is this loser?"

The man reached out one large, calloused hand and grabbed Tate by the shoulder. "I said leave the lady alone."

"And if I don't?" Tate said.

"Then this loser is going to stuff you back in that helicopter."

A shadow of fear crossed Tate's face. "If you don't take your hand off me, I'll sue you for assault. I'll take that grimy shirt off your back."

Pixie pleaded, "Go away, Spencer. Go back to New York. Leave me alone. You've hurt me enough without causing any more trouble."

Tate ignored her and stared at the man. "Do you know who I am?"

"I'd say you're an asshole."

Tate scowled. "I'm Spencer Tate."

"You've proven my point."

Tate raised his chin and turned to Pixie. "You're making a huge mistake. You'll regret this."

"The only thing I regret is ever agreeing to marry you."

Tate turned to go, then paused and spat out scornfully. "Why I ever thought you'd be anything more than trailer trash, I don't know."

Blood rushed to Pixie's face. "Haven't you hurt me enough already?" she asked softly. "Just go."

"Oh, I'll go. And when you wake up in the morning, you'll still be cheap, and I'll be Spencer Tate. Don't bother calling." Tate thrust his hand out, palm up. "I want my ring back. It's the least you can do after blowing a hundred grand."

Pixie pointed her finger at Tate. "Fat chance."

"The ring, Pixie."

Pixie folded her arms across her chest and shook her head.

"Okay. If that's the way it's going to be. Just wait."

"What about my windshield?" the man asked.

Tate pointed at Pixie and grunted. "Let her pay for it. She's already cost me enough money."

Soon, the sound of rotors whirring struck up and the Sikorsky rose above the pines and began streaking away.

Pixie watched the helicopter disappear as another sad chapter of her life closed. Elrod and the man looked skyward as the helicopter disappeared in the chilly, late afternoon air.

Pixie fought tears and stood with the man and Elrod in awkward silence. The man looked at Pixie, confused, seemingly trying to make sense of what he had witnessed.

Pixie turned to him and said, "What are you staring at? Haven't you ever seen trailer trash?"

"That's not what I was thinking."

"You'll get your money. I'll pay for your windshield."

The man's expression clouded. "I don't want your money."

"Don't be silly. Now go on home to your sweet thing and forget you ever met me."

A few seconds later, he was gone.

"Who was that?" Pixie asked miserably.

"Caleb Gray."

"I couldn't have him looking at me with those sad brown eyes like I was some charity case."

"You sure that's what he was doing?"

"I don't like pity, Elrod."

"That may be true, but if you see him again, you might want to know a few things."

"Why is that?"

"He don't have no 'sweet thing' to go home to." Elrod looked down and shuffled his feet for an instant before adding, "His wife was killed a few years ago in a car wreck."

Pixie looked away and swallowed.

"She taught at the elementary school."

"Oh, Elrod. I'm a damned fool."

"You didn't know, but you sure as hell put your foot in it."

Pixie stepped toward the house. She could feel her heart sink. "You'd better go, too. I ain't in the mood for lobster anymore."

"Don't be too hard on yourself."

She turned away in the afternoon shadows, fighting tears as she made the short walk to the Stringer Cottage. "Why not?" she called out to Elrod as he made his way down the path to his truck.

Caleb brushed the chunks of glass off the truck's seat with the back of his hand. He was still trying to make sense of what he witnessed. He recognized her immediately. She was the woman in the bikini in front of the Stringer Cottage, waving like a Hollywood star. When the jerk told her she was trailer trash, Caleb wanted to rip him apart, but he knew better than to enter someone else's affairs. Still, he saw the look of vulnerability and hurt on the woman's face and felt a longing. He even had to fight the instinct to gather her in his arms and tell her things would be alright. Yet he had the feeling that she could fight her own battles. As he finished brushing the glass shards off the seat, her words echoed in his ears. She had told him to go home to his sweet thing. There was nothing sweet anymore about going home.

Pixie wandered through the cottage and finally settled in the porch room in a wicker chair overlooking the sea. The sun was lowering across the bay, and the gulls were circling a lone lobster boat heading back to Spring Harbor. She'd felt alone before, but she always had her work to fall back on. After the inevitable train wreck of her relationships, she would lose herself in the bottom line of her real estate business. Now she was forty years old and upon Spencer's urging, had sold her business. There was nothing to distract her from the mess she'd made and the fear of middle age. In the mornings before she dabbed on her makeup, she could see the subtle lines forming around her eyes and the occasional strand of gray hair. She didn't want to end up alone and unloved. The thought frightened her.

She thought back to the man standing on her lawn with his honest face and rugged looks. There was a profound sadness about him that should have tipped her off. Pixie cursed herself. She'd stuck her foot in her mouth, and he'd bolted like a wounded deer. Now she felt as alone as she had ever felt. Her grand plans of having a lobster with Elrod had vanished as quickly as Spencer Tate's helicopter had roared away toward the horizon.

Pixie had surprised herself when she refused to give Spencer back his ring. The diamond held no allure. It was as if she needed a glittering symbol of failure to make certain it never happened again.

Chapter Six—Bugger Off

A wave of disappointment struck Dirk Peters when he realized Utami had purchased an economy class ticket for his flight to Maine. Now that he'd agreed to destroy the entire lobster industry, he expected big things – at least economy plus. Instead, he was booked on an airline he'd never heard of, where the seats were designed for hobbits. To make matters worse, during take-off at LAX, the 34-year-old Boeing 767 blew an engine and came to a screeching halt a few yards from a chain link fence. While the airline tried frantically to locate another plane, Peters sat in the terminal bar and drank his second vodka.

Peters tried to recount Marley's instructions. They'd been simple and direct. The mission to Spring Harbor would be a scouting trip. Peters' cover would be that he needed a well-deserved respite from the glare and hype of Hollywood by taking a restorative seaside holiday in a place that no one had ever heard of. He would size up the town, look for points of vulnerability, snap compromising photos, as Marley put it, of "crustacean abuse," and dig up as much dirt as possible to help fuel the eventual invasion of angry, self-righteous, oily-haired, sign-carrying, chanting activists who would descend on Spring Harbor like a school of piranhas. And if everything came together, as Marley promised, Dirk Peters' name would be synonymous with the likes of Gandhi, Mandela, and Mother Teresa. Film offers would come pouring forth and Dirk Peters' star would shine again.

Fortunately, Marley had given Peters enough of an advance to pay his rent. Goldberry had backed off when Peters had smugly transferred money into his landlord's Venmo account. The downside was that Marley mentioned several times the importance of deniability. Peters was never to utter Utami's name. *Ever.* For the operation to succeed, Peters had to operate as if he were protecting a state secret. The drama of being a lone agent, as if he were MI-6, had caused Peters to relish the role, until Marley had told him that if upon the miniscule chance the operation backfired, Dirk Peters was on his own. Peters' expression had soured until Marley had assured him over margaritas on the patio at *Fia* that Peters had nothing, absolutely nada to worry about.

Peters put aside creeping doubt with another gulp of his martini and heard the shrill attendant's voice over the loudspeaker requesting passengers to return to the gate. He polished off his drink, slapped down enough cash to pay the tab but not a penny for a tip, and slid out of his chair. As he exited the bar, to his delight, a redhead, early thirties, lightly freckled, wearing tight jeans and a low-slung blouse, beckoned him with a smile. He moved to her like a dog in heat.

Peters was about to ask if she wanted his autograph – the perfect line to ensure a woman knew he was famous – when she pointed and said to his horror, "I'd like a corner table."

Peters scowled and tried to hide his burning cheeks. How his star had fallen. It was wretched enough to be pitching bogus erectile dysfunction remedies on late night TV, but maître d' at an airport watering hole?

"Bugger off," he grunted, brushing past her. "I've got a bloody flight to catch."

Seven hours later, Peters' plane touched down with a thud at LaGuardia. His head pounded and his mouth felt like the Sahara. He'd guzzled two vodkas on the flight east, trying to ignore the senile idiot next to him who kept calling him Carl and asking when they were going to land in Des Moines.

Peters instinctively glanced at his watch to see how much time he had to catch the puddle jumper to Bangor. Except that he didn't have a watch. His prize Rolex had been pawned like everything else. Peters promised himself that when he returned to stardom, he'd buy a Patek Philippe, one of the most expensive watches in the world. No, not a watch. That was too common a term for a masterpiece like a Patek – an exquisite timepiece that would make heads turn. It was like wearing a Maserati on his wrist. He felt a stir in his groin thinking about what was to come. All he had to do was create a row in a town he'd never heard of only a few days before and destroy a way of life. Simple. Those blokes wouldn't know what hit them.

On his way to the gate, Peters passed a lobster tank sitting in front of a restaurant. The lobsters were crammed like sardines in a tin. Despite his pounding head, Peters stopped, and with a sly grin, pulled out his phone. He quickly snapped photos of the trapped and desperate crustaceans and was about to hustle to his gate when he heard a shout.

"Hey, you!"

Peters spun and spotted a bald, middle-aged man waddling toward him through the crowd with a bulbous nose and a gut that bounced like a chunk of Jello.

"I want my money back."

"Bloody hell," Peters thought. "What now?"

The man pointed his finger at Peters as people streamed past in the terminal walkway. Peters could see the purple veins crisscrossing the bloke's nose. "That stuff you've been selling gave me a rash." The man quickly glanced at his crotch.

Peters was incredulous. "You put it on your knob?"

The man turned red and his voice fell to an angry whisper. "My wife says it looks like a spotted salamander. It won't go away."

Peters smirked. "You're supposed to take it orally diluted with water, you idiot."

The man looked confused.

"Read the directions."

"I can't. They're written in Chinese."

"Get a translator, you twit." Peters pushed him with the palm of his hand. "Now get out of my way."

"Hey, you shoved me," the man protested, trying to regain his balance as Peters hurried away. The man shook his fist. "I'll sue you. I promise. My doctor says I have second degree burns!"

Peters disappeared in the throng of passengers and headed toward his gate. He felt dizzy, and his head throbbed. He realized the only way he was going to survive the trip to Bangor was to have another drink.

Elrod stood on a step ladder with drops of perspiration peppering his forehead and ran a steamer across hideous green wallpaper that had been pasted on the kitchen walls when Eisenhower was president and bobby socks were the rage. The wallpaper fell in folds as Pixie watched with glee as the Godzilla-colored paper crumpled to the floor. After Spencer had returned to New York in a huff, Pixie had attacked the Stringer Cottage's kitchen with a vengeance. She and Elrod had torn up the scuffed linoleum floor and counters, taken the ancient refrigerator and stove to the dump, and ordered enough paint to cover the hull of the *Queen Mary*. In the pantry, Pixie had set-up a hot plate, a microwave, and a mini fridge to hold her over until the kitchen project was finished.

As Pixie explained to Elrod, this was the beginning. The entire Stringer Cottage was going to be transformed. Powder and puff. Bright and airy. Modern kitchen and baths. Comfy furniture. New appliances and the crème de la crème, the cedar shingled exterior, now a weathered gray from years of harsh weather, was going to pop. Pixie had chosen a soft, creamy pink, which for an instant had made her forget her woes. She imagined her house by the sea, in a place as far away from the glitz of Dallas as she could have imagined, taking on new life, guided by imagination and her and Elrod's sweat.

Elrod wiped the perspiration off his forehead with the back of his hand and climbed off the step ladder.

"You're not stopping, are you, Elrod?" Pixie asked, a frown forming.

"Yup."

"Bless your heart. We're almost finished." Pixie looked at her caretaker with one hand on her hip and a smudge of plaster on her cheek. "How are we going to get this project done if you're always taking breaks?"

"That steamer ain't light."

Pixie sighed. "Oh, hell bells. I guess I'll finish the job if you aren't up to it, Elrod."

"Fine by me. I've been on that ladder all morning."

"And you're doing a great job. We're making progress."

Elrod groaned and rubbed his shoulder.

Pixie pursed her lips as she swept her eyes across the demolished kitchen before her eyes settled on her caretaker. "Do you think I'm trailer trash, Elrod?"

Elrod took a step back.

"That's what Spencer called me. You heard him."

Elrod wiped his forehead and leaned against the dust-covered counter. "Just because someone calls somebody something, don't mean it's true."

Pixie shook her head. "I've tried all my life to forget I grew up with nothing. We ate enough mac and cheese to grow horns. My momma stripped. She left us alone at night to fend for ourselves while she worked. By that measure, maybe I am trash."

He raised his eyebrows. "You don't look like trash to me."

"I've tried to forget Port Arthur. But every time I start feeling like I'm breaking free, I get reminded that I'm still that girl living in a trailer without running water with a momma who spent her money on cigarettes and whiskey and fed us dirt." Pixie turned and gazed out the window. "You ever want to throw your arms in the air and give up, Elrod?"

Elrod shrugged and placed the wallpaper steamer on the floor.

Pixie said, "I don't mean give up remodeling the kitchen. I mean about life."

"Once in a while."

"Like when?"

Elrod looked away. "When my wife, Emma, died."

"But you didn't."

"Nope."

"Life goes on."

"Yup."

"What's that saying? Life is for the living."

"Makes sense to me. You can't live if you're dead."

"True."

"That fella who climbed out of the helicopter . . ."

"Spencer?"

"He wouldn't last three seconds out there fishing." Elrod pointed toward the ocean. They could see the bay from the kitchen window. "He's never seen a real day's work. I looked at his hands. Smooth as silk. Not a callous. He's no one to be calling anyone anything."

"He makes fifty-six million dollars a year."

"That don't buy respect in my book." Elrod shook his head.

"What does?"

"A good heart. That's gold. Worth more than money."

"You think I got a good heart?"

"You bought Millbridge Island sight unseen and saved it from being ripped apart. And you did it to save Delvin's hide after he took up with another woman."

"I did, didn't I?"

"What did you see in Spencer to begin with?"

"Now that I think about it, I got no clue. I guess with Spencer I got caught up in an idea of myself."

"Maybe it's better to be yourself than to try to be an idea of yourself."

Pixie sighed. "I guess I was trying to be someone I ain't."

"And maybe that's the same problem you're having with men."

Pixie scrunched her nose and brushed a wisp of hair from her forehead. "I'm going after the wrong kind of man?"

"Most likely."

Pixie looked down for a moment and asked, "You got any nominations for Mr. Right, Elrod?"

Without pause, Elrod said, "Caleb Gray."

His certainty caused the air to rush from Pixie's lungs. For a moment, she was speechless. "The one who told Spencer off, and I told to hit the road?"

"That's the one."

"He looks like damaged goods."

Elrod stayed silent for a moment. "Reminds me of someone else."

"Who?" Pixie asked.

Elrod shrugged and reached for the steamer.

Chapter Seven—My Fellow Loser

Dirk Peters hated cats. Most of all, he detested the smell of cat food. Standing in the cramped parking lot of Oceanview Motel on a cold, rotten, drizzly morning, every time he took a breath, he noticed a fishy smell, like stale tuna. He'd arrived in Spring Harbor late the night before after picking up a horrid rental car at the airport. Utami had rented Peters a yellow Chevy Malibu with 105 thousand miles, and he'd thrown a fit. The bored man at the counter with glassy eyes and missing teeth, kept twirling a pen in his hand and glancing at his phone as Peters, with his head throbbing, pleaded for an upgrade.

Now Peters stood in the rain with a hangover and studied the hideous car. The sound of gulls filled the air, and the breeze smelled odious, like a rotting dish of Meow Mix. He started to regret his decision to join forces with Marley when he spotted a delivery truck rumbling by the motel. Painted on the side was a grimacing lobster standing on a diving board ready to jump into a pot of boiling water. The words stenciled beneath the image made Peters break into a sly smile, and for an instant, forget his doubts.

Mackerel Cove Lobster Co. Take the plunge! Where we sell 'em and you boil 'em!

It was all going to be too easy, Peters thought.

He pulled his car keys out of his pocket, opened the door, and grudgingly climbed into the Malibu. Soon, Dirk Peters, of Hollywood infamy, was driving through Spring Harbor, headed into town in search of a Bloody Mary.

To his dismay, Peters saw that Spring Harbor was a mixture of a few restaurants, trinket and t-shirt hawking shops, a hardware store, a couple of rundown seaside motels, and faded, white clapboard homes. The Methodist Church sat on Main Street, while less than a quarter mile away, a scattering of docks and wharves lined the harbor. Lobster boats and a few trawlers swung on moorings in the light breeze. Wire lobster traps were stacked on rotting wharves while gulls circled above. As he drove past the harbor, the smell of bait fish infiltrated the car. Peters crinkled his nose in disgust. Only a few years before, Peters had been riding on Rodeo Drive in his gleaming Jag with Aglaia Hecht, a fabulously stunning German actress, with the world in the palm of his hand.

After parking by the Chamber of Commerce, a Federalist mansion on Main Street that sorely needed paint, Peters walked into the Widow's Watch Restaurant and eyed the bar. The Widow's Watch overlooked the harbor and served the usual fried seafood, tapped and bottled beer, and generous slices of homemade blueberry pie. The restaurant and bar were empty in the mid-morning but for a middle-aged man with narrow eyes, a fleshy stomach, whisker tufts sprouting from his chin, and sandy blonde hair below his collar that was graying at the temples. The guy sat at the bar's far end on a wooden stool and glanced at Peters. Without hesitation, Peters ignored him and sidled to the other end of the bar where he eyed the vodka labels with loving scrutiny.

The bartender was about to ask Peters what he was drinking when the man took a sip of rum and said out of the side of his mouth, slurring his words, "I know who you are. Friggin' Dirk Peters."

Peters braced for the onslaught, thinking back to the idiot in the airport who put ERECTO LIFE drops on his meat puppet.

"Dude, I loved *Bango and Dash*." The man pounded his fist on the oak bar and gulped his drink.

Peters felt his neck relax. He broke into the smile that cinematographers once adored. Peters loved adoration, even from a sozzled bloke.

"I've seen that flick three times. Is Kala Dix as hot in real life as she looked in the movie?"

Peters nodded. What he didn't reveal was Dix had the worst halitosis on the planet. When Peters kissed her in the famous boardwalk scene, he thought he was going to retch. It was as if she had dipped her tongue in a septic tank.

"What is Dirk Peters, I mean THE Dirk Peters doing in Spring Harbor, Maine?" the man asked.

"On holiday," Peters said, sticking to the script Marley had given him.

The man rolled his eyes. "You're kidding, right?"

"I'm not."

"Spring Harbor?"

"I thought it would be a refreshing change of scenery."

The man pondered Peters' words as the bartender asked what Peters wanted to drink. "Bloody Mary," Peters said, "and make it stiff."

When Peters turned back to face the man, he was met with a stare of incredulity. The guy pressed. "You could have gone anywhere. Spring Harbor?"

Peters realized the man wasn't going to let it go.

"I needed a holiday." Peters shook his head mournfully. "There was a woman," he said dramatically.

The man grabbed his drink, slid off his stool unsteadily navigating the bar, and plopped down next to Peters. "A break-up, huh?"

"Exactly," Peters said. He was moving into full actor mode. Marley had been adamant. Stick to the talking points.

"That sucks."

"It does, mate."

"We're alike, you and me."

"And how's that?"

"I owned this town. I was practically mayor," he whined.

Here it comes, Peters thought. A delusionary tale spun by a sod. The thrill of being recognized began to fade.

"I had Spring Harbor by the balls. But I get a divorce, my kid starts hating me, and I'm accused of sending harassing texts to a school employee. Who is a total bitch, by the way."

"Sounds awful." Peters could have cared less. He needed a drink to put out the pounding between his ears.

"You don't know." The man shook his head and took a sip from his highball glass. His eyes turned to burning hatred and the whine turned venomous as he spat, "I lost everything, like you."

"Me?" Peters asked, nearly falling off his stool.

"That's right. I've seen you on late night TV."

"Bloody hell," Peters thought. "Here we go again."

"We got things in common. You know that, Dirk? How do you go from a killer movie like Bango and Dash to selling drops to slab on your pecker?"

Peters' face grew red. "You don't put the drops on your knob, it's an oral medication."

"Whatever . . . we had the world by the short hairs. *Alphas.* Now look at us. Two guys sitting at a bar with no life."

Peters ran his hand through his lush hair and muttered, "Speak for yourself."

"Come on, Dirk. You think I don't read *The Enquirer* while I'm in the checkout line? If you were still a star, you sure as hell wouldn't have washed up in Spring Harbor. Don't bullshit a bullshitter."

The blood ran out of Peters' lips. Only the prospect of a stiff Bloody Mary and the echo of Marley's warning to lie low kept him from lashing out. Peters glanced impatiently as the bartender mixed his drink. Earlier in the year, *The Enquirer* had run a story about Peters throwing a tantrum in front of a handful of TV executives. He'd auditioned for a minor and recurring role as the daft neighbor next door in a dubious sitcom called *Sick World* and never received a call back. In a desperate fit, he'd barged into a meeting at CBS headquarters, made an idiot of himself, and had to be dragged out of the building by two burly security guards. And this is the picture the loser beside him had in his head of what Dirk's life had come to.

"You were living the dream and now look at you. . . like me. Washed up. Ruined. A pariah. I mean what do we do after the world gives us the middle finger, Dirk? I'll tell you. We get revenge. We mess up people. We go to the dark side."

The man studied Peters' face as the bartender set the Bloody Mary on the bar. Peters snatched the drink and took a gulp. He felt the alcohol slide down his throat in a numbing wave and shivered with delight.

"Look at me," the guy said, tapping himself on the chest. "Boozing in the morning. Boozing in the afternoon. Boozing at night. I haven't taken a shower in two days." He sniffed his armpit. "I don't own a razor. I'm not even sure if I brushed my teeth this week." He raised his glass and said, "Cheers, my fellow loser!"

"Loser?" Peters snapped. Peters wanted to tell the bloke that he was on an important mission, one that would change the world. If he played his cards right, Peters was about to become one of the most famous activists on the planet. Plus, he was going to get rich. *Very, very rich.* At the least, that was the plan.

"Don't get touchy, Dirk," the man said. "You gotta hit bottom before you can pick yourself up."

"Stephen Covey?"

"No. Dr. Phil."

"Bloody hell."

"We could do a lot of damage together, Dirk. You know that? Take our revenge on a world that's trying to toss us on the scrap heap."

Peters' eyes were beginning to glaze over. He reached for his drink to take a sip when the guy said angrily, "I want to destroy this town."

"Destroy the town?"

"Blow it up."

"How?"

"I got ideas. Believe me." The man rubbed his hands together.

Peters leaned back in his chair. He pondered his next words carefully. He could hear Marley whispering in his ear to be discreet. "Remember," Marley had warned. "You're under cover. A pathfinder. We need to know what we're getting into before we send in the troops."

Peters pursed his lips and asked innocently, "You like lobster?"

The guy sneered. He pointed toward the picture window behind the bar with a view of the harbor. A lobsterman dressed in foul weather gear and rubber boots riding in a skiff headed toward his boat in the rain. A black lab stood in the bow with its nose to the wind.

"Hate it." He thumped his palm on the bar.

"Really?"

"And I hate the bastards who catch 'em."

Peters perked up and subtly nodded toward the lobsterman heading out into the harbor in his skiff. "Why?"

"I hate everyone, Dirk. It doesn't matter who they are. I despise everyone in this rotten town, including lobstermen, clammers, wormers–"

Peters shifted gears. "Do you know where I can get a boat?"

"Why do you need a boat?" The guy slurped his drink.

"Touring."

"You can pay for a ride on the Argus along with the other tourist suckers," he said.

"I prefer my own vessel."

"I got a boat," the man said. "Matter of fact, Dirk, I live on it."

"What kind of boat?"

"A 1968 Lyman Express Cruiser."

"Does it float?"

"Hell, yes. It runs, too. Most of the time. Sure, it needs paint and varnish and has a little rot, but she's a beauty."

Peters peered out at the harbor. Marley had wanted him to take pictures and video of lobstermen in the act, hauling those poor, pitiful crustaceans aboard for slaughter. Peters could imagine the images going viral on TikTok as he gave a soulful, dramatic narration, and the entire world, because of Dirk Peters, waking up to the horrors of the industry.

"How much would it cost me to rent your boat?"

The man broke into a smile. His eyes twitched. "Now you're talking. For you, Dirk, five hundred dollars an hour."

"That's larceny."

"Fuel, Dirk. Wear and tear. Labor. Expertise."

"Expertise?"

"It's hard work navigating around the coast of Maine. One screw up and you're in big trouble. You're not hitting sand in these waters, Dirk. Granite. The graveyard of the sea."

"I'll pay you fifty dollars and nothing more."

"An hour?"

"That's right."

The man leaned back with a pouty face. "Sixty."

It wasn't his money, but Peters had about enough. Peters said, "Take it or bloody leave it."

The man closed his eyes and put his head down as if he were making a life-altering decision. "Okay. Okay. For you Dirk. I wouldn't do it for anyone else. Got that? But for you, it's a deal. When do you want to go?"

Peters shook his head as rain poured in sheets across the harbor. "When the weather clears."

"Okay."

"The boat is seaworthy, right?"

"I told you she's a beauty."

"By the way, what's your name, mate?"

The guy reached for his rum, took a chug, and slowly stuck out his hand. "Maddox, Horace Maddox." His narrow, pinched eyes darkened. "And remember, I once owned this town, Dirk. And believe it or not, I'll own it again."

The toilet paper in the Stringer Cottage resembled 80-grit sandpaper. Whoever purchased it – most likely Delvin – had bought the cheapest stuff on the shelf. Being tortured by toilet paper that felt like a belt sander reminded Pixie of her childhood. Her mother's one-stop shopping had taken place at Penny General, where she snapped up discarded brands with her meager earnings. Pixie vowed she'd never subject herself again to cheap toiletries like Shine Bright toothpaste or food packed in dented cans and plain cardboard boxes where only the "miracle" of salt and hot sauce made it edible. It was one of the things that drew her to Spencer. When she was riding in the League's corporate jet or staying at five-star hotels in London or Dubai, she'd nearly forgotten her hard scrabble childhood. And it wasn't that she couldn't afford luxury herself. But his presence had made her feel like royalty until she discovered that she wasn't his only princess.

Pixie had made a trip to the IGA and left Elrod huffing and puffing, sweating and cursing, holding the wallpaper steamer in the torn apart kitchen. She'd wanted no part of driving Elrod's smelly pickup and settled on the nearly restored 1958 Eldorado Brougham, which was about as "stylish" a ride as she'd imagined. She'd broken into a pretty smile when people waved at her as they passed. Pixie had a package of Charmin Ultra Gentle, shampoo, conditioner, and a horde of other items crammed into her shopping cart as she wheeled down the narrow aisle in the cramped IGA that sat up the street from the high school and a dilapidated gas station. She paused for a moment after spying a bottle of her favorite wine sitting on the top shelf above shelves of hard liquor. She lifted on her tippy toes to reach it when she heard a man's smooth and sophisticated voice utter, "Please, allow me. "

Pixie turned. The man broke into a glamorous smile that caused his crystal-clear blue eyes to sparkle. He had a square jaw and luscious blonde hair. He reached up and grabbed the bottle off the shelf and handed it to her.

"Anything else I can help you with?" he asked, sounding like an elegant blend of Ralph Fiennes and Daniel Craig.

Pixie studied him. She detected a whiff of alcohol and noticed rings under his eyes, but he was . . . she struggled to think of a descriptor . . . and settled on beautiful, as if he was a porcelain figurine that could chip or shatter. He didn't seem real.

"Dirk Peters," the man said with that fabulous British accent.

"Hiya, Dirk Peters," Pixie replied.

The man paused and seemed disappointed, as if Pixie should have responded more favorably.

"Anything else I can assist you with?" he asked.

Pixie noticed how he checked her out to see if she was wearing a ring. She recognized his hungry look. She'd seen it thousands of times before when she'd danced. In the clubs, she had felt the testosterone fill the air like an atomic charge, setting off an ozone-like haze. "Now that you've made sure I'll have a glass of wine this evening, I'm all set thanks to you."

Peters grinned. Charm oozed from every pore. "A glass of wine sounds lovely. Are you looking for company?"

Pixie laughed. She thought about his offer for a moment as a means of taking her mind off Spencer when alarms sounded in her head. "Not tonight."

A wave of disappointment passed over Peters' face. "I'm a wonderful dinner companion. Full of wit and occasional wisdom."

"I'm sure."

"And in a town like this," Peters swept his eyes across the nearly empty, cramped, and poorly lit grocery store, "good company, I imagine, is hard to find."

"Well, it just got harder for you," she said. "I'm all tuckered out. I'll be in my jammies before the sun sets."

"May I ask your name?"

"Pixie."

"Pixie who?"

"Pixie McGee."

Peters broke into a smile. "How lovely."

"You think? My momma named me after a stripper. They were amigas. Tight as ticks."

"Your mother was in burlesque?"

"Hell no. She stripped. Right down to her birthday suit, and lord knows what she did when the show was over."

The man drew back, startled. "I get the sense you're jesting with old Dirk."

"I ain't jesting."

"Well, Pixie sounds lovely to me."

Pixie smiled and tapped her forefinger on her lip. Men were all the same. "So would Eunice and Bertha as long as they had a big chest and a nice caboose."

Dirk smiled to acknowledge the point. "Maybe so, but I still say there is something about 'Pixie' that appeals to me."

"C'mon, Mr. Peters. Pixie is a cheap name, right up with Trixie, Dixie, Candy, and Krystal, but it's mine. No one names their daughter 'Pixie' unless they live in dirt. My momma barely finished eighth grade. To her, Pixie sounded glamorous, like a movie star. I'm saddled with it. Some days I wonder if she'd named me Ashley or a simple Sue, would my life have taken a different road."

"Perhaps we could discuss that over wine?" He flashed what was undoubtedly his most winsome smile Pixie's way.

Unfortunately, his glibness raised unwelcome images of Spencer. Pixie had had enough. "No offense, but who names their kid Dirk?"

"What do you mean?"

"Dirk the twerk. Dirk the lurk. Dirk the jerk. Dirk rhymes with smirk too," she added, though by then his face was already crestfallen. "Just joshing. Dirk's a lovely name."

Peters ran his hand nervously through his thick hair. "Seriously, what's wrong with Dirk?"

Pixie took a step back and put the wine bottle in her cart to indicate her desire to end the conversation.

"Seriously?" Peters pressed.

Pixie shook her head. "I was having fun. It's a peachy name."

"Peachy?" Peters looked horrified.

"Right up there with Dagwood, Deron, and Dean."

"Those are ghastly names."

"Why'd your momma and daddy name you Dirk anyway?"

"They didn't. I did."

"You did?" She laughed.

"I'm an actor. It's my stage name."

Pixie smiled slowly. "An actor? It figures."

"Haven't you ever heard of Dirk Peters?"

Pixie rarely went to the movies or watched TV. She'd been too busy growing her business. She had little time for leisure. "Nope."

"*Bango and Dash*?"

"Sorry."

"Perhaps you saw me on *Hawaii Five-O*?" he asked with growing desperation.

Pixie shook her head and smiled. "What's your real name?"

Peters paused before finally mumbling, "Archie."

"I see why you picked Dirk."

Peters leaned forward. "Truly, you don't know who I am?"

"Not a clue."

Pixie noticed disappointment cloud Peters' eyes.

"You sure you won't have a drink with me? Dinner tonight?" he asked, sulking.

Pixie shook her blonde hair. She was tired of men and their fragile egos and insecurities and infidelities. She imagined good ole Dirk wanting more than a glass of wine and a porterhouse steak, and she wasn't about to be the dessert for another insecure, egotistical man. The scars were far from healed. "I'm all tuckered out, Dirk. Thanks, but no thanks."

"Will I see you again?"

"Spring Harbor's a one-horse town. I suppose."

Peters managed a broken smile. "We'll take a raincheck."

Pixie grabbed the handle on her cart and said, "Adios, Dirk," and with a swift push, she moved down the aisle leaving Dirk Peters of Hollywood infamy in her tracks.

Chapter Eight—Dirk the Jerk

After his foray to the Widow Watch and meeting Horace Maddox, Peters had decided to pick up liquor to bring back to the motel. Then his eyes fell upon her. She was reaching to grab a bottle of wine when Peters swooped. The woman was simply stunning. Marley had given Peters a litany of no-no's, but he never said Peters couldn't shag.

Then she'd made fun of his name. Worse, horrifyingly, she had mocked it in that Texas twang. It had made Peters' head spin. He chose Dirk while watching a 1960's black and white surfing movie called *Beach Safari* in his cockroach-infested flat in torn skivvies. Dirk had been the hunk that all the girls were drooling over, and he thought it a fitting name for what he envisioned for himself. There wasn't an actor alive in Hollywood with the name Dirk. He thought it would stand above the crowd of desperate blokes hoping to land a part. To his ears, Dirk Peters had a nice ring, a quick cadence that would make Hollywood directors' heads turn.

As he walked out of the IGA with a bottle of vodka, his head was spinning with doubt. *Dirk the Twerk? Dirk the Jerk? Dirk the Lurk?* And to add insult to injury, she'd refused to have a drink with him. His mind began to spin in a froth of insecurity. Had the name Dirk plunged him into Hollywood's sewer? If he'd chosen Stone or Clay or Barrett, would he be in a ghastly fishing town near the polar ice cap?

Peters noticed that the rain had stopped, and the clouds looked puffier, as if the sun might break through the scud. Gulls shrieked as they circled above while he made his way to the mustard-colored Malibu. Peters squinted as he looked up at the flock of herring gulls swooping back and forth. He loathed birds. He didn't like cats either, but he liked that cats devoured birds. If only birds ate cats too, there could be a battle to mutual extinction. He was about to shake his fist at the feisty gulls when a wet splat landed on his shoulder. Drowning in doubt, he couldn't help wondering, if he hadn't chosen Dirk, would these horrors be happening.

As Pixie rumbled back to Millbridge Island in the Eldorado, she thought about her encounter with the Brit. From the get-go, he'd struck her as shallow, insecure, and possibly conniving. He was a charmer, but he was the type whose charm would end once he had managed to get her clothes off. She knew immediately she'd gotten under his skin when she made fun of his name. Dirk the Jerk. A man worth something would have laughed it off and accepted her joshing for what it was. She thought back to the man standing on her lawn as Spencer called her trailer trash. He oozed a quiet confidence. Elrod said his name was Caleb Gray. Caleb was a name carved out of trust, strong and enduring. Like granite. Even when she put her foot in it, he didn't get his underwear in a bunch. He just turned and left. As he should have done, given she was a dumbass.

Pixie slowed down and gazed at the harbor as she drove to the Stringer Cottage. She stared at the Atlantic beyond, gray and vast, the rocky coast and islands, the gulls circling. She was a long way from Port Arthur and the glitz of Dallas. Spencer had gone for her throat and called her trash. For an instant, she wondered if it was true. She thought back to Caleb Gray standing on her lawn with wounded eyes. She'd told him to go back to his sweetie. It wasn't the only time she'd stuck her foot in her mouth, and as she neared the Millbridge Island bridge, she sadly acknowledged that it probably wouldn't be the last.

Peters woke with the sun peeking through a slit in the curtains and a slice of pepperoni pizza glued to his pillow. After his encounter with the Texas Queen in the IGA, he'd gone back to his motel room and nearly polished off the vodka. Now, filled with disgust and self-loathing, he peeled the pizza off the pillow. His hangover was massive: thirst, headache, biliousness, fog, aches and pains, and worst of all, a desire for a Bloody, which, even in his addled state, he knew would only perpetuate the endless cycle of self-harm he was inflicting upon himself. Peters wiped the sleep from his eyes and reached over to the bedside table, fumbling for his phone. He smelled of sweaty sheets and festering tomato sauce. It was a new low among a long, sordid list.

Peters squinted at his phone. He had two texts. The first was from Marley checking in, the second was from Maddox.

I'm at the dock. Where are you? Come on Dirk. We had a deal

...

Peters shot up. *Bloody hell.* He was late. He'd forgotten that he chartered the boat and was supposed to be at the town landing at 9 am. He struggled out of bed and was immediately hit by a tsunami of dizziness. He was about to lurch to the bathroom when he stopped in his tracks and spied the bottle of vodka on the water-stained dresser. Fighting the nausea, he reached for the bottle and took a swig.

Thirty minutes and four aspirins later, Peters stumbled down the rampway at the town dock, heard the *pop, pop, pop* of a backfiring motor, and spotted Maddox standing over an open engine box near the stern of the boat engulfed in a billowing cloud of smoke. Peters rubbed his eyes and stopped in his tracks. The Lyman was named *Fortune* and bobbed up and down in the light wake. The boat's blue hull was chipped and scuffed and the bright work around the cabin was cracked and peeling. The canvas Bimini covering the flying bridge was torn and faded. Worse, above the waterline, the boat had a handful of crudely cut wooden *dutchmen* patched over rotted planks. Adding to the appearance of unseaworthiness, the Lyman looked bow heavy, as if she was ready to plow under rather than effortlessly ride the swells. Peters could hear Maddox cursing, as he waited on the ramp to see if the smoking engine would ignite the fuel tanks.

Oblivious to Peters' presence, Maddox, dressed in grease-stained khaki shorts, a sleeveless t-shirt, and a shabby wide brimmed fishing cap, shook his fist at the ancient Chrysler Crown and kicked the engine box before turning and seeing Peters at the top of the rampway. Maddox yelled above the engine's monstrous clamor, "What are you waiting for, Dirk? Let's go, buddy boy."

Peters thought about reversing his steps and heading for the motel and more sleep but reminded himself that he'd foolishly given Maddox $100 as downpayment for the charter. Reluctantly, he took a step forward, and soon Maddox was casting off lines and the smoking vessel was lurching across Spring Harbor on a clear warm morning toward Frenchman's Bay.

Maddox stood at the flying bridge's wheel with a beer in one hand, peering at an array of broken gauges before turning to Peters. "What do you want to see, Dirk? Seals? Puffins? You want to catch stripers? I brought fishing tackle." Maddox pointed at tangled rods resting in two rusty outriggers.

Peters shook his head and looked around for life jackets. Seeing none, he grabbed a beer from the Styrofoam cooler resting next to Maddox as the boat sluggishly weaved between pot buoys dotting the harbor entrance. "Lobsters."

"Lobsters?"

Peters took a sip and swished the beer around. "I want to see how lobsters are harvested," he said. "I'm fascinated."

Maddox's eyebrows rose above his sunglasses. Sunlight poured through the torn and flapping Bimini. "You chartered a boat to watch these idiots catch lobster?"

"Righto."

"BORING . . . You see one trap hauled, you've seen a million. Besides, lobstermen are assholes."

Peters peered through his Vuarnets at Maddox, still fighting a queasiness that wasn't being helped by the chop. "What makes them such assholes?"

"Oh, they strut around town acting tough, cry about how hard and dangerous their job is and how they don't make enough money. Boo hoo." Maddox took a chug and killed his beer. He crushed the can in his fist and tossed it over his shoulder into the harbor. "Poor? Ha! They buy new trucks all the time, own hunting camps, and go to Florida in the winter. Tough life, huh?"

Peters nodded.

"And look at this." Maddox pointed to dozens of brightly painted pot buoys bobbing up and down. "You practically can't get in or out of the friggin' harbor without snaring your propeller. These idiots dump their traps everywhere. They don't care that everyone else has to run a minefield. Last year, my prop got tangled in a line, and I had to go overboard. Overboard, Dirk! The water was cold as shit. Freezing."

"Oh, my."

Maddox reached for another beer. "I could have died."

Peters noticed the wind was picking up as the boat left the harbor and entered the bay. He could feel the Lyman sluggishly push against a light chop. "Bloody hell, I hope I don't heave," he thought.

"If I had my way," Maddox continued. "I'd cut every trap off from here to Lubec. I'd bankrupt those bastards. Everyone's worried about global warming killing the lobster industry. Nothing would make me happier than seeing these guys go under. They're a big reason why this town is a dump."

Peters perked up. "How so?"

"Diversification, Dirk. Haven't you heard of diversification? It's basic economics. This place has relied on the lobster industry for too long. If people had listened to me, we'd be the Palm Beach of the north. Luxury homes . . . upscale dining . . . a golf course to rival Augusta National . . . We could host the U.S. Open . . . and industry, Dirk. Industry! We'd be home to tech startups and flocks of people wanting to work remotely."

"What about winter?" Peters asked, suppressing a burp.

"We'd create the largest ice festival in the world. We'd have concerts and build a huge indoor water park. Maddox World! How does that sound?" He grinned. "And nature. Look around." Maddox swept his hand and gestured to the islands beyond. "People go to Newfoundland all the time to see the Northern Lights. You can see them from here, Dirk. Sure, not always, but once in a while. Plus, I got connections, buddy boy. An old fraternity brother works for the NHL. We could host the Winter Classic every year on the harbor front. Imagine, the Bruins playing the Canadiens in Spring Harbor, Maine. It would be spectacular!"

"Bloody delusional," Peters muttered.

Maddox frowned. "What did you say?"

"Bloody brilliant," Peters said above the grind of the engine.

Maddox broke into a smile. "It is, isn't it? I have ideas, Dirk. But nobody listens anymore." His expression darkened. "They wrote me off. Shunned me. But I'll show them."

Peters noticed a distant lobster boat between two small islands and pointed. "Over there."

Maddox snatched binoculars that hung on a hook from a strip of warped mahogany. He took his hands off the wheel and focused on the lobster boat. The cabin cruiser began to drift off course, pulling to starboard toward a crop of ledges that jutted above the water outside the harbor entrance. Peters' nerves started to contend with his queasiness as the boat began to veer toward the seaweed-covered rocks.

"Caleb Gray," Maddox spat.

"What about him?" Peters asked, fighting off the urge to lunge for the wheel and correct the boat's course.

Maddox scratched his chin, oblivious. "He thinks he's better than everyone else. High and mighty. Bigshot lobsterman. Before his wife got killed, he testified in front of the Senate."

"The Senate?" Peters repeated, indicating with his hand what lay before them. As the ledges grew closer, he imagined the sickening crunch of wood striking granite and being hurled off the flying bridge into the icy water.

Oblivious, Maddox continued. "That's right. They were grilling him about lobstermen killing whales."

Peters couldn't stand it anymore. "Maddox!" he yelled, pointing straight ahead.

"Jesus, Dirk!" He grabbed the wheel and spun it hard, and the boat began to fishtail away from the rocks. "Why didn't you tell me earlier? You're my crew. My eyes and ears. You trying to get us killed?"

Peters found himself thrown against the side of the bridge which sent his beer flying. His shoulder struck one of the metal poles that held the Bimini. He groaned out a couple of choice words.

A few seconds later, the boat slid past a sinister looking ledge and was back on course toward the distant islands. "That was close," Maddox said, snatching another beer from the cooler as if nothing had happened. "Next time, stay alert, buddy boy. Hear me? You could have cost us bigtime."

Peters rubbed his shoulder. Clearly, Maddox was nuts, Peters thought. Peters was about to remind Maddox that he was a paying customer, not a hired hand, when he thought back to what Maddox had said about whales. "You were saying about whales?" Peters asked, flexing his shoulder to make sure nothing was broken.

Maddox turned to him, the corroded binoculars swinging from his neck on a worn leather strap. "Murderers . . . all of 'em . . . Gray lies through his teeth. Tells the senators he's never even seen a right whale. He goes through this sad sack song and dance about how the whole Maine economy will be ruined if lobstering is banned. When if they'd listened to me years ago, no one would care. The whole town would be rich."

"Hmm."

"Do you think I care about whales, Dirk? Harpoon 'em all I say." He took a chug of beer and wiped his mouth with the back of his grease-stained hand. "But I hate lobstermen worse."

Peters tried to point, but his shoulder burned. "Let's go see what Mr. Gray is up to."

"You really want to see how a lobster is caught?"

"Yes."

"I told you, Dirk, BORING . . . Wouldn't you rather fish for stripers?"

Peters shook his head.

"Go out to Seal Island? See puffins?"

"I detest birds." Maddox was beginning to irritate him no end. Marley had warned him against tipping his hand, so he didn't want to seem overzealous, but Maddox clearly didn't understand the idea of a charter.

"Okay. Okay," Maddox said, pushing the throttle down hard as the boat lurched forward belching smoke and making a terrible racket as the pistons banged up and down. "Let's see what this baby will do."

Chapter Nine—Why Boil Them Alive?

Caleb Gray looked up from his trap and saw Maddox's stink pot clunking across the bay billowing oily smoke. Maddox was always up to no good. Since being accused of harassing behavior and going bankrupt after a string of bad investments, Maddox had become a shady figure – a man of dubious schemes – and had clearly gone off the deep end. Caleb had had a few run-ins with Maddox over the years. The last of a prominent Spring Harbor family who had made its money in banking and real estate, Maddox had tried to purchase a large swath of the Spring Harbor working waterfront and turn it into an upscale hotel, restaurant, shopping, and condominium complex. Caleb and other lobstermen attended the town hearings and made forceful arguments against Maddox's plan. If Maddox had gotten his way, he would have destroyed the lobstermen's way of life. Caleb remembered after the project was defeated, Maddox had thrown a tantrum outside the Town Hall and had threatened to ruin Caleb. He braced himself for what was to come.

Caleb slid the bait bag into the wire trap and kept one eye on the boat plowing toward him. He secured the trap, gently pushed the throttle forward, made certain the line didn't tangle as the trap slid down the gunwale and plunged off the stern. With gulls swooping above hoping for bait scraps, he made a wide, smooth circle, his Yanmar six-cylinder, turbo-charged marine diesel engine purring, and headed to the next trap. Looking for his next lime-green pot buoy, Caleb reached down to pick up his gaff. The gaff was three inches longer than the one he'd used for years, and just now he saw the first scratch on its stainless steel-tipped hook. His attention was pulled away, when he noticed on the Lyman's decrepit flying bridge that Maddox was with a man he didn't recognize.

What a disaster, Caleb thought. Maddox's boat was listing to port, she was bow heavy, and the decades old engine was burning way too much oil. It sounded like the pistons were going to rip through the rotting lapstrake hull. Before he'd gone under, Maddox used to fly around Frenchman's Bay in a sleek Cobalt R8 runabout acting like a bigshot. Maddox lost the boat like everything else. Now he was living on the Lyman Express Cruiser that had been sitting for years in an overgrown field on the side of Route One.

As Maddox's boat grew closer, Caleb noticed the other man scampering down from the flying bridge to the stern. Caleb turned away and wrapped the trap's line around the hydraulic hauler's cylinder. While the trap rose to the surface, Caleb got a strong whiff of burning oil and fell into the shadow of Maddox's flying bridge. The boat was only a few yards from the *Mary G.* Caleb turned to see Maddox standing by the wheel drinking beer and sneering at him, while the other guy was pointing a phone at Caleb.

"Little early to be drinking, Horace, isn't it?" Caleb asked before pulling the trap out of the water and resting it on the gunwale as his boat gently rode the chop.

"What's it to you, Gray?"

Caleb nodded at the man who pointed the phone at him. "Who's your friend?"

"None of your business."

"It is my business when someone's pointing a camera at me."

"It's not against the law."

"No, but it's bad manners."

The other man broke into an ameliorating smile. Even though the guy was wearing sunglasses, for some reason Caleb thought he recognized him. He looked oddly familiar.

"I'm utterly fascinated by lobsters," the man said in a rich British accent. "I hope you don't mind me capturing the experience."

Caleb shrugged and opened the trap. Usually, he didn't mind the tourist boats when they pulled close so the passengers could observe a "real live" lobsterman. It was part of being a good representative for the industry and state. Caleb realized that many of these people were spending their hard-earned money to take a vacation on the Maine coast and experience its pleasures. But Maddox? A whole different story. Besides, who in their right mind would climb aboard Maddox's scow?

"You're burning too much oil, Horace," Caleb said as he casually began to toss shorts back into the water. "Shorts" was the age-old term for lobsters that didn't meet the size requirement.

"What's it to you?"

"Your engine's burning out."

The British guy interjected. "Doesn't it hurt the lobsters when you yank them from the trap and hurl them back?"

Caleb looked up. The man was still pointing the camera at him. It was an odd question. "No."

"How do you know?"

"'Cause lobsters don't have nervous systems like we do." Caleb was doing his best to be patient.

"Unlike whales and porpoises and whatever else you murder," Maddox said with a sneer.

"That doesn't happen, Horace. You and I both know the environmentalists dream up all sorts of things."

Caleb noticed after he said the word "environmentalists," the British man smiled thinly and kept pointing the phone at him. Caleb pulled a small crab from his trap and tossed it overboard before grabbing another lobster. "This one's a keeper," Caleb said to the British guy and held the arching lobster up for the camera. He was trying to be instructive even though Maddox was incredibly annoying. "Hardshell, too."

"Hardshell?" the Brit asked.

"Its exoskeleton. It hasn't shed yet. In the summer, lobsters begin to lose their shells and become shedders. Some people like to eat soft shell lobsters. They think the meat's sweeter."

"Hmmm . . . Why boil them alive?"

The way the man asked the question set off alarms. Caleb squinted at him and said, "because that's the way they taste best."

"But isn't it cruel?"

No wonder he reacted as he did when Caleb referred to the environmentalists. "Compared to what? A meat-packing plant?"

"It's more than cruel," Maddox spat, throwing his empty beer can overboard and grabbing another one. "It's criminal."

"Why is that, Horace?" Caleb asked, shaking his head as he watched the can float away.

"Would you boil a live chicken? Toss a bleating lamb into a cauldron of bubbling oil?"

"It's not the same."

Horace broke into a mocking expression. "Oh, not the same. Did you hear that Dirk? Not the same! How do you know, Gray? Have you ever asked a lobster what it feels like to be boiled alive?"

"This is an inane argument, Horace." Caleb peered at the other man for a moment. Maddox had called him Dirk. Dirk . . . *there was something familiar about the man.*

"Is it?" Maddox spat.

Caleb noted Maddox's contempt. Over the years, the lobster industry had faced numerous challenges, including pressure from environmental groups pushing for stricter rules. In response, lobstermen made concessions. For decades, the industry had been a model for successful regulation, with measures like size and trap limits. But there were still protests. Caleb had been chosen as one of the spokesmen for the Maine commercial lobster industry. He traveled to Washington multiple times, dedicating himself to understanding the arguments on the other side. Despite resistance from fellow lobstermen, he supported changes he believed were reasonable: trap limits to prevent overfishing, weakened fishing lines, seasonal closures, trawling up to reduce the amount of vertical rope in the water, marking gear for accountability, and funding for research into alternative fishing gear to protect endangered whales.

While there had been a few documented instances of whale entanglements with fishing line, whale strikes in shipping lanes was by far a more frequent occurrence, and yet there had been almost no serious measures to regulate ship routes and vessel speed in waters where endangered whale species congregated. Caleb viewed himself as a pragmatist. He loved whales and found all instances of accidental death deeply regrettable, but he also regretted how endangered Maine lobstermen had become. He had adamantly pursued a solution to protect his brethren from the ravages of dwindling stocks, warming waters, Canadian fisheries, and foolhardy regulations. Over time, he'd grown disillusioned with the process, worn down by stubborn and proud fishermen, overzealous conservationists, and shortsighted politicians. After Mary's death, he lost the drive to continue as a spokesperson. He simply didn't have it in him anymore.

Caleb studied Maddox for a few seconds and glanced at Dirk. "I think you've taken enough pictures."

"He can take as many as he likes," Maddox said, taking a swig of beer and glancing at his passenger. "Isn't that right, Dirkster? We're on the high seas. Last time I checked, Gray, I didn't see a no trespassing sign."

The British man oozed, "I can't speak for the captain." He shot a dubious glance at Maddox. "But please know, mate, I'm not trying to be disrespectful. Just fascinated by your way of life and these creatures."

Caleb nodded.

"How many traps do you fish?" The man was still holding up the phone.

"Six hundred. That's the limit."

Maddox interjected. "They'd have more but the state tried to slow down the killing machine. These guys," Maddox pointed his beer at Caleb as the boats drifted side-by-side, "would do anything to make a buck. Isn't that true, Gray?"

"At least we come by our money fairly, Horace. This is honest work and a renewable resource. If you had your way the natural beauty of much of our coastline would be destroyed. I for one am glad you got shot down."

Maddox's expression darkened.

Maddox crushed the beer in his hand and foam squirted out of the can. He said menacingly, "Just wait. I'll own this town again."

Caleb bit his tongue. He wasn't going to take Maddox's bait. He'd said his piece. He was about to reach into the trap for another lobster when he heard a loud, guttural blowing sound and a splash of water. He turned his head to see a minke whale bearing down on his boat, then back to Maddox and the Brit, who had whipped their heads around and now watched with open mouths as the whale steamed toward them. Instinctively, Caleb grabbed his gaff.

"Bloody hell," the Brit shouted, still holding the phone in front of him.

"Christ," Maddox shrieked from the flying bridge.

As if drawn to the Lyman and Maddox by radar and Neptunian gods, the whale veered from the *Mary G.* and took aim at Maddox's ramshackle vessel. Caleb watched with fascination as the whale arched its back, rising and falling, water spouting from its blowhole. Sighting minkes wasn't uncommon. Caleb always felt a sense of awe when he spied whales. They were majestic, nearly always docile, and often curious, swimming past his boat while he hauled traps. He marveled at the beauty of the mammals and never took for granted the stunning world of wind, sky, and water where he made his living. But this sighting felt different as if the minke wanted to avenge some great and mysterious wrong. Caleb wondered if Maddox had harassed the minke earlier on one of his drunken jaunts.

Caleb wouldn't put it past Maddox to have chucked a beer can or shot a flare at the whale, which seemed hellbent on taking aim at Maddox's boat.

Caleb noticed Maddox's face grow ashen. The Brit still held his phone in front of him with one hand and had clamped the other to one of the outriggers. Even as the minke neared Maddox's boat Caleb felt sure that it was playing chicken and would veer away at the last instant, but then the minke hit the Lyman broadside and he heard Maddox shrill, "Holy shit, Dirk!"

An eight-ton mammal ramming a wooden hull made a sickening, splintering sound. With fascination and mixed with a tinge of horror, Caleb watched Maddox fly off the swaying bridge and land with a splash into Frenchman's Bay. The whale sounded before rising again between the drifting boats. Instinctively, Caleb reached across his lobster trap and bent over the side holding his steel gaff like a spear to fend off the angry minke. But after wreaking havoc on the Lyman the leviathan sounded a few feet from the *Mary G.* and disappeared into the murky depths.

Stunned, Caleb tossed the gaff away and took inventory. The Lyman listed heavily to port, taking on water. Blood poured from the Brit's nose as he staggered away from the stern, while water poured over the gunnels and Maddox flailed in the bay shouting for Caleb to rescue him. Caleb had an image of a whale coming from the deep and devouring Maddox in one slurp, in a manner reminiscent of his favorite children's book, *Bert Dow, Deep Water Man.* Except any sensible whale would spit Maddox out like festering sushi.

"Help me, you idiot," Maddox shouted, beginning to paddle toward the *Mary G.* For an instant, Caleb considered pushing his throttle down and leaving Maddox and the Brit in his wake. Instead, he angled his boat toward Maddox, pulled Horace from the icy waters, and a few minutes later, had rescued the desperate Englishman from Maddox's sinking boat.

After Caleb radioed the Coast Guard to report the incident, the three of them watched in silence as the Lyman slid beneath the oily waves. Maddox sat on the engine box with smoldering eyes wrapped in an old wool blanket, and the Brit leaned against the foc'sle holding a bloody towel against his nose while still clutching his phone.

Without a word, Caleb pushed the throttle forward and headed to Spring Harbor. He couldn't wait to get Maddox and the Englishman off the *Mary G.* Like bait fish, they stunk to high heaven. Rotten to the core. And with the delay, he would be out until dark hauling traps.

Chapter Ten—*La Nuit Est Pour Les Amoureux*

Pixie smiled when the waitress, a pretty young thing with rosy cheeks and a bundle of chestnut hair, took her order. Pixie was going to finally eat her lobster – a lobster roll smeared with hot butter on a toasted bun. On a Friday evening, the bar at Ebb Tide was boisterous and packed at the end of the work week. Elrod sat across from her transformed by a subtle smile and a clean shirt. He told her he hadn't been "out carousing" since Davis had left for Arizona. Pixie had noticed Elrod's face open up when all heads turned as they walked into the restaurant. Pixie was no stranger to the attention, but she was especially happy to see how much it pleased Elrod to be with her in that moment. She had worked him hard. She owed him a memorable night on the town.

Ebb Tide sat on one of the wharves next to the ferries that ran daily to a scattering of outer islands. Along the wharf, barnacle-covered lobster traps sat piled high, and inside the restaurant, a nautical theme carried the day: brightly painted pot buoys hung on the walls along with black and white photographs of four-masted schooners from bygone years. Through the windows, patrons had views of the harbor and islands dotting Frenchman's Bay. Pixie and Elrod sat in a corner booth, the table made of reclaimed pumpkin pine, which glowed warmly in the evening light.

Pixie raised her eyebrows when Elrod ordered a Moxie with his hamburger. She said playfully, "I thought I was going to get you drunk and have my way, Elrod."

She was enjoying the faint blush that was creeping up Elrod's weathered cheeks when she felt a hand on her shoulder and winced when she discovered the Englishman standing beside the booth with a bruised nose, bleary eyes, and a drink in his hand.

"Ah, Pixie," he slurred. "What a pleasant surprise."

"Dirk the– "

Peters pursed his lips and held up an unsteady hand. "Please . . . how about we pretend that silly conversation never took place."

"Fair enough."

"I thought you might need some amiable companionship."

Pixie's eyes grew steely. "I have it. Meet my compadre, Elrod."

"Younger companionship," Dirk said sloppily, but in that silky accent it clearly betrayed his arrogant entitlement. Pixie saw he was well on his way to being totally skunked. Ignoring Tibbetts, he said, "If you don't mind . . .," plopped into the booth beside Pixie, and pushed his knee against hers. His presumption made her want to stab him in the crotch with her fork.

Instead, Pixie said through a cold stare, "Well, sit with us at your own risk. I may not be as charming as I was the other day. What happened to your shnoz?"

"A slight boating mishap."

Pixie pulled away and settled back uncomfortably. She was used to pushy men and delighted in showing them she could be as hard as titanium. She knew how to handle them, especially from her dancing days when she'd have to fend off groping hands and unwanted kisses. She also enjoyed beating men at their own game. In the real estate world, her male competitors refused to take her seriously until they woke up one day and discovered she'd stolen the North Dallas market. Spencer wasn't any different. One evening, sitting in his luxury condo with floor to ceiling windows overlooking a pulsating Manhattan skyline, he'd tossed up his hands trying to understand a complex new salary cap system proposed by the Players' Association. After he'd gone to bed, Pixie had carefully read the document. In the morning, she'd explained the complexities of the proposal as Spencer sat transfixed. Men saw all that blonde hair, heard her speak with that throaty Texas twang, and wrote her off as brainless. Pixie remembered Mrs. Washburn, her high school math teacher, pulling her aside after Pixie had told her she didn't think she could afford college. Pixie thought Mrs. Washburn was going to cry. "Oh, Pixie," she'd said, frowning, "what a shame." Mrs. Washburn had a lot to do with what Pixie had become, because those words burned at Pixie's ears until she did something about it on her own.

Peters took a gulp of his drink and settled his bloodshot eyes on Elrod. "Three's a crowd, Grandpa. Don't you think it's past your bedtime anyway?"

"Still working on my Moxie."

"If you aren't careful, they might switch the lights off and lock you out of the retirement home."

Elrod stared blankly at Peters.

"Leave Elrod alone," Pixie broke in.

Peters smiled thinly. "Just having a little fun with the old geezer."

"Elrod, this is Dirk. We met at the grocery store yesterday."

"I know who he is," Elrod said.

For an instant, Peters looked confused. "You know who I am?" he asked hopefully.

"That's right."

Peters paused before breaking into a knowing grin and an inebriated glow. "*Bango and Dash*?"

"Nope."

"*CSI*?"

Elrod shook his head.

"*Appalachia*?"

Elrod shook his head again.

"Who am I?" Peters asked, throwing up his arms.

"A dickwad."

Pixie burst into laughter and said, "You asked for it. I should have thought of that one yesterday. Dirkwad."

Peters scowled and snatched his drink with a shaky hand. He stared at Elrod. "Bugger off. Can't you see I want to be alone with the lady."

"Not unless the lady says she wants to be alone with you, and somehow, I don't see that happening."

"You tell him, Elrod," Pixie said.

Peters leaned back and ran his hand through his thick hair and said dramatically to Pixie, "Have it your way. I thought we might seize the serendipity of our meeting to get to know one another better, but perhaps you prefer your men old and wrinkled."

Pixie snapped, "Mind your manners, Dirk the Lurk."

"You're a fine one to talk of manners." Peters looked at her unsteadily.

"Now it's time for you to go, Dirk. Hear me?"

"Go?"

"That's what I said."

"But the night is young. We are," Peters said with a woozy Cary Grant-like flair, "getting to know one another." He draped his arm around Pixie's shoulders, stared deeply into her eyes as if the cameras were rolling, pulled her close, and drunkenly slurred, "*La nuit est pour les amoureux . . . The night is for lovers.*"

Pixie reached for her fork, about to treat Peters' thigh as if it were a chicken-fried steak, when she did a double take. Caleb Gray stood across the restaurant, wearing oilskins and waders. He looked tired, and clearly he'd just stepped off his boat from a long day hauling traps. Their eyes met for an instant, and Gray glanced at Peters and back to Pixie with a glimmer of disgust. In a sudden flash of horror, she realized Gray thought she was with Dirk Peters. With Dirk Peters! *Hell bells.* In a panic, she felt the impulse to shove Peters out of the booth, race across the crowded restaurant, and tell Gray it was all a mistake. But it was too late. Gray did an about face and was gone.

Pixie and Elrod sat in silence as Peters, his head resting against the back of the booth, his mouth hanging open, snored in between deep, uneven breaths.

"He sure is a prince," Elrod said, scratching his chin, before taking a sip of Moxie.

Feeling her heart sink at the thought that she now had two strikes with Caleb Gray, said, "I'd kiss him if I was sure it would turn him back into a toad."

Elrod shook his head and put his soda down. "He's got trouble written all over him."

Pixie nodded.

"As sure as the sun shines."

"You need to steer clear."

Pixie sighed, flashing back to Gray standing by the door looking at her with disapproving eyes. "You can be sure of one thing, Elrod. I ain't going to be Dirk the Jerk's princess."

Caleb walked to his truck and swore as rain began to patter against the pavement. He hadn't had time to fix his windshield. He was going to get soaked on the drive. It had been a long day. After dropping the Englishman and Maddox at the dock and speaking with the Coast Guard officer-in-charge and a brainy and suspicious Department of Maine Resources marine biologist about the whale strike, he'd headed back out to fish. When he'd finally returned to the harbor as storm clouds gathered from the south, he'd gone into Ebb Tide to order take-out. He'd spotted the Englishman and wanted no part of Dirk Peters or, for that matter, the woman who he'd met at the Stringer Cottage. She'd looked at him with surprise, and he thought, alarm, as Peters nestled beside her, his arm tucked around her shoulders. It was difficult for Caleb to comprehend why she'd be with men like the jerk who'd arrived in the helicopter, or Dirk Peters, who struck Caleb as a vain and shallow lightweight. But he never pretended to be an expert with women. It didn't matter anyway. Did it? But there was something about the woman that suggested that the scene in the booth wasn't what it seemed. She struck Caleb as nobody's fool, but there she was nestling with Peters. It didn't make sense. But what did? Caleb had watched a minke whale obliterate Maddox's boat hours earlier and only a few years before, the love of his life was ripped away on an icy January morning.

He shook his head and put his truck in gear. As he pulled out of the Ebb Tide parking lot, the rain began to blow in heavy sheets, pelting the roof of his pickup and drenching him through the opening caused by the shattered windshield. It was going to be a wet and hungry drive home.

Peters stumbled to the motel vending machines, filled a plastic bag with ice, and bought a soda, hoping the fizz would temper his dreadful headache. He couldn't remember how he made his way back to his motel room the night before, but it didn't matter. He vaguely recalled sitting with that woman and an old man. What mattered was spraying a fire extinguisher on a raging headache and chewing a handful of antacids for his stomach, which bubbled like a pot of rancid bacon fat.

Bleary-eyed, Peters had noticed two missed calls from Marley. When Peters returned to his room, he fell onto the lumpy mattress, placed the ice bag on top of his head, sipped his soda, and punched up Marley's number. The early afternoon light sifted through a slit in the curtains, partially illuminating a room that smelled of mold and dirty socks.

Peters took a deep breath and hit the call button. A few seconds later, an irritated Marley answered.

"Where have you been, Dirk?" Marley asked, nearly breathless.

"It's been a bustling morning," Peters lied, trying to sound alive and alert, as if he'd been awake since the crack of dawn.

"What happened?"

"What do you mean?" Peters sat up. The rickety bed groaned.

"It's all over the news."

"Bloody what?"

"The whale, Dirk. I send you to Maine on a clandestine mission and you end up on CNN."

"Huh?"

"You were supposed to be fact-gathering. Tell me how you happen to be on a boat that gets attacked by a whale?"

"Happenstance."

Marley went silent for an instant. Peters could tell Marley was trying to gather himself. "Don't you see the implications?"

Peters' head began to pound harder. He'd popped four Tylenol – damn his liver – and the large dose of acetaminophen hadn't eased the throbbing. "What bloody implications?"

Marley stammered, "Whales are supposed to be victims, Dirk. Not the enemy! People all over the world are asking what you and that other bloke did to incite an attack."

"Nothing. Truly. I was simply observing the lobsterman, gathering facts."

"Tell that to our friends at Greenhaven. They want to launch an investigation."

"Well, then they're fools."

"Don't you see, Dirk? Greenhaven is supposed to be on our side. Not sending crazed activists to Spring Harbor to investigate what actor Dirk Peters did to piss off a whale."

For an instant, Peters closed his eyes.

Marley grunted. "We have our PR people working overtime, Dirk. Behind the scenes. Luckily, no one knows you've been retained by Utami . . . unless . . ."

"I've betrayed nothing," Peters interrupted. But then he began to wonder what he might have revealed in a drunken stupor the night before.

"This is hard, Dirk, but because of this . . . *this incident* . . . we're thinking of contacting Alejandro Hiadro."

"What for?" Dirk felt bile begin to bubble in the back of his throat.

"To replace you."

"Replace me? With that ass?" Peters could see Marley's thinking. A few years earlier, Hiadro had narrated an inane documentary about rescuing the tiger salamander from extinction. Peters and Hiadro had a past. They had gotten into a scuffle at a blowout bash in Malibu. The struggling actors had begun to detest one another after they found themselves competing for the same dismal roles. Hiadro had sneered at Peters and called him a *cabron* after Peters had purposely spilled his drink on Hiadro's girlfriend, a flighty actress who'd won a minor part on one of Disney Channel's shows. Soon, they began tossing a few mistimed punches hoping for someone to break up the fight before, God forbid, they bruised a cheek or suffered a black eye – *or egad, split a lip.* Peters reached to check on his swollen nose.

"This is serious. Understand? Very, very serious. A provoked whale attack could become a major international incident."

"I'm telling you, the bloody beast attacked us."

"Dirk . . .," Marley said, as if he were addressing a wayward child. "Optics, my boy. Optics."

Peters fell silent.

"The investors at Utami are very upset, Dirk. Your situation is delicate to say the least. Whatever you do, don't do anything else stupid. Hear me? Lay low until we think of a way to extract you."

"I'm not in bloody North Korea."

"You might as well be."

"Now that you mention it, it feels a bit that way, yes."

"I got to go now, Dirk. But understand how serious this is. It made the front page of *The New York Post*."

"What was the headline?"

"Call me Dirk, Brit Pitchman Incites Whale Attack."

"Pitchman?" Peters asked, aghast.

"I have to go, Dirk. Remember, don't do anything stupid. Understand? Stay away from the media – especially TMZ. Those blokes will tear you apart."

Marley rang off. Peters slowly reached for the clicker and snapped on CNN. The banner scrawl on the bottom of the screen flashed, *Actor Dirk Peters Involved in Maine Whale Attack.*

Despite himself, and despite how much it hurt to do so, Peters managed a smile. "Actor." That was much better. And he loved publicity, any publicity.

Actor Dirk Peters . . .

He loved the sound of it. But his pleasure dissipated as he thought of *The Post.*

Pitchman . . .

He simply could not live with that moniker, no matter how accurate.

With glazed eyes, he stared at the TV as the female anchor with poofy blonde hair and enough makeup to paint the hull of a cruise ship, turned to the story on the coast of Maine.

British Actor Dirk Peters was involved in a serious incident off the Maine coast yesterday. In a rare attack, his vessel was struck and sunk by a minke whale. The captain of the charter boat, Horace Maddox, refused to be interviewed, but denies any wrongdoing. Peters was unavailable for comment, and a spokesperson for the actor couldn't be reached.

"That's because I don't have a fookin' spokesperson," Peters grumbled. His agent had deserted him a few years before.

Seconds later, a Department of Marine Resources biologist wearing wire-rimmed glasses was being interviewed on a wharf overlooking Spring Harbor.

Reporter: Do minke whales normally attack vessels?

Marine Biologist: Hardly ever.

Reporter: Then what might cause such an event?

Marine Biologist: Provocation. The whale might have felt endangered, especially if it was protecting its calf.

Reporter: What would provocation entail?

Marine Biologist: The boat got too close. The passenger tried to touch the whale with his hand or an object. Or worse, someone on the boat tried to harm the whale.

Reporter: Harm it?

Marine Biologist: That's right. Stick it with a sharp object. Throw something at it. Or worse . . .

Reporter: What could be worse?

Marine Biologist: Shoot it.

Reporter: Shoot it?

Marine Biologist: That's right.

73

Reporter: Who would do that?

Marine Biologist: Someone deranged. Someone who doesn't respect these amazing mammals.

The camera cut to stock footage of a sinister factory whaling ship in rough, overcast seas firing explosive harpoons at an unsuspecting whale.

Reporter: What is the penalty for provoking or harming a whale?

Marine Biologist: Fines up to $50,000 and a year in prison if convicted. The laws for harming whales aren't tough enough. Maybe this incident will wake people up to the harm mankind inflicts on these magnificent creatures.

Peters swore, grabbed the clicker, and flipped the television off. He hadn't done a bloody thing to the whale. He was innocent, and he was being painted as a psychotic criminal. He shivered thinking about the implications of spending a year in some American dungeon. He'd heard stories. He gulped. With his looks, he wouldn't last a week.

On a whim, Peters reached for his phone. His head felt like someone was pounding a hammer into his temple. For the first time, he checked his video feed and found the footage he'd taken of the lobsterman hauling traps the day before. He forwarded the video to moments before the whale struck Maddox's boat. He watched with growing interest as the tumultuous scene unfolded. Despite the whale plowing into the vessel, Peters marveled at the way he'd been able to keep the camera steady.

And then he saw it. He shot up off the bed and began pacing around the cramped room running his hand through the hair that once made women swoon. He watched it again and again. It was a gift from heaven. Out of context, the video depicted a damning narrative for the lobsterman. Marley would be ecstatic. Utami would soar, and if Peters played it right, it wouldn't be long before Dirk Peters and his hair would be making women swoon once again on his way to becoming a very, very rich man.

The first floor of the Stringer Cottage looked like a bomb had burst. Furniture piled in corners, drop cloths covering the floors, and wallpaper peeled off to reveal glue-stained, eighty-year-old plasterboard. The kitchen was ready for granite counters and paint, and Pixie had ordered new stainless-steel appliances to replace the ancient stove and refrigerator. The first-floor bathroom would be next – a new vanity, fancy sink, pretty paint, and a fresh coat of polyurethane on the pine floors.

Pixie was putting the finishing touches on a kitchen cabinet when she heard a knock and set her paint brush carefully on a paper towel. When she opened the door, a Fed Ex man held out a thin cardboard envelope and asked her to sign for delivery. Pixie eyed him carefully, as if to say, "how'd you find me?" and moments later, after he'd left, peeled open the package to discover an envelope addressed to her in a severe font with the venerable law firm Garner, Winston, and Burr. The letter read:

Dear Ms. McGee,
RE: DEMAND FOR RETURN OF ENGAGEMENT RING AND REIMBURSEMENT FOR DAMAGES

We represent Spencer Tate in the matter referenced above and are writing to demand immediate action regarding the return of his engagement ring, as well as reimbursement for damages resulting from a reckless and spendthrift evening at Ferrar.

As you are undoubtedly aware, Mr. Tate and you recently concluded what was intended to be a joyous and celebratory evening, culminating in your committing an irresponsible and egregious act. Regrettably, the events that transpired thereafter have necessitated our involvement.

It has come to our attention that while dining at Ferrar, you engaged in a series of extravagant expenditures, which included, but were not limited to, an exorbitant bill incurred at Ferrar, totaling a staggering sum of $118,751. Furthermore, despite the termination of the engagement, you have failed to return the engagement ring to Mr. Tate, a possession of sentimental and considerable financial value.

It is our client's position that these actions constitute a breach of your fiduciary duty to exercise reasonable care in handling shared assets and a reckless disregard for the financial well-being of both parties involved. Consequently, we hereby demand the following:

1. The immediate return of the Cartier engagement ring to Mr. Spencer Tate. Failure to comply with this demand will result in legal action to recover the ring.

2. Reimbursement to Mr. Tate in the amount of $137,751.05, representing the expenses incurred at Ferrar and unauthorized use of the League's Gulfstream G550 due to your reckless behavior.

Please be advised that should you fail to meet these demands within 30 days, we will not hesitate to pursue all available legal remedies to secure the return of the ring and seek restitution for the damages incurred.

We trust that you will take prompt action to remunerate our client as specified above.

Sincerely,
Cornelious Burr, Esq.
Managing Partner
Garner, Winston, and Burr

Pixie crumpled the letter and tossed it on the dusty kitchen floor. So, Spencer couldn't walk away. The bill from Ferrar, the engagement ring, the cost of using the League jet, they added up to piddly in his world of rarified air. His net worth was staggering. He had to have the last say by sticking it to Pixie because no one gives the middle finger and walks away from Spencer Tate. The Cartier ring meant nothing to her, but for some reason, she knew she'd fight to keep it to hold Spencer accountable for his philandering and lying ways. As for Ferrar, the exorbitant bill served Spencer right. The man stood her up to roll around with some cheap floozy. Let Spencer set his hounds loose. Let him threaten her with highfalutin' lawyers. She looked out the kitchen window at the Atlantic and at the gray, billowy storm clouds building on the horizon. If that's the way he wants to play it, fine, Pixie thought. Spencer wasn't threatening a pauper. She could easily write a check for the dinner – and to buy the ring if she wanted it, for that matter. But it was the principle, and besides, a good fight might be just the thing. She'd punch back.

She gritted her teeth and started to scheme, but suddenly she felt an empty, hollow feeling wash over her. She thought about the night before and Caleb Gray turning away and leaving the restaurant after he spotted her with the Dirkwad. When he'd left Ebb Tide, she'd felt a visceral tug, as if she wanted to follow him into the night and more. *Much, much more.* She knew she'd never felt anything as deep and primordial with Spencer. Pixie tried to shake off the feeling of longing. But it wouldn't go away, like the letter crumpled on the floor, reminding her that life was loaded with disappointment and heartache.

Pixie picked up her paintbrush and turned to the unfinished cabinet. She'd do what she always did, bury herself in something to make her forget. It was an age-old remedy. And with a sigh, she knew in her heart it wasn't working.

Then it struck her. Pixie broke into a mischievous smile, set the paintbrush aside, and reached down and picked up the crumpled letter. Spencer wasn't going to get the last word. *No siree.*

Pixie left the house and climbed into the Cadillac and soon found herself at the fish counter at the IGA. Myrna Thompson, who wore cat glasses and had worked at the grocery store for as long as anyone could remember, wrapped a mackerel in butcher paper and handed the fish to Pixie. "There you go," Thompson said. "Broil it, honey, and it won't be so oily."

"I'm not cooking it," Pixie said with a grin.

Thompson shook her head. "You going to make that sushi? I hear you can get worms. Not me. I cook everything."

"I've got something else in mind."

Thompson gave her a quizzical look as Pixie headed to the checkout.

In the parking lot, Pixie popped open the Brougham's ancient trunk and opened a small cardboard box. She took the letter Spencer's attorney had sent and wrapped it over the butcher paper so the print was face up and secured it with a strip of packing tape. She placed the wrapped mackerel in the box and taped the box shut. She took the folded sheet of paper with the address she'd written in curly swirls before taping it on the front of the box.

Ten minutes later, in the tiny white clapboard post office tucked off Main Street, the postmistress eyed the package and sniffed suspiciously. "Would you like to send the package Priority Mail?"

Pixie pursed her lips and said, "How about by dog sled?" She smiled. "What's the slowest delivery you got?"

The Postmistress gave her a quizzical look. "Ground. It can take a week to ten days. It depends."

Pixie tapped her fingers lightly on the counter. "That's just the thing this baby needs."

The Postmistress sniffed again and read the name on the mailing address. "Spencer Tate."

Pixie pulled a credit card out of her purse and handed it to the woman. "That's right. I'm sending him a little reminder of the good times we had."

The postmistress studied the package and sniffed once more. "Cologne?"

Pixie grinned. "From Paree." 'Paree, Texas,' Pixie thought to herself with a smile as she turned to leave.

Chapter Eleven—The Marine Institute of the Pacific

The Board meeting for the Marine Institute of the Pacific had ended, and Senator Jonathan Tyler stood on the institute's terrace overlooking Hacienda Bay drinking a Chateau Montelena from a landfill-bound plastic cup. He chatted with a socialite who'd married the CEO of a multi-billion-dollar Silicone Valley tech company as the hazy sun set over the Pacific. The woman had made her own mark as a philanthropist who supported a myriad of environmental causes while she and her husband's carbon footprint spread like sewage as they danced around the world in a corporate jet.

Tyler had won a heated election running as an environmentalist with Green Party leanings. He had all the bonafides: drove a Prius, had solar panels installed on the roof of his home, took back country camping trips to Zion with his family, wore faded flannel shirts to the local hardware store on Saturday mornings, and made sure he and his wife championed organic farms by buying produce at local farmers' markets.

No one knew about his dirty secret, the hidden investments that had been meticulously chosen. His portfolio included petrochemical, oil and gas, and mining and metal asset holdings. He'd secretly invested in a venture capital multinational real estate company that was mired in controversy, trying to develop a large parcel of rainforest in Costa Rica to build a luxury hotel complex which included a golf course through the jungle. And his commitment to use his office to hamstring the lobster industry had yielded him a large, undisclosed stake in Utami, a company he had high hopes for, especially after he'd pressed the institute to publicly call for a ban on lobstering. If the data on their impact on whales was a little dubious, well, he wasn't counting on many votes from lobstermen anytime soon. He was happy to masquerade as Green because that's what wins elections in California, but he was damn sure not going to let his nest egg languish due to squishy politics.

Since they had been in constant contact after that fool actor was involved in the whale strike, it was no surprise when he felt his burner phone vibrate and saw that Marley was calling him. He stepped away from the socialite with a glance at his phone and an apologetic shrug as if to say, *always politics, a Senator's cross to bear*, and took Marley's call on the far side of the terrace.

"I think we've got something big, Jonathan," Marley said with excitement. "Very, very big."

Tyler pushed the phone closer to his ear. "What's going on, Marley?"

"This could seal the deal. It's devastating." Marley gave a high-pitched laugh.

"How so?"

"I'll send you the video."

"To my ghost account."

"Righto."

"And Marley . . . It doesn't matter if we bring that industry to its knees if you produce lobster meat that tastes like shit."

"Don't worry. We're working on it."

"You better be."

"Wait until you see the footage. It's smashing."

"Send it."

"Will do, old boy. Will do."

Tyler stepped away from the railing and looked out at the bay. He noticed a sea otter swimming in the kelp below. He felt a warm hand on his wrist. It was Sandy Francois, the institute's director. She smiled at him knowingly and subtly tapped her watch. A divorced woman in her early forties, she had dazzling blue eyes and short cut auburn hair set-off by high cheekbones. Soon they would rendezvous in Santa Cruz at a hotel tucked away from the harbor. Tyler tried to hide his excitement and said, "our man at Utami has something for us."

Francois smiled. "I hope it's good."

Tyler nodded. Francois had been an excellent accomplice.

"Will I have all of you tonight?" she whispered, a smile pursing her lips.

"Every bit."

"Delicious," Francois murmured before sauntering away to the other side of the terrace.

The call came the next day from Lou Farnham. Caleb was on the wharf repairing traps when his phone buzzed. It had been too rough to fish. Heavy, overcast clouds hung above, and the wind swept from the northeast, churning up white caps in the bay.

"Have you seen it?" Farnham asked, his voice a mixture of expectation and triumph.

"Seen what, Lou?" Caleb had dealt with Farnham before. Over the years, Farnham had covered a variety of stories for *The Bangor Times*, including the continuing saga of the lobster industry. Farnham relished fomenting scandal.

"You have a problem. A big problem, Caleb."

Caleb felt his neck stiffen. "Is that right?"

"You've hit the bigtime. You're trending on the internet."

Caleb frowned.

"Every environmental group wants your head."

Caleb grunted and put one foot up on a trap. He felt a chill race up his spine. He tried to steady his voice. "Tell me more, Lou. What bullshit are you slinging today?"

"Oh, this story is real. And it smells bad. Real bad. Seems you provoked and tried to kill the whale that sunk Maddox's boat. Tried to harpoon it with a gaff."

"Not true."

"The video suggests otherwise. And the Englishman painted a grim picture. Do you have a statement for me?"

Caleb's mind raced. He thought of the Brit videotaping when the minke struck Maddox's boat. Caleb had grabbed the gaff out of instinct.

Farnham sighed. "I suggest you get your side of the story out before the feds lock you up. You want to go on record?"

"Not a chance."

"Suit yourself. I've already spoken to the higher-ups in Augusta, not to mention Greenhaven."

"Go away, Lou." Caleb remembered how Farnham had pursued him at the Senate hearing. He could tell the reporter smelled blood in the water. "Find someone else to harass."

Farnham gave a short laugh. "Suit yourself."

"Do me a favor."

"What's that?"

"Don't call me anymore." Caleb punched off his phone and felt his pulse beating hard. He typed his name and did a google search. His heart began to sink when he discovered the video had gone viral.

When he watched the clip, his hands began to shake and the blood rushed to his face. The sequence of events was deceptive. The Brit narrated in dramatic tones as the footage showed Caleb gripping the gaff by his ear, as if he were throwing a javelin at the minke, which was no more than a few feet from the *Mary G.* In his other hand, he held the lobster he'd been showing to the Englishman. The lobster's back was arched and its claws extended as if Caleb was squeezing the marrow out of it. Caleb had the look of the hunter. His eyes were steady, his jaw set, and neck muscles taut. Anyone who watched the video would think he was determined to kill, a modern-day Ahab. And as the whale began to sound under Caleb's boat, the video stopped, leaving the deadly impression that he had plunged a gaff into a minke whale.

Caleb thought of the time-tested truism: *no good deed goes unpunished.* He'd been hauling traps, minding his own business, when Maddox and the Brit had shown up. He'd rescued them after the whale strike and been repaid with lies. Caleb took a deep breath and looked past Frenchman's Bay to open water. His first instinct was to find that Englishman and pummel him. His second was to climb aboard the *Mary G.* and head to sea. Instead, he grabbed his work gloves and pliers and started up the rampway to his truck.

Fifteen minutes later, Caleb's heart sank when he spotted the Bangor news station vans parked in front of his house. He stepped on the brakes and came to a halt. The media hung like buzzards on the hard-packed dirt road that ran past his century old two-bedroom Cape. An overgrown bed of orange and yellow daylilies sprinkled with blooming catmint that Mary once lovingly tended ran along the front of the home, and next to the work shed, lobster traps were stacked nearby. Caleb's instinct told him to turn the pickup around before he was spotted and drive away. Previous encounters with Lou Farnham taught Caleb that the media would try to pin him to the wall. He'd learned that perception became truth. He suspected that there was nothing he could say that would alter the image now ingrained in viewers' minds of him towering over the minke with a gaff in his hand.

As Caleb turned his pickup around, he could hear his phone blowing up. Texts poured in and the cell rang intermittently as he pulled onto the empty Old Bangor Road. Then suddenly, his phone went silent. He knew on this stretch cell phone coverage died. He was trying to get his head around what his next move should be when he saw a dog lying in the ditch that ran along the road. It was as big as a bear cub with black fur, rust-colored paws, and a splash of white on its chest. Caleb didn't recognize it. He pulled over and hopped out of his truck. One of the dog's hind legs splayed unnaturally, and it was bleeding from several wounds, but it was clearly alive as it panted heavily. Undoubtedly, the Bernese Mountain Dog had been struck by a car.

Caleb knelt and noticed the dog didn't have tags and looked emaciated. There was no shine on its fur and the dog didn't raise its large head when Caleb reached out and patted it. "You're in rough shape, old boy. I need to get you to a vet."

As the overcast skies gave way to rain, Caleb gently picked up the dog and carried the animal back to his truck. Despite his care, the dog gave a short yelp when he laid him on the bench seat. The rain started to pick up and was now collecting on the dash. Caleb closed the passenger door and walked around to the driver's side. When he turned the key in the ignition, he heard a grinding sound. He tried to start the engine again and cursed when he was met with silence. Caleb knew immediately it was the starter. He shook his head and looked at the dog with growing panic. Caleb's heart started to beat hard, as the injured animal brought back a memory Caleb had buried for years. He'd been a boy when Tack, the family mutt, had broken away from its run and sprinted across the road. A neighbor didn't have a chance to swerve. Tack died as nine-year old Caleb held the dog in his arms with tears streaming down his cheeks.

Caleb softly patted the dog and told himself it wasn't going to happen again. He thought for a moment and realized waiting for a car to pass on a deserted road was a non-starter. He would carry the dog a quarter mile to Millbridge Island and see if Elrod Tibbetts was at the Stringer Cottage.

He hopped out of the truck and a minute later was walking in the driving rain across the Millbridge Island bridge with his adrenaline running high and a dying Bernese Mountain dog in his aching arms. He felt the cold rain on his cheeks. "Hang in there, old boy. I'm going to get you help."

Caleb swore when he didn't see Elrod's truck in the small dirt parking area. The vintage Cadillac Eldorado Brougham sat alone with its gleaming white walls, polished chrome grill, and shiny tail fins. Caleb had heard that Elrod put hours and hours into lovingly restoring the car with Davis, the football coach, and his assistant. He wondered if the woman was there, but hoped like hell the Englishman wasn't. Caleb wasn't sure if he could contain his fury if he came face to face with the Brit.

Lights were on so he sloshed up the path to the cottage. His shoulders burned and his clothes were soaked and heavy when he approached the kitchen door and called Elrod's name. He waited a few seconds, called again, and heard footsteps above the pouring rain. The door swung open and she stood in front of him with her blonde hair in a ponytail, a smear of white latex on her cheek, holding a paintbrush in one hand.

For an instant, her azure eyes sparkled when they met his, but when she noticed the dog's back leg and dire condition, they winced with concern. "Oh, my," she said, retreating as Caleb moved out of the rain and entered the kitchen. He was immediately hit by the smell of fresh paint and polyurethane as he stood on a drop cloth holding the dog and dripping water.

"Is Elrod here?" Caleb asked.

The woman shook her head and gently put her hand out and rubbed the dog's ear. "Bless your heart. What happened?"

"I found him in a ditch. My truck died, and I need to get him to a vet." The woman turned and quickly set the paint brush down. She grabbed a raincoat and the car keys hanging on a hook near the door and said, "I'll drive you."

"You don't have to do that. I can take the old car if you think it would be alright."

"Don't be silly. You need help, and I'm happy to do it." She ran her hand along the dog's-soaked head. "You poor thing. We're going to get you all fixed up."

Caleb stood frozen as she tugged on her coat.

"What are you waiting for?" she asked. "Chop, chop."

With the dog resting on one of the drop cloths in the Brougham's spacious back seat, they soon headed off the peninsula. There was no veterinarian in Spring Harbor. The closest vet was fifty minutes away in Bangor. Caleb rode in his soggy clothes as the woman sped past a farmhouse and a field of purple and white lupine bending in the wind and rain. The Cadillac's wipers beat as the woman clutched the large 50's-era steering wheel and craned to see over the dash. Elrod had done a beautiful job restoring the car, which now smelled like a blend of leather, vinyl, and wet fur.

Caleb alternated between checking on the animal and stealing surreptitious glances at the woman. She was glamorous, even with paint smeared on her cheek and her light almond-colored hair clasped in a ponytail. The delicate straight nose, sculpted cheekbones, small hands, the clearest skin Caleb had seen despite the faint crow's feet around her deeply pooled eyes, which sparkled with hints of blue and green. She had a steeliness about her, too. Never mind the twang and the "shucks." She was a force to be reckoned with. He'd seen it with Mr. Important, with his helicopter, and just now as Caleb stood on the Stringer Cottage lawn. The woman didn't mince words. She wasn't necessarily imperious but had an air of command.

The image of her and the Englishman at Ebb Tide made no sense. Whatever could she see in that vain and manipulative man? To get his mind off the Brit, he turned once again to check on the dog, who continued to pant and give an occasional yelp of pain. He thought about trying to strike up a conversation, but he didn't know where to start.

Mary had been the only one who could break through his introversion. She'd been playful with him during high school. Out of the blue, in the spring of their senior year, she'd asked him to the prom. He'd been dumbfounded. At the end of prom night, after the music stopped and the gym emptied, they'd found themselves sitting on the granite bluff on Millbridge Island, shoulders nearly touching, looking at the cold stars and the sliver of moon casting a thin light on the sea. He felt overwhelmed by her nearness and the fresh, clean smell of her hair when she shocked him, blew him away, by whispering that she loved him in a voice beyond her years. It was full of warmth and conviction, empathy and insight, as if she knew his strengths and limitations, assessed them, and was now offering her pronouncement in his favor. In that moment, he knew he loved her too and that there would never be anyone else. And there hadn't been.

Caleb awoke from his reverie with the awareness that they were moving at an alarming speed. The Brougham's massive 330 HP V-

8 hummed. He glanced at the speedometer and saw the woman had the car racing at 85 mph. He wanted to close his eyes.

"Don't kill us," he said finally after she navigated a subtle curve.

A smile crossed Pixie's lips. "You don't think I can drive this queen?"

"That's not what I said."

"I drove an Indy car once. Had that buggy going 165." She paused and tapped the steering wheel with her forefinger. "Twenty-five glorious laps at Texas Motor Speedway. Bing Cleaver said I was a natural."

"Bing Cleaver?"

"You never heard of Bing? One of the most famous drivers on the circuit? Mr. NAPA Auto Parts? Bridgestone tires? Whew. Where have you been?"

Pixie paused.

"Ole Bing wanted to date me bad. He kept calling and calling. I didn't want nothing to do with him. But that didn't stop me from asking to drive his car. One day he invited me to the track and handed me a helmet with a smirk. I said, 'Just you watch.' He kept on smirking as if to say, 'you won't break 60.' After I finished the last lap and tugged my helmet off and shook my hair loose, his mouth was hanging open like I'd kicked him you know where. He asked, 'where'd you learn to drive?' I just smiled and let him ponder. I don't have time for men who underestimate me."

"This isn't an Indy car, and these roads aren't a track."

"No. But we have our poor friend in the backseat. Trust me, darlin'. I'll get us there."

Caleb noticed a bend approaching. He was about to say something when the woman turned to him and said, "You going to ask how I learned to drive?"

"How?" Caleb asked, putting his hand on the dash and bracing himself as the woman took the curve.

"Karts." She glanced at him as they sped by another farmhouse perched on the side of the road. Behind the house and barn, a large field led to a stand of pines bordering the property. "One of my momma's friends, and believe you me, she had a lot of 'friends', took me to the dirt track. I learned fast. He didn't have a dime to his name, but he loved to race karts. When my momma finally kicked him out, I felt bad. He was one of the few I liked."

Caleb braved a glance at the dog. The Berner took short, uneven breaths. Its eyes were closed and its soaked head rested on crossed paws. Caleb looked at his phone. Earlier he'd turned off the notification volume. The texts were piling up. He had six missed calls. In a moment of resignation, he switched off the cell. He imagined a news helicopter circling his house and was thankful that the news stations in Bangor were too small to own one.

Pixie turned and asked, "How come you haven't asked my name? I'm nearly offended." She smiled. Her teeth were even and a brilliant white.

Caleb shrugged.

"Well, It's Pixie. It's not much, but it's what my momma gave me. I've done the best I can with it, but sometimes my best falls short, Mr. Caleb Gray."

A look of surprise crossed Caleb's face.

"Elrod told me your name. I'm sorry I barked at you on the lawn with Spencer. Sometimes I forget my manners."

"No apology needed."

"I'm sorry that Spencer damaged your truck. He's a rat."

Caleb nodded.

"And I'm ashamed of what I said to you. Elrod said I stepped in it. It's not the first time."

Caleb glanced at her. "How would you have known?"

"I wouldn't have. But it was a dumbass thing to say anyway, given I didn't know a thing about you." She gave him a quick glance before navigating another turn. "I'm sorry about the missus."

Caleb nodded.

"She must have been a special woman. I can tell. I know these things. You have that look."

"What kind of look is that?"

"It's a look that says you're solid and real. Special women gravitate to that look. I know it. In my experience, they see it and value it before the man even knows it about himself. Tell me the truth, she made the first move, didn't she?"

The dog gave a short groan. Caleb turned his head to check on the Berner. He was glad of the interruption because his heart was too full to allow an answer. Pixie said to the dog, looking in the rearview mirror, "Oh, honey, you hang in there. Hear me?" Pixie punched the accelerator. The car started moving even faster. The fields and occasional houses were a blur as the Cadillac raced off the peninsula. Pixie tightened both hands on the wheel, concentrating. Caleb gripped the handle on the door.

Suddenly, Caleb had to know. He blurted, "Are you seeing the Englishman?"

"Oh, gawd. No."

Caleb stayed silent.

"I may have bad taste in men, aka Spencer Tate, but Dirk the Lurk?"

Caleb broke into a smile.

"He sidled up next to me stinking drunk and put his paw around me. But even I'm smart enough to steer clear of snakes like Dirk Peters. In my dumbest moments, I wouldn't have fallen for Dirk the Lurk. He ruined my dinner." She sighed. "My whole life I've attracted hound dogs. Spencer Tate included."

Caleb felt an urge to tell Pixie what the Englishman had done to him. He wanted to tell her about the video and the trouble in which he found himself. But he grew up in a home where you didn't share your troubles. His family mirrored the cold, rugged granite coast where they'd made their living for generations. You took whatever life dropped at your feet and dealt with it. Alone.

"I thought you two . . .," Caleb said, his voice drifting away.

"Thought what?" Pixie's voice rose.

"Might have had something going."

Pixie took her eyes off the road and glanced at Caleb for an instant. He noticed her eyes narrowing and boring into his as the rain swept down and the wipers slapped back and forth. "I misjudged you. I didn't think you were capable of jealousy."

Pixie's words struck Caleb like lightning. "Jealousy?"

"I call it like it is. And it warms my heart, darlin'."

Caleb blushed. He felt self-conscious, as if she'd returned him to the awkward teenager he'd been.

Pixie smiled. Her eyes crinkled, and she reached over and touched his arm. Her fingers were soft and warm on his wrist. *Electric*. As quickly as she'd reached over, she pulled her hand away and placed it on the steering wheel. "Don't mind me. I'm just joshin' you. Now let's get this poor thing to the vet."

Chapter Twelve—Ahab

The animal hospital sat up on a hill off the Old Bangor Road and overlooked a narrow stretch of the Penobscot River. The vet had converted a century-old Victorian home surrounded by leafy hardwoods that dripped in the rain.

Pixie and Caleb entered the reception area which was once a sprawling sitting room. The area was decorated with ornate crown molding and a large open-hearth fireplace that looked as if it hadn't been lit in years. Linoleum had been slapped over what had once shown white oak. A half dozen people sat in orange plastic chairs lining the room with their dogs and cats, waiting for the vet. An older woman with a kind face and arthritic fingers kept a lime-green parrot in a cage at her feet, shouting, "Tiki, Tiki, behave!" – while the parrot stalked angrily back and forth on its rung, shrieking as if it was high atop a kapok tree in the Amazon. Every time the bird squawked, a German Shepherd would let out a guttural, intimidating growl, and strike up a symphony of howling dogs and hissing cats.

Caleb held the injured Bernese on his lap while he and Pixie waited. The damp Bernese lay still in Caleb's arms with its eyes closed, its breathing uneven and labored. Caleb glanced at his watch. They'd been waiting for nearly thirty minutes. Caleb looked around the waiting room. The other animals didn't seem to be in life-threatening situations. Not wanting the stricken animal to die in his arms, he was about to gently give the dog to Pixie and ask why the delay when she beat him to it, rising from her chair and approaching the receptionist with a steely look. Caleb heard some low murmuring and then Pixie's voice rise. "Chop, chop," she said for the whole room to hear, and with that the receptionist quickly disappeared into another room behind her office.

Pixie turned to Caleb and shook her head. "Sometimes you gotta light a fire."

The old woman with the parrot pursed her lips and said, "You tell that woman, honey!"

Pixie smiled and said, "It won't be long now."

Pixie was right. Within a minute, Pixie and Caleb were led into a room with a vinyl-covered examination table, a medicine cabinet, and a small metal table on which a canister full of cotton balls rested.

On the wall hung a large, framed photograph of two sleek Irish Setters racing across a snow-covered field.

"What happened?" the vet asked when he came into the room. In his early fifties, he wore blue scrubs and wire-rimmed glasses beneath a shock of graying hair.

"I found him on the side of the road. He got hit by a car. He's starving, too."

"Where'd you find him?"

"Spring Harbor."

The vet raised the dog's eyelids. "Jaundiced." He turned to Pixie. "Does your husband always do good deeds?"

"A regular Boy Scout," Pixie answered, flashing a smile at Caleb.

Caleb said, "We aren't married."

"Sorry," said the veterinarian without looking up from his examination.

"Oh, but doesn't he wish," Pixie chirped. "He's been trying to get the nerve to slip that ring on for years."

Caleb felt his cheeks redden. "She was kind enough to drive me after my truck died."

The vet leaned over and manipulated the dog's injured leg. The Berner yelped. "Sorry," the vet whispered to the dog. "We'll get you fixed up."

"Is he going to be okay?" Caleb asked with concern.

"I'm going to stabilize him and get him into surgery this afternoon. He's got some broken bones, and he's underfed and hurting, but he'll make it." The vet shook his head. "How anyone could treat an animal so cruelly . . . I see it all the time."

Caleb was about to ask more questions when the receptionist opened the door and beckoned to the vet. "Can I speak with you for a moment?" she asked.

The vet raised his eyebrows and left the room. As Caleb caught the muffled sounds of a conversation on the other side of the door, Pixie sighed and gently rubbed the Berner's ears. Caleb noticed a white stripe on Pixie's lightly tanned finger where her engagement ring had been – the ring Spencer Tate had demanded she return before calling her "trailer trash."

Caleb knew trailer trash. The woman next to him was anything but. She looked spectacular in her faded jeans, white t-shirt, and ponytail. She wore small diamond earrings and the splotch of paint on her cheek completed the portrait. No, not trailer trash. That was for sure.

Pixie looked up and smiled. "Thank goodness he's going to be okay," she said. Caleb nodded and realized with a flash that Pixie was right. When he'd seen her with the Englishman, he'd felt a jolt of anger, so much so that he had to leave Ebb Tide. He'd told himself that it was just his dislike for the Brit, but now he realized he wasn't being honest. And then with this dog throwing them together by fate had Caleb wondering if it was time for him to reenter the world. Pixie's joke had truth to it.

A moment later, the door swung open and the vet and the receptionist came into the room. With narrow eyes and an angry expression, the vet tapped on the phone he was holding and held the screen in front of Caleb. To Caleb's dismay, the minke whale video began to roll.

Stunned, as if the air was sucked from the room, Caleb took a step back. As the video played, the vet's face showed his disgust. Caleb noticed that Pixie's eyes grew confused as she watched.

"Do you hunt whales for fun, Mr. Gray?" the vet asked, his voice full of malice.

Caleb was too shocked to speak. He grew angry as he heard the Englishman, in that ludicrous voice, narrate the video. Caleb could feel the tips of his ears grow hot and his neck stiffen.

"You're an internet sensation. Over a million hits. Whale hunter," the vet sneered. "Talk about cruelty. Guys like you give lobstermen a bad name. You ought to be ashamed."

"I didn't hurt the whale. I had no intention of throwing the gaff. The video distorts what really happened. And that Englishman is lying through his teeth."

The vet rolled his eyes.

"I'm telling the truth."

"Tell that to the feds. I hope they lock you up." The vet pulled the phone away from Caleb's face and set it on the metal table. "I don't like you. As a matter of fact, I detest you, but that won't stop me from treating the dog. You can go now. The woman can stay, but I don't want any part of you. Understand?"

"I didn't hurt the whale," Caleb said, his face darkening, his fists tightening.

The vet pointed at the door. "Out."

"Hold on," Pixie said, pointing at the vet with a wisp of hair in her eyes. "Didn't you hear him?"

"I heard him," the vet said, "and I don't believe him."

"If a tiger was running at you all hot and bothered, and you had a spear in that hand of yours, wouldn't you raise it in defense?"

"A minke whale's not a tiger. It's a docile mammal until it's provoked."

"You weren't on that boat, so you don't know. And you're taking the word of the internet over a man who's gone to great lengths to save a dog he found by the side of a road? How can you call yourself a man of science?"

"Ridiculous," the vet mumbled, shaking his head. "You're asking me to trust you instead of my eyes. I know what I saw in that video." He looked at Caleb. "Go."

Caleb glanced at Pixie and at the Berner, whose breathing was growing even more labored and painful, and said, "I'll be in the car." He turned to the vet. "You can think anything you want, but I didn't harm the whale."

The vet stared at him stonily and turned to the dog in silence.

Twenty minutes later, as a thunderstorm swept through, bending trees and driving curtains of rain across the gravel parking lot, Pixie ran to the Cadillac with her hood pulled tight and hopped into the car. Without a word, Caleb tossed his phone between them on the bench seat. He'd checked his messages. Friends wanted to know what happened, a few environmental crazies had found his number and left scathing, threatening voicemails, and to top it off, he had calls from the state police in Augusta, and Ed Pratt, Spring Harbor's Police Chief.

As Pixie pulled out of the lot, she said, "Well, the good news is that poor old pooch is going to be okay, the bad . . ."

Looking straight ahead, Caleb said, "Thank you for standing up for me back there."

"'When you're in a pickle, hop out of the jar,' my momma used to say."

He glanced at his phone sitting and rubbed his temples. "Over a million hits and counting and a call from the state police."

Pixie frowned. "What in God's green earth happened?"

Caleb shook his head. "The Brit's lying about what happened. I just don't know why."

"Tell me more. Don't hold nothin' back."

Caleb turned to her. His head throbbed and his mouth felt dry, but as rain pounded on the roof of the Cadillac, he began to recount the story.

Dirk Peters couldn't get enough of the video. He'd watched it dozens of times, enchanted by his mellifluous narration and astonished by the internet sensation he'd created. Beyond Instagram, the footage of the whale had exploded on TikTok and run wild on news feeds around the world. In a few short hours, Peters had gone from actor "has been" to celebrity whistleblower. He'd already done interviews on KTTV in LA and, to his delight, the BBC World Service. Around the globe, Dirk Peters was becoming a household name . . . again. He was being portrayed as heroic. The man who risked his life to film a brute about to spike a whale with a gaff. When asked if the lobsterman had indeed impaled the leviathan and caused the whale to ram Maddock's boat, Peters coyly recounted how he wasn't sure but thought he'd seen a slick of blood in the water. Better yet, Marley and the powers at Utami were ecstatic. The video was beyond their wildest dreams. Greenhaven and the rest of the fist-shaking, tree-hugging mobs wanted Caleb Gray's head, not to mention a harpoon driven through the lobster industry's heart.

Suddenly, he heard a pounding on the motel door. "It's me, Dirkster. Maddox. Open up, buddy boy."

The elation Peters felt tumbled away. Peters wondered how Maddox had found him. Peters pulled the covers over his head and pretended to sleep. He could hear Maddox's breathing and the shuffle of feet.

Maddox's tone sharpened. "I know you're in there, Dirkster. The lady at the desk told me. There's no hiding from Horace Maddox." Maddox pounded on the door again. "I got nowhere to go. I slept in my car last night."

"I'm bloody napping. Come back later."

He'd had enough of Maddox. Peters had grudgingly thrust a few dollars in Maddox's hand after the boat had met Davey Jones' locker but then had extricated himself from his company as fast as he could.

"I thought we were buddies. I thought we had each other's backs," Maddox snorted. "So that's the way it's going to be? Huh? Huh, Dirkster? I thought you were bigger than that. A stand-up guy. Was I ever wrong."

"Can't you let a man take his rest?" Peters knew he'd need to deal with Maddox at some point, but Marley hadn't given him any guidance, so stalling seemed like the best plan.

"Hmmm. You're a big shot now. An internet sensation. Filmed a whale attack with that idiot Caleb Gray holding a gaff in his hand. And oh boy, the voice over, Dirkster. First rate. Sounded like a National Geographic special. Poor whale minding its own business and this moronic lobsterman picks a fight. It makes for a great story except . . ." Maddox's voice trailed off.

Peters tugged the sheets down and raised his head. "Except what?"

Maddox gave a sinister laugh. "Except that it's not true. It's total fiction, Dirkster. You don't want that to get out, do you? Dirk Peters, Hollywood star, big shot, made the whole thing up. See how much of a big kahuna you'd be then."

"Easy, Horace. I thought I was doing you a favor, mate. Didn't you say you wanted to obliterate the lobstering industry? You don't want to back out when we've just started do you?"

"Try me. I lost my boat – a tragedy – my life possessions, my . . . dignity . . . and all I'm asking for is a small helping hand from someone who I thought was my buddy. And now you turn your back on the one person who knows what happened yesterday and is willing to go along with it for a small price."

"Define 'small price'?"

"One hundred grand."

"What!" Peters shot off the bed and flung open the door. Maddox stood in front of him unshaven with bloodshot eyes and reeking breath. "That's insane."

"Is it?" Maddox smiled thinly.

"Blackmail."

"Call it what you want. But it's a small price to pay for your reputation, Dirkster. Imagine if the story got out that Dirk Peters lied about a whale attack. Made up the whole thing at the expense of a pitiful lobsterman. You'd never work again. Kiss Hollywood goodbye. Adios. You'll be living in a cockroach-infested apartment in Tijuana. Eating tortilla crumbs out of the gutter."

"You wouldn't dare."

"Oooooh, try me."

Maddox pushed past Peters and sat down in a torn stuffed chair near the curtained window and put his feet up on the water-stained, scuffed coffee table. "One hundred grand, Dirkster, and it's our secret."

Peters ran his hand nervously through his hair. It would have been so much easier if Maddox had drowned. "I haven't got anything like that kind of money. If I did, why would I be in this fleabag?"

"I don't believe you."

Peters pointed to the empty bottle of cheap vodka on the dresser. "You think I'd be drinking that piss if I had money?"

"Come on, Dirkster. You were a Hollywood star."

"Right. I was."

"Really?" Maddox raised his eyebrows.

"I barely have one hundred quid to my name," Peters' lied.

Maddox drew a breath and rubbed the whiskers on his chin. "Then you got a big problem, Dirkster. Big."

"Are you that desperate?" Peters knew the answer before he finished his words.

Maddox pointed his finger and sneered. "Last night I slept in a 1994 Ford Escort parked behind the dumpster at the IGA. You're talking to a real-life desperado, Dirkster. You better fork over the money or else I'm calling CNN and telling them you're a phony. A big liar. I'm sure they will pay nicely for that story."

Peters put his head down and sat on the edge of the bed across from Maddox and stared at the floor.

"It's only money."

Peters looked up. Only money. He thought about calling Marley and confessing about Maddox. Surely, Marley would meet Maddox's demands? But Peters had foolishly launched the video portraying himself as a hero without thinking about how easily Maddox could undermine the whole fabrication. It was the work of an amateur and Marley would be frothing. Peters would no longer be the golden boy.

As his mind raced, he took a deep breath. Maddox leaned back, rubbed his fingers together, and squinted like a wretched facsimile of a mafia don.

Maddox finally asked, "What's it going to be, buddy boy?"

Peters felt the best solution would be to handle this on his own. He'd promise Maddox a small percentage of his stake in Utami. He'd tell Maddox everything and hope the crazy bloke wouldn't spill the beans.

After Peters had finished recounting to Maddox his conversations with Marley and his agreement with Utami, Maddox leapt out of his chair, wrapped him in a horrifying hug, and with sour, rummy breath that made Peters recoil, exclaimed, "We got a deal, Dirkster!"

Pixie slowed down when she spotted the police cruiser parked on the shoulder of the road behind Caleb's broken-down pickup. She was still processing what Caleb had told her about the whale strike. Caleb, in a shaken voice, asked her to stop.

"It's Ed," Caleb said. "He's wondering why my truck is sitting on the side of the road in the rain with a broken windshield."

Pixie pulled over and watched as the Spring Harbor Police Chief, wearing a blue raincoat and a peaked hat covered in clear plastic like a custom-fitted shower cap, climbed out of his SUV and walked across the road.

As Caleb rolled down the window, Ed said, "I thought it was Elrod in the Caddy." He smiled at Pixie. "You're not Elrod. That's for sure."

Pixie noticed a mole on the side of Ed's face. The officer, middle-aged and undoubtedly weary from the trials and tribulations of being a small-town cop, wore a pained expression.

"What happened to the truck, Caleb?" Ed asked.

"A bad starter."

"The windshield?"

Caleb glanced at Pixie. "A rock kicked up and shattered it."

"The whale?"

"A long story."

Ed frowned as rain lightly pattered on the pavement in the late afternoon. "You've got news vans in front of your house."

Caleb nodded.

"They smell blood." Ed leaned closer to the open window. His voice hardened. "Did you gaff the whale?"

"I didn't touch it."

"That may be, but the state police are looking for you."

Caleb pointed to his phone. "I know."

"You've caused quite a stir."

"The Englishman's lying."

Ed nodded. "Do you have a lawyer?"

"No."

"They're thinking about putting out a warrant for your arrest."

"I figured as much," Caleb said, sighing.

"Arrest?" Pixie said to Ed. "Are you joshin'?"

"I wish I was." He looked at Caleb with concern and looked back at Pixie. "Caleb's in some hot water, Ma'am."

"Like a lobster," Caleb said with a hint of anger.

"Turn down the heat," Pixie said. "He's an innocent man. I've met Dirk Peters. He's a skunk."

Caleb said, "Toss Horace Maddox into the pot and it stinks even worse."

Ed nodded again. "Caleb, I've known you all your life. I don't for a second believe you gaffed a whale. But my advice is that you get a good lawyer and stay away from the media. In the meantime, I'm going to pretend that I never saw you."

"I appreciate it, Ed."

"The state police want to know what happened. The longer it takes to find you, the grumpier they're going to get. They got the environmentalists all over their backs. The governor even went on the record saying they should throw the book at you. I suggest you get that lawyer soon and have him or her give Augusta a call before their underwear gets too tight."

"Then what?"

"The state police interviews you. They weigh the facts. They–"

"Arrest me?"

"Maybe. Maybe not."

"The video's a lie."

"I believe you." Ed shook his head. "But this whole thing is out of my hands."

Pixie frowned, her eyes narrowing. "I watched the video with my own eyes, and there's not a teeny-weeny bit of evidence that my friend here threw that spear into that whale's hide. It's all a popcorn fart in a hurricane. A witch hunt. Officer, why can't you call off the dogs?"

"They're not my dogs to call off. If some people get their way, you'll be locked up in Thomaston, Caleb, or worse."

Ed reached through the open window and put his hand on Caleb's shoulder. "Get a good lawyer."

"And?" Caleb asked.

"Don't talk to the state police until you do."

Ed glanced over his shoulder at the broken-down pickup across the road. "You want me to call a tow truck?"

Caleb shook his head. "I'll call, Ed."

"I figure you got enough problems. It's the least I can do."

"Thanks, but no thanks. I got it."

Pixie leaned over. "I got one more itty-bitty question for you, officer."

Ed smiled. "Please call me, Ed."

"What happens when you find out ole Dirk Peters is a lying snake?"

The Spring Harbor Police Chief frowned. "Caleb could sue for defamation I suppose, but that's hard to prove, what with the video and its being Caleb's word against his. Seems like that would be a hard road to travel, as dissatisfying as that sounds."

Pixie looked at Caleb and turned back to Ed. "I'm no stranger to hard roads." She touched Caleb's arm. "Are you?"

Ed took his eyes off Pixie and glanced at Caleb. "Like I said, get a good lawyer." The Spring Harbor Police Chief stepped away, gently patted the hood of the Cadillac, and walked across the Old Bangor Road in the soft rain to his SUV.

Caleb rubbed the back of his neck. Pixie noticed his eyes were red and his face colorless. "Would you mind taking me into town?" he asked.

"What for?"

Caleb's eyes clouded. He gritted his teeth. "I'm going to find that bastard."

Pixie gave him a knowing smile and said, "Darlin', now you're talking. Don't get mad. Get even."

Chapter Thirteen—The Force

If Maddox called him Dirkster one more time, Peters was going to explode. Dirkster that. Dirkster this. Dirkster, buddy boy.

The two of them sat at the bar, peas in a sodden pod, downing rum and cokes, while the patrons at the Widow's Watch kept their distance and eyed them suspiciously. By now, Peters had seen clearly how much the townspeople detested Horace Maddox, and he didn't blame them one bit. Unfortunately, he now received the same baleful, even threatening glares from a few of the patrons. On the positive side, by early evening, the whale video had three million views on TikTok and counting.

Maddox reached unsteadily for his drink before sucking the rum and coke from a straw and wiping his mouth with his grimy t-shirt. He glanced around the Widow's Watch and broke into a sloppy grin. "Do you feel the hate, Dirkster? Ooh, frosty in here, isn't it? But they don't dare mess with us. You know why?" He slapped Peters on the back.

"Pray tell." Peters was cursing himself for divulging his "arrangement" with Utami. "And bloody stop calling me Dirkster," he added sharply.

"Come on, buddy boy, don't be so thin-skinned. It's a term of endearment. After all, we're business partners."

Peters rolled his eyes and looked up at the ceiling as if asking for lightning to strike.

"You know how *The Force* works in *Star Wars*?"

Peters reached for his drink and took a sip. What rubbish he thought. *The Force.* He loathed *Star Wars*, especially because he'd failed to land a part in *The Force Begins* eight years earlier. Russell Finch, that sniveling, backstabbing Australian jerk, won the role.

"*The Force*," Maddox leaned back and smiled, oblivious to Peters' mounting hostility. "It surrounds us, Dirkster. We got this town by the balls. People don't know what to think. They have no idea what's going to hit them. A huge tsunami . . . an earthquake . . . a gigantic asteroid . . . a horde of flying tiger monkeys. We got the power of the cosmos right in our hands."

Peters watched Maddox take a huge pull on his rum and coke through a candy-striped straw. Peters cursed under his breath.

Maddox was bloody nuts, and he now had Peters' future in his hands. A few times that evening, Maddox had uttered the name Utami loud enough to jeopardize the whole operation. The final time, Peters had clamped his hand over Maddox's rum splattered lips and kicked him in the shin.

Maddox leaned over and whispered in a conspiratorial tone, "The crazies are going to start circling this town. All the environmental nutsos. There'll be demonstrations. Riots. Lobstermen will be fleeing for their lives. With the money from you know who, Dirkster, I'll start building venture capital and this town will be at Horace Maddox's mercy." He tilted his head back and laughed. "All because of a stupid whale."

Peters noticed the bartender had stopped wiping the glass in his hand and looked past Peters with alarm as a hush swept through the bar. Peters glanced over his shoulder and saw the big man coming.

It was Caleb Gray.

Caleb spotted Maddox and Peters at the bar and cut through the restaurant. He moved swiftly with his fists clenched and tips of his ears burning. Just when he was about to ride the surge of adrenaline to fling himself at Peters and pummel him, he felt a tug on his arm. He whipped his head around and realized Pixie had grabbed him. He paused long enough to extricate himself only to find that she had leaped ahead so she could get the first piece of Dirk Peters.

Startled, he watched as Pixie stuck her finger in Peters' face and tear into him. Then, when Peters called Pixie a "bimbo" in that silky, cynical British accent, he watched in amazement as Pixie reached across the bar, clutched an empty beer bottle, and whacked Peters over the head.

The 'tong' sound of bottle on skull silenced the conversation at the bar. The bottle hadn't shattered, and Pixie held it in her hand.

Peters' eyes grew wide before they rolled back in his head and he tumbled to the floor.

Maddox leapt off his barstool and turned to Pixie. "You killed Dirkster!"

"All I did is give him a little love tap. It's what you do when you hope to knock some sense into thick heads."

Maddox snatched his drink, took a long sip, and wiped his mouth with his sleeve. His eyes flickered with recognition as he stared angrily at Pixie. "I know who you are, Ms. Deep Pockets. You bought Millbridge Island and the Stringer Cottage. You helped screw me outta that deal. Now you've killed my buddy, the Dirkster. You murdered a Hollywood legend."

"Legend my ass," Pixie said, holding the bottle as if it was a hammer.

Caleb knelt and felt Peters' pulse while a crowd pushed around him. He looked up at Pixie. "He's not dead."

"Of course he's not," she said. "If I wanted to kill him, I'd have broken the bottle on the bar and gone for the jugular. I'm sorry to say that I've seen it done, and it ain't a pretty sight. You don't spend years in clubs without witnessing your share of fights. But I'll say this. He's going to have a helluva headache."

Maddox said, "I saw it with my own eyes. Assault and Battery with a deadly weapon."

"Oh, shush before you get yours." Pixie raised the beer bottle as if to strike.

"You wouldn't dare," Maddox said, stepping backwards.

"Try me. You're as much of a skunk as he is."

Caleb stood up, reached over and gently took the bottle from Pixie. He snatched the rum and coke out of Maddox's hand and dumped the icy drink on Peters' face. Maddox shrieked, "My drink."

Moments later, the Brit began to stir.

Caleb grabbed Pixie's elbow. "Let's get out of here. Nothing good is going to happen if we stay."

Maddox pointed his finger, "You owe me a rum and coke, Gray."

"I owe you a beating, Horace, so count yourself lucky."

Maddox shook his fist at Caleb. "You're both going to jail. They're going to throw away the key if I have anything to do with it."

Caleb heard a distant siren. Spring Harbor's finest was on the way. He grabbed Pixie's elbow. "Let's go."

Pixie gave him a grin. "Party pooper."

As they drove out of Spring Harbor, Caleb asked, "What was that?"

Pixie pursed her lips and gripped the wheel. "He picked the wrong time to call me a name. That rattler ain't going to speak to me like that. Spencer was bad enough."

"A beer bottle?"

"He had it coming."

"You could have killed him."

"He's dang lucky. If that barstool weren't so heavy, I would have hit him with that."

"I could have handled it," Caleb said.

Pixie's eyes narrowed. "Why do you boys always think it's your right to 'handle' everything?"

"What do you mean?"

"Shield the little woman from the world with a hefty dose of testosterone. Keep us from getting our hands dirty." She turned to him. "I spent my whole life dealing with turds like Dirk Peters. I'd still be living in Port Arthur and working behind a register at Winn-Dixie if I couldn't handle myself. Besides, you got enough problems without adding an Assault and Battery."

"That's not what I was saying."

"Maybe. But let's leave it at this . . . Dirk the Jerk got a dose of Texas justice."

"A dose alright . . ." Caleb's voice drifted away. He thought about the state police and the conversation with Ed Pratt. He thought with alarm about the siren that grew louder and louder as he and Pixie fled. It was rare to hear a siren in Spring Harbor. The town police department was Pratt and a 20-year-old deputy with acne.

"I bet you never thought you'd be running from the police with a former stripper."

"I never imagined a lot of things until today."

Pixie turned to him. "Was she beautiful, Caleb?"

Pixie's question took his breath away. He nodded.

"You think I'm cheap?" she asked, her eyes beginning to well.

"No," Caleb whispered. "I think you're amazing." He felt his cheeks burn after he said it and so turned to look out the passenger window. In the fading light, he saw a trawler headed out to sea with its running lights glowing. He felt a deep stab of emotion and wanted to fold Pixie in his arms, and tell her how he felt, but instead, he shifted the subject. "Now we both need to get a good lawyer."

Pixie quickly brushed a tear from her cheek. "I suppose. I guess that's what you do when you're in a heap of trouble."

Outside of Harrington they stopped at the Quarter-Moon Motel. A handful of disheveled cabins bunched closely together in the woods, the Quarter-Moon had seen better days. The clerk, an old man with a shiny pate and a pocket protector full of pens, had taken cash without blinking, given Pixie and Caleb the last vacant cabin, and handed Caleb the key with a knowing look, as if to say, son, the walls are paper thin and the bed springs squeak. *If you're going to do it . . .*

The decision to spend the night at the Quarter-Moon had been made after Pixie and Caleb found a state trooper's SUV and a lone news van parked in front of Caleb's house and figured Ed Pratt would be looking for them at the Stringer Cottage. Pixie had spun the Eldorado around and, after a conversation, they'd decided to hunker down for the night, park the Cadillac behind one of the few motels lining Route 1, and face the authorities in the morning. Caleb had checked his phone and noticed two missed calls from Ed Pratt and a call from the state police in Augusta. Caleb's plan was to call a lawyer and turn himself in at the state trooper barrack in Bangor in the morning. Pixie was going to let Ed Pratt find her. She was going to proclaim self-defense, make a stink, and see if the Spring Harbor Police Chief had it in him to bring charges. She figured as soon as Ed spoke with Peters, he'd want to clobber the arrogant twit too.

She'd found herself in a similar situation when she was twenty and dancing at a club in Dallas. An inebriated customer had leapt on stage and came at her wide-eyed with his hands out like a Svengali. Before the club's bouncer could set his hands on him, Pixie hit the drunk between the eyes, knocking him down. After the initial shock of watching an exotic dancer flatten a middle-aged man with a pot belly and thinning hair pasted across a pink scalp, the club patrons gave Pixie a standing ovation. Two days later, the man had the gall to press assault charges. She'd discovered he was a shameless ambulance chaser from Oklahoma City attending a legal conference in Las Colinas. A judge dismissed the charges as ridiculous.

Pixie gave a soft whistle when she entered the tiny cabin. The pine board walls glowed in the soft light from an overhead fixture, and a tired dresser was shoved against the wall across from a sagging twin bed. She smelled moth balls. "Well, I'll say this, it ain't the

Ritz," she said, squinching her nose. She turned to Caleb and pointed at the bed. "It's going to be a tight fit."

Caleb nodded. "I'll sleep on the floor."

"You afraid of Pixie McGee?" she asked with feigned horror. "I rarely ravish men on a first hideout."

Caleb stayed silent.

Pixie said, "I'll keep my hands to myself. Scout's honor."

Pixie went into the bathroom and said, "Built for a Lilliputian." She ran the faucet in the sink. After a few seconds she poked her head around the door. "At least we got hot water." She paused and brushed a wisp of hair from her eyes. "I got paint on my cheek and I smell like a mule. I'm taking a shower." Pixie noticed that Caleb continued to look grim. She was feeling the stress, too, but she'd learned long ago that you had to face life's troubles with a sunny heart and a big smile. She wasn't going to rise from the dirt just to let skunks ruin her life.

Pixie closed the bathroom door and took off her clothes, gently folded them and laid them on the small vanity next to the sink. She glanced at herself in the mirror. *Still pretty, very pretty, but forty. No longer young. She noticed a strand of gray at the scalp. Crow's feet at the corners of the eyes. A smile line. A smidgen of extra weight at the hips.*

In the cramped shower stall, the hot water and soap felt miraculous and ten minutes later she was drying off. She put on her t-shirt and panties and walked out to an empty room. Caleb was nowhere to be seen.

She was about to climb into bed when Caleb slowly opened the cabin door and held out two chocolate bars. A look of surprise crossed his face and he averted his eyes. "We never ate dinner. This is all the motel clerk had."

Pixie took her candy bar and placed it on the nightstand. Caleb peeled the wrapper and devoured his in a few bites. When he was done, Pixie pointed to the bathroom and held her nose. "Your turn."

"Alewives," Caleb said, frowning. "I loaded bait this morning."

A few minutes later, as she heard water beating against the metal shower stall, she slid in between the sheets onto the lumpy mattress. The bedspread smelled like disinfectant. Pixie sighed and wondered if Caleb would climb in next to her. The thought of him sleeping on the floor depressed her. She wanted to feel him – feel his arms wrapped around her, to be held tight. That's all. Spencer always had needs to fulfill, but he rarely held her. She should have seen the red flag. She'd deluded herself into thinking he loved her when she should have realized she was merely another shiny object in his toybox. Looking back, she now realized that getting her to sell her business so that she could be at his beck and call was another red flag she had chosen to ignore. And there were a few hints at his unfaithfulness even before the whole thing with the Brazilian cutie gave her the cold dose of reality she needed to recognize what a fool she'd been.

What a train wreck. Pixie pursed her lips in disgust. She thought back to smashing Peters over the head with the bottle. In hindsight, she knew that it wasn't really Dirk she was hitting, it was Spencer. Dirk was an asshole, and she hated what he did to Caleb, but mainly she was channeling her fury at Spencer and all the men who came before who tricked her into believing that they cared for the woman she was, when what they really wanted was the tasty "bimbo" they could enjoy and dispose of when they had their fill. Delvin was an exception, she supposed. And now what did she have to show for years of scratching and clawing her way out of that moldy trailer in Port Arthur? Money for sure. It certainly wasn't respectability. A few years earlier, *Lone Star* had published a feature article on her real estate business. They referred to her as the stripper who'd danced her way to the top. Somehow, they'd found an old photo of her prancing onstage. She had to acknowledge that she was never going to be able to escape her past.

Pixie heard the water stop in the shower and sighed. It felt good when Caleb had used the word *amazing* to describe her. Amazing could mean many things. Yet, she didn't feel amazing. Anything but. She felt empty and tired. Used and discarded. Alone. She thought back to the monstrous engagement ring sitting in a pine drawer at the Stringer Cottage, a symbol of yet another flunking grade on the report card of love.

When Caleb emerged from the bathroom wearing boxers, Pixie stole a glance and noticed he didn't have an inch of fat. He was lean and muscled from years of physical labor. A deep scar ran along his shoulder. She patted the place on the bed beside her.

"I'll sleep on the floor," he said.

"You sure? I'll curl myself into an itty-bitty ball."

Caleb walked over to the tiny closet and pulled a blanket off the shelf and an extra pillow. "It's better this way."

Seconds later, after Caleb had settled next to the bed, Pixie snapped off the table lamp and sighed. Impulsively, she asked, "Will you tell me about her?" Pixie rolled on her

side and propped herself on an elbow. She put her chin in her hand and looked down at him.

"I can't," he said, stumbling for words.

"Too much hurt?"

"It does no good. It won't bring her back."

"A shame."

"What about you?" Caleb asked softly, his voice hoarse from exhaustion. "Who's Pixie McGee?"

Pixie put her head on the pillow and stared at the ceiling. "I thought I knew. But now?"

"Spencer Tate? You deserve better."

"Do I? I'm a dumbass when it comes to men."

"I meant what I said."

"What's that?"

"You're a force of nature. I've never been with a woman who hit someone over the head with a beer bottle. The look on Dirk Peters' face." Caleb gave a short laugh.

"In hindsight, I shouldn't a done it."

"Probably."

"But I did. I crossed that threshold and now—"

"Trouble."

"It becomes me." Pixie sighed. "Two fugitives on the run," Pixie added wistfully.

"Bonnie and Clyde."

"Thelma and Louise."

Caleb turned on his side. "I hope the dog's okay."

"I'll fetch the poor thing in a day or two. That's if I'm not in jail."

They fell silent for a bit. Seemingly not wanting the conversation to end, Caleb said, "You smacked Peters hard, not that he didn't have it coming."

"Not hard enough."

Caleb suddenly spat out, "Why the video? Why the lie? Peters was asking a lot of questions before the minke struck Maddox's boat."

"What kind of questions?"

"Garden variety about lobstering, but with an edge, like he had an agenda."

"What kind of agenda?"

"I'm not sure. But I didn't like it."

They both fell silent. Pixie heard Caleb's steady breathing. After a minute, Pixie broke the silence. "Your wife must have been a special woman."

"She was."

"You're lucky you had that kind of love." She paused. "Will there be anyone else?"

Caleb hesitated and said finally, "For a long time I thought that part of my life was over, but now I'm not so sure. There may be somebody."

A wave of disappointment washed over Pixie. She managed to say, "Well, she's a lucky woman."

"I haven't told her though."

"Why not?"

Caleb's voice grew soft. "I'm not sure, but maybe because I don't ever want to lose someone I care for again."

They fell silent and soon Pixie heard Caleb's breathing betray the rhythm of sleep. She tried to close her eyes and drift away, but she kept wondering about the woman that Caleb loved and the hurt that kept him from embracing life again.

Chapter Fourteen—Greenhaven

The state trooper barrack was a squat and ugly building located only a couple of hundred feet beyond Bangor International Airport's perimeter fence. Caleb sat across a laminated conference table from a veteran trooper with brushy hair and reading glasses tipped on the edge of his nose. He sat back in his chair and said, "Over the years, I've investigated crazy things, Mr. Gray, but never a person accused of harming a whale."

"I told you I didn't provoke the whale or endanger it."

"And I heard you." The trooper flipped through a file. "You have no record. You've never been given a citation for speeding. Nothing. You're squeaky clean. What happened?"

Caleb recited the story. He'd made the decision earlier to put off calling an attorney. He told himself he had nothing to hide, but he also knew he'd have a difficult time paying lawyer fees. He'd woken up in the morning with a sore back and a stiff neck from the pine floor and felt a pang of regret as he saw Pixie sleeping with her thick hair mussed on the pillow and noticed the shape of her breasts and curve of her hip under the blankets. The night before, he'd desperately wanted to tell her he cared for her, but the words wouldn't come out. His ability to express himself was imprisoned in a tangle of emotions.

After Caleb finished, the trooper leaned forward. "It may be like you say, but regardless, you riled up a hornet's nest by picking up that gaff, Mr. Gray."

Caleb frowned. He began to regret not having a lawyer by his side.

"The Governor isn't going to have it. She's livid. She's got people around her who want your head, especially with an election coming up. She's under pressure to show she's tough on protecting the environment. Especially after her little episode."

Caleb shook his head. Two years earlier, the Governor was caught on video throwing an empty McDonald's bag out the back window of her limousine while she was being chauffeured to a July Fourth celebration in Presque Isle. The incident had caused an uproar. She'd been trying to reestablish herself as environmentally conscious ever since.

"What are you telling me?" Caleb asked.

"We're going to pursue this case."

Caleb frowned. "You're going to arrest me?"

"Not yet. Right now, I need to inform you that you are officially under investigation." The trooper rose out of his chair and walked across the room to a small folding table in the corner and grabbed a newspaper sitting on top of it. He turned and tossed the newspaper in front of Caleb. "You've got big problems, Mr. Gray."

Caleb felt his pulse begin to race. It was a full-page black and white frame still in *The New York Times* of Caleb holding the gaff like a spear with the lobster clutched in the other hand, looking enraged as the minke neared the *Mary G*. The advertisement read:

Stop the Slaughter. Act Now.

Last year, 1,364 whales were reported slain worldwide for commercial purposes. That's the beginning. Countless more were needlessly slaughtered by criminal harvesters from the Southern Ocean to the Gulf of Siam. For decades, Greenhaven has fought to save endangered species across the globe. For a few dollars a month, we can continue our efforts to save the planet. Invest in your world at Greenhaven.

Caleb's stomach began to roil. The trooper shook his head and put his chin in his hand. "Full-page ad in *The New York Times*?" He paused. "You've hit the bigtime, Mr. Gray." He smiled thinly. "If I were you, I'd keep a low profile."

Twenty minutes later, Caleb walked across the parking lot under a cool, cloudless morning and climbed into the Cadillac. Pixie turned to him and said, "No handcuffs?"

"Not yet anyway."

"You live to see another day."

"I guess," he said, shaken.

Pixie looked at him closely. "But the posse is closing in?"

"Real fast."

"What happened?"

As Pixie pulled the car out of the parking lot, Caleb began to recount the conversation. When he told her about the Greenhaven advertisement, she grimaced and whispered, "Sweet Jesus." She gave Caleb a sympathetic glance. Then she said, "Well, my turn to be grilled."

Ed Pratt was waiting for them at the Stringer Cottage. He sat in one of the Adirondack chairs next to a stone wall lined with bursting patches of daylilies with a view of Frenchman's Bay.

"I forgot how pretty it is here," Ed said, lifting himself up as Pixie and Caleb walked across the scrubby lawn dotted with granite outcroppings. "Elrod and I figured you'd show up sooner or later." Ed pointed to the far side of the house. Elrod was on a ladder scraping chipped paint from a second-story window.

"I had business in Bangor," Caleb said, shaking his head.

"I know. I got a call from my state trooper friends," Ed said. "Between you and me, the Governor's on the warpath. She's livid. She's got people around her who want your head, especially with an election coming up. She's under pressure to show she's tough on protecting the environment. Especially after her little episode."

Caleb shook his head.

Ed looked at Pixie. "What's your story, Ms. McGee? A beer bottle?"

Pixie broke into a sweet smile. "Can we say he had it coming and leave it at that?"

"Nope. What happened?"

"Dirk the Jerk called me something shameful. If he'd called your significant other that, you'd a hit him over the head, too."

Ed said, "No, Ms. McGee, but then I have other ways of getting even. And I'm not the focus of the investigation. What did he call you?"

"I'm not telling."

A cloud of frustration washed across Ed's face. "So, after he said what he said you grabbed a beer bottle and hit him?"

"Served him right," Pixie said defiantly.

Ed shook his head and turned away. A lobster boat plied across the bay followed by a stream of shrieking gulls. He focused again on Pixie. "I'm sorry he called you a name, but it doesn't warrant you attacking him physically."

"It wasn't an attack. More like a love tap."

"He's got a concussion, Ms. McGee. Witnesses said you knocked him out cold."

Caleb interrupted. "I'd say he was dazed, not unconscious, Ed."

Pixie said with pursed lips, "I was defending my honor. Besides, have you talked to the man? If you have, you oughta know by now that Dirk Peters is a snake."

Ed gave a brief, knowing look. "He's threatening to press charges."

"Go figure," Pixie said. "What a darn surprise."

Ed's eyes clouded, and he looked at the lobster boat chugging toward Jonesport.

Caleb said, "Come on, Ed. Peters was asking for it."

"Case closed," Pixie added.

Ed turned to Pixie. "To the law, it doesn't matter what he called you. You can't resort to physical violence to right that wrong. Did Peters put his hands on you? Touch you before you struck him?"

"Would it make a difference?" Pixie asked, pursing her lips.

"Did he?"

Pixie smiled, a twinkle in her eye. "Come to think of it, he put his hand on me like this." She reached out and put the palm of her hand on Ed's wrist.

"You sure?" Ed asked.

"As sure as the sun rises."

"Help me God?"

"Hope to die."

Ed smiled warily. "Did you feel threatened?"

"That junkyard dog has been trying to jump my bones since I met him in the grocery store. Caleb here witnessed him mauling me while I was trying to have a nice meal with Elrod. He can confirm that. Let's just say I was tired of him getting handsy with me, shall we?"

Ed nodded briefly. After a moment, he said, "We're going to let this little matter sit, and hopefully it'll go away, especially after I tell Peters that you might file a harassment case as a counter charge. But no more hitting people with beer bottles, Ms. McGee. Understand?"

"Gotcha."

"Promise? No more trouble."

"I'll be on my best behavior."

Ed took a step back, turned to Caleb, and shook his head. "I'm sorry about the *Mary G.*"

Pixie noticed the confusion spreading across Caleb's face.

"What are you talking about, Ed?" Caleb asked.

"I thought you knew."

"Knew what?"

Ed frowned and shuffled his feet. "The state impounded her until the investigation is over."

"Impounded her?"

"That's right. The boat's got more tape wrapped around her than a Christmas present."

"Are you kidding me?" Caleb's face reddened. "I've got six hundred traps to haul and bills to pay."

"I'm sorry, Caleb."

"Not as sorry as I am."

"I hope you got a good lawyer."

"How can those wolves do that?" Pixie asked.

Ed shrugged and rolled his eyes. "The state can do pretty much whatever it wishes. From what I hear, the Governor wants Caleb's head. Sounds like she thinks it would look better on your gaff than on your shoulders, Caleb."

Caleb looked away angrily toward the bay. The sun sparkled on the water like crystal shards.

"They can't do that to the *Mary G.*, Ed." Caleb snapped, whipping his head around, his fists clenched.

"Don't do anything stupid, Caleb," Ed warned.

"Like rip that little English weasel apart?"

"I'm going to pretend I didn't hear that." Ed stuck his fingers in his ears.

"Pretend all you want," Caleb grunted. "No one's going to steal my livelihood."

The golf ball-sized knot on the crown of Peters' head throbbed and the light filtering through the slits in the motel room curtain struck his eyes like daggers. The moment the bloody bimbo hit him was still a blur, as was the aftermath when the paramedics arrived and eventually led him woozily out of the bar. They'd declared a grade-two concussion, kept Peters overnight for observation in hospital in Bangor, and sent him back in the morning to Spring Harbor in Maddox's dilapidated car as Horace, behind the wheel, polished off a six pack during a terrifying drive to the coast.

Yet, somehow, despite the lump on his head and being coerced to reveal Utami to Maddox, Peters felt elated. On his phone, through concussed eyes, he'd seen Greenhaven's full-page ad in *The New York Times* and realized that his mission to Spring Harbor had succeeded beyond his wildest expectations. Caleb Gray had become a symbol for outraged activists. There were already renewed cries to ban lobstering and send the bloke away to prison for life, or worse, for "attacking" the whale.

As far as Peters was concerned, he'd bloody done his job. Now it was time to collect. He'd lived up to his end of the bargain. He wanted his payoff and to escape this wretched town. At the bar the night before, he could feel the cold stares, 'the serves you right' looks as he was wheeled out of the restaurant. He'd implicated one of their own and now all hell was about to break loose. He needed to get out of Spring Harbor. Fast. Surely Marley would shower him with praise and extricate him before someone could do serious harm. God forbid they mess with his face, especially now that he was poised to retake Hollywood as a heroic whistleblower.

Peters recalled the actor Montgomery Clift, the heartthrob who'd suffered a disfiguring car accident in the 1950s. Despite a handful of movies afterwards, where directors shot Clift at delicate angles trying to minimize the damage to his face, the actor's career plummeted. The thought of Clift made Peters shiver.

Peters squinted painfully and grabbed his phone. Impulsively, he punched up Marley's number and after a few rings, heard the man from Utami's voice. Peters' elation grew as Marley indeed showered him with praise: *Splendid. Masterful. Brilliant. Smashing.*

After Peters made it clear that he no longer felt safe in Spring Harbor, Marley cleared his throat and said, "But you're not done, old boy."

"*What?*"

"We need you to stay the course. There are rumblings. Something big on the way."

Peters' chest tightened. "Are you bloody kidding me? Three million views on TikTok? What more can you people possibly want from me? Who knows what will happen if I stay. It's going to get dangerous here. It's easy enough to say 'stay the course' from California."

"Show some courage, Dirk. No one's going to lay a finger on you."

Peters touched the knot on his head and winced.

"Something's brewing. Last night Greenhaven tweeted about a protest. A big one."

Suddenly, Peters sat up in bed and pushed the phone closer to his ear.

"Buses full of fire-spitting demonstrators descending on Spring Harbor. Something's in the works. We need you to stay. We need you to be front and center, leading the charge."

A smile crossed Peters' face.

Marley said finally, "Keep your ear to the ground and eyes open. We're watching and listening on our end. Stay on your toes. Keep stirring the pot." Marley began to chuckle. "The boiling pot that is. All thanks to you."

"I'm risking my life, mate. There better be combat pay."

"Not to worry, Dirk. We'll take good care of you. Remember, old boy, Utami is going to be a smash hit."

After Marley rang off, Peters climbed off the sodden mattress and went to the window. He squinted painfully as he peeled the curtains back and scanned the empty motel parking lot. He started to fantasize about being the center of the protesters' attention. But then his fantasy shifted to the reality of a rabid mob of torch carrying townspeople descending upon the bloke who turned the world against Spring Harbor and helped destroy a way of life. A shot of fear raced down his spine. He needed something to protect himself in case it turned ugly.

He glanced at his wallet sitting on the dresser. He remembered passing a ramshackle hunting and fishing store on the outskirts of town. He would take no chances. Peters always wanted a pistol with a shoulder holster concealed beneath his Pronto Uomo blazer. And he was in America, where buying a gun was no more difficult than buying a ham sandwich. Maybe a 44 Magnum like Clint? Peters smiled. If people dared to touch him, he'd delight in watching their faces when he opened his blazer and revealed the "heat" he was packing.

Sandy Francois ran her finger down the nape of Jonathan Tyler's neck and kissed him softly on the lips. The day before,

115

Francois had made the flight to Washington to lobby in the halls of Congress for sustainable seafood practices, a thinly veiled euphemism for attacking the industries that Utami was hoping to replace.

Riding the delicious wave of publicity surrounding the whale-killing, lobster-slaughtering fisherman, Francois eagerly looked forward to her meetings with Washington's power brokers. Tyler had tried to arrange for Francois to meet the President, but the Commander-in-Chief declined. The world's most powerful man was winging his way on Air Force One to New Orleans for a campaign fundraiser at the Ritz-Carlton, where the $10,000-per-plate dinner to help re-elect Governor Montrose Beauregard would feature a sumptuous Cajun Crawfish and Shrimp Etouffee.

The night before, Francois had taken an Uber to Foggy Bottom and entered the Watergate as she always did, through a side entrance, slipping into Tyler's apartment unseen. Francois' sundress quickly fell to the floor and Tyler, with his family 3,000 miles away in San Francisco's Pacific Heights, ravished the institute director, their moans of delight drowned by the roar of planes taking off and landing at Reagan National.

After kissing Tyler, Francois nestled against the two-term Senator and said, "It won't be long now."

Tyler nodded and laid his hand on Francois' hip. "Marley said it could be big."

"Marley's always saying that," she scoffed.

"But this time he may be right."

"I got a call from Healthy Farms yesterday."

Surprised, Tyler lifted his head and turned to Francois. "Why didn't you tell me?"

Francois smiled. "I thought I'd wait. The cherry on top of the hot fudge sundae." She propped herself on an elbow, kissed him, and brushed her fingers across his smooth chest. "It was Angus." Angus Hartley was the founder and CEO of Healthy Farms, which prided itself on organic brands and sustainable practices, and then charged outrageous prices that only the wealthy could afford. *On sale, a pint of organic, handpicked Peachy Blue Chilean blueberries for only $10.99!* "The video pushed him over the top. He's going to announce on Monday that Healthy Farms is banning the sale of lobsters."

116

"That will be the third major chain."

Francois purred, "Devastating, isn't it?"

Tyler pulled Francois close in the tangle of sheets. "There'll be more."

"All thanks to that idiot lobsterman."

"Who is he?"

Francois said, "Who cares?"

"Does he have a name?"

"Gray, I think. Caleb Gray."

Tyler blinked, as if for an instant he was trying to place the name. "Well, Caleb is in hot water. Real hot."

"Scalding."

Tyler nibbled Francois' ear and whispered, "Should we turn to more important matters?"

"What do you have in mind?" she cooed.

"I want you again."

"How?"

Tyler grinned devilishly. "Slathered in warm butter."

"With a squirt of lemon?"

"Exactly."

"It sounds delicious."

"Oh, it will be," he said pulling her on top of him, his voice tinged with lust. "A gourmet meal."

Chapter Fifteen—Grand Heron

Swathed in yellow tape, the *Mary G.* sat tied up between the *Elsie B.* and *Our Sons*, three stout, broad-bowed lobster boats bobbing gently in the light northwest breeze. Over the years, the fishing fleet dwindled as the state grew older and fewer young people took up the trade. Fifty years earlier, numerous lobster boats and trawlers dotted Spring Harbor and the Gulf of Maine while the industry thrived. At first, the locals scoffed at the notion of climate change, but now they accepted reality as the data poured in from oceanographic research tanks, which showed the temperature in the Gulf of Maine rising faster than nearly any body of water in the world. Maine lobstermen wondered how long it would be before lobsters clawed their way north to colder waters, and an enduring way of life vanished.

Pixie and Caleb walked down the steep rampway at low tide. Gulls circled above and an osprey, perched in a nest atop a navigational spindle at the harbor's mouth, chirped excitedly as its chicks fed. Caleb's brow furrowed in anger when he saw the impounding tape wrapped around the *Mary G.'s* wheelhouse. He climbed aboard and started tearing away the tape.

"Oh, darlin'," Pixie said, standing with a hand on her hip and frown pursed on her lips, watching Caleb. "If they weren't going to throw you in jail before, it's a sure thing now."

Caleb gave a defiant look as he balled a long strip of tape in his hands. "Climb aboard."

"Are we running from the law?"

"You'll see," he said, tossing the tape into a bucket by the engine box and putting out his hand to help Pixie over the gunwale.

Soon the Yanmar struck up and the *Mary G.* moved swiftly out to sea on a cloudless afternoon. When Caleb looked back, he imagined a state trooper standing on the dock shaking his fist in anger. But the only eyes watching the *Mary G.* were a flock of gulls hovering above, hoping for scraps of bait fish.

The swells picked up a few miles off Isle au Haut. The island, perched on granite and topped with stands of pine, rested several miles off the coast and soon fell astern of the *Mary G.* Caleb held the wheel and looked back as the mainland faded. Pixie sat on the engine box with her face uptilted and her eyes closed, as if she didn't have a care in the world, sunning herself as the boat gently rode the swells.

When Ed Pratt had told Caleb his boat was impounded, Caleb felt his throat constrict. They could accuse him of harming a whale and breaking a federal law, threaten to bring charges, but they weren't going to take the *Mary G.* He had hundreds of thousands of dollars invested in the boat, traps, and gear, and like all Maine lobstermen, a streak of fierce independence. They weren't going to wrap yellow tape around the wheelhouse and tell him to go home with his tail between his legs to wait until some bureaucrat in Augusta or Washington decided his fate.

He turned and saw Pixie dozing under the mesmerizing effect of the swells and the purr of the engine. She looked serene and especially beautiful the way the sunlight was striking her face. She wore jeans, one of Caleb's sweaters he'd dug out of a footlocker, and no makeup other than her bright red lipstick. Once again, he wanted to tell Pixie how he felt. He could even feel Mary, the love of his life, begging him to live again. But the tangle of emotions he was feeling were just too hard to sort through. How could he even begin to express his heart when everything he was feeling was all jumbled? And now this. What had he just done?

What a mess. It was starting to dawn on him how foolish and impulsive it was to take the boat. They'd come after him hard now. He knew that. A sudden movement caused him to turn away from Pixie. He saw water shoot from a blow hole and the majestic arch of the back. The curved dorsal fin told Caleb the whale was a minke, and soon he saw two others alongside, swimming in a pod. Caleb realized that part of what made him so angry from being falsely accused of harming a whale was the primordial awe and wonder he felt whenever he was in their midst. He loved these creatures and would be the last person on the planet to harm one.

Caleb throttled back. He stepped away from the wheel, tapped Pixie on the shoulder, and pointed. She rose off the engine box and put on her sunglasses. She smiled and said, "They're beautiful."

Caleb nodded. He looked at her and felt a wave of affection. The sweater fell to her thighs and her blonde hair, clasped in a ponytail, glistened in the sunlight. She radiated beauty – he felt as if an electric charge had struck him.

"Sometimes they run in pods of two or three," Caleb said, turning back to the whales about fifty yards off the *Mary G.'s* starboard beam. "In the Arctic, they can swim in pods of a few hundred."

Pixie touched his arm and smiled. "Caleb Gray. Where are we going? France?"

Caleb pointed east. "To a special place." He paused and reached for the wheel. "Because I don't know where else to go."

Grand Heron Island rose out of the Atlantic like a fortress. Twenty-three miles off the Maine coast, the one square mile island found fame when the British frigate, *HMS Restless*, shipwrecked during a February gale during the War of 1812. Stranded, the few survivors nearly froze before they were rescued by an American brigantine and imprisoned in Machias.

Caleb brought the *Mary G.* to the lee side of the island and carefully steered the boat into a narrow cove. A wharf rested on barnacle-covered pilings a few hundred feet from the inlet's entrance, and a small, weathered Cape, the warped cedar shingles blackened by decades of harsh weather, sat amidst a stand of wind-battered firs.

Caleb could smell pine and juniper mixed with salt, and brought the *Mary G.* carefully into the wharf, where after a few turns of the wheel, throttle bursts, and a cleated spring line, the boat came to rest.

"I feel like I'm at the end of the world," Pixie said. "Where are we?"

Caleb stepped onto the wharf and reached out to Pixie. She clasped his hand and lifted herself off the *Mary G.* "Grand Heron."

"A little island getaway?"

"It's been in the Gray family since 1764."

"You own it?"

Caleb smiled thinly. "You're not the only one who can call an island home."

"But I got a bridge, electricity, and indoor plumbing."

"True."

"And Elrod."

"Another huge plus."

Pixie swept her eyes across the island. "No one's gonna find us here. It's like we're outlaws disappearing into the Sierra Madre."

Caleb suddenly realized the flaw in his plan. He'd forgotten about their cell phones, and so foolishly left an electronic trail to the island. "Oh, they'll find us," he said, with a wave of his phone. He desperately wanted a couple of days on Grand Heron to ponder his situation and to figure out a way to make things right not only with the law, but with Pixie. Caleb looked west toward the horizon. "I just brought more trouble on the both of us."

Pixie sighed. "Well, until it comes, let's enjoy paradise."

After stepping along inland trails to see parts of the island, they sat silently on the rocks overlooking the cove and ate peanut butter on saltines they'd found in the Cape's narrow pantry as the sun set in brilliant mixed hues of orange, yellow, and purple. *A summer sky.* They had picked wild strawberries for dessert. Pixie and Caleb chewed off the tiny crowns, tossed them into a tidal pool a few feet below as sculpins darted back and forth, nibbling the stems. When the sun finally slipped below the waves, they spotted the outline of a freighter running hard to Halifax and minutes later the cabin lights of a cruise ship bound for Bar Harbor. They sat in silence as stars twinkled into view like millions of diamonds glittering across the heavens.

"I made a promise to Mary," Caleb said, staring at the stars radiating above. "She loved the island. More than anyone."

"What was it?" Pixie asked.

"To give the island to the Land Trust. She wanted it to be untouched. A sanctuary. Since I was the sole owner after my parents died, I signed the papers after she was killed. The island goes to the Trust upon my death."

"Preserved for the ages?"

Caleb nodded. He turned to her. His words were sharp. "Ever since we saw the whales today, I've been thinking."

"About?"

"Why Peters would set me up. What's in it for him? He doesn't seem like he could care about anyone but himself. He's vain, egotistical– "

Pixie interrupted. *"Selfish, shallow . . . a jackal."*

"He'd be the last person to care about a whale or the ethics behind lobstering."

"Notoriety? Fame?"

"Maybe."

"If we're putting our detective hats on, I'd say money, because by the look of him, he hasn't got any. I can see it in his eyes. Dirk Peters needs cash."

"So why make me into some kind of Ahab?"

Pixie sighed. "Like I said, money. Someone's putting him up to it."

Caleb shook his head. "He's barking up the wrong tree. I'm a nobody. I have a mortgage, a half million dollars in bank loans on the boat and trap stock, and an old truck with a broken windshield."

Caleb could see Pixie give a half smile. "And soon a sweet dog that's gonna need a lotta love and two heaping meals a day."

"And vet bills."

"Fur on the couch."

"Mud on the carpet."

"Fleas."

"That's if I'm not locked up somewhere."

Pixie shook her head. "Ole Dirk is up to something."

"But what?"

"I don't know, but one thing's for sure. He ain't the mastermind. The man is a dang fool."

"I need to find out what's going on."

She gave him a sympathetic look. "You mean '*we*'?"

"Ed practically said you were free and clear. No need dragging you back into this."

"Honey, I'm in this too deep to go skipping back to Dallas as if nothing happened. I'm shamed about all that's happenin' to you, but these last two days with you have been just what I needed."

Pixie's shoulder brushed against his as he spotted the sharp trail of a meteor shooting across the sky. Caleb felt a wave of emotion, an urge to kiss her mixed with a bolt of fear. He felt awkward. He could tell she sensed his desire and clumsiness.

Caleb was about to brush his lips against hers when the threatening whine of a fast-approaching boat dashed his ardor against the rocks. Caleb pulled away as the beam of an LED light revealed that the vessel was making a beeline toward the island.

"We have friends," Caleb said, kicking himself for forgetting to switch off his phone. Couldn't those bastards have allowed him a nice moment before they hauled him away?

"Officers in blue, I assume?" Pixie asked.

Caleb shook his head in disgust. "The Coast Guard. Unless I miss my guess, I'm going to be their prisoner until the state police meet us in Spring Harbor."

Caleb was right. The Coast Guard seized the *Mary G.* and Pixie and Caleb were whisked back to Spring Harbor in the response boat while two enlisted men followed, bringing the *Mary G.* home. Two state troopers and Ed Pratt were waiting for them on the dock with flashlights in hand in the early hours of the morning.

"Dumbass," Ed said as the state troopers cuffed Caleb and led him up the ramp.

"Where are they taking him?" Pixie asked, desperation in her voice.

"Bangor," Ed said.

"When can I get him out?"

"When, and *if* bail is set."

"If?"

"The Governor has a hair up her ass, Ms. McGee. A big one. They might throw away the key."

"That's ridiculous," Pixie said, feeling her anger rise.

"Tell that to the Governor."

"I might do that," Pixie said, her voice rising.

Chapter Sixteen—The Crazies Are Coming

With no sleep the night before, Ed Pratt was on his third cup of coffee staring disbelievingly at his computer screen as sunlight filtered through the window next to his cluttered desk. The email had been sent by a fringe eco-terrorist organization called Fighters for a Free Animal Planet, and they'd threatened to burn Spring Harbor to the ground. They referred to the town as the Axis of Evil. The missive was a sinister heads up from an organization that prided itself on hit-and-run destruction across the globe. Fighters for a Free Animal Planet had recently torched a large meat processing plant in Iowa and three of the chief organizers, caught and convicted of domestic terrorism, were spending their days plotting the downfall of humanity in Leavenworth. Undaunted, those that remained carried on. A Russian factory ship sunk in the Baltic. A fish market blown apart in Tokyo. A government game official overseeing the Saskatchewan moose lottery kidnapped and found hanging naked by his feet from a rafter in a remote, abandoned outfitter's camp. He was fortunate to be alive.

Now Spring Harbor. Alarmed, Ed rubbed his brow. He took threats seriously and reached for the phone. He needed to call the state police and FBI. First, however, he made a call to Almira Babb, the bird-like matriarch of Spring Harbor who ran the Chamber of Commerce with an iron fist and then to Van Burnham, the head selectman who'd overseen the town for forty years. Ed's calls were met with alarm. When he finally put down the phone, he noticed the email from Fighters for a Free Animal Planet had vanished. He clicked his mouse a handful of times in disbelief. Moments later, his computer began to make an unnatural whirring noise. His screen went black, and after a couple of seconds, the laptop let out a flatulent burst and died.

Ed looked up at the ceiling and sighed. It had been a long night, and now it was going to be a longer day. Ed believed in law and order, and Spring Harbor was in the bullseye of a gathering storm. He cursed under his breath. "Caleb Gray, what have you done?"

The man they called Roarsh sat at his grimy desk in his strip mall office in Alexandria, Virginia and stubbed his cigarette into a butt-filled ashtray. The batteries in the cheap smoke detector had been removed long ago, and smoke hung in the fluorescent-lit room in a gray cloud, as his co-worker, the woman they called Kiki, sat across from him in a metal folding chair with a computer on her lap. She wore ripped jeans, a flannel shirt, and her dark, stringy bangs fell so low that the main feature of her face was a nose ring large enough to snare tuna.

Roarsh and Kiki had worked together before. They were the organizers. The facilitators. The op directors. Disenchanted with the world, they'd dropped out of a small, pricey, liberal arts college and fell into the warm lap of Greenhaven. They brought people together and made sure the trains ran on time. They staged the protests, rented buses, procured signs, ran social media, and made sure there were plenty of bullhorns so the message could be heard loud and clear.

Roarsh reached for another cigarette, lit it with a plastic lighter, and smiled at Kiki. "This is going to be big."

"As big as North Dakota?"

"Bigger."

"Sick."

"Not to mention all the celebrities."

"Who's the dude who started this?" Kiki asked.

"A loser. The bigwigs in corporate already put together a dossier. A dude named Caleb Gray."

"RIP."

"Exactly. The mother is going to hang. I heard they arrested him this morning."

"Did he really kill a whale?"

"Does it matter?"

Kiki shrugged. "Guess not."

"It's all for the cause. Two birds in one stone, the assholes who murder whales and the lobster industry."

Kiki reached over and pulled Roarsh's cigarette from his lips and took a drag. "When's the date?"

"Soon. Real soon."

"How many protesters?" she asked, handing back his cigarette.

Roarsh smiled thinly, took a drag, and picked a piece of tobacco out of his teeth. "Brace yourself."

"Dude, how many?"

"Looks like 15,000 easy."

"Fifteen thousand? You're shitting me?"

"I am not."

"Are we going to be able to pull this off?"

"After all this time you doubt me, Kiki?" Roarsh grinned.

"I'm hungry," Kiki said, changing the subject and rubbing her stomach.

"Sushi?"

Kiki broke into a thin smile. "You know we're not supposed to eat anything that moves, Roarsh. We signed a pledge."

"When did that ever stop us?"

"What are you suggesting?" She raised an eyebrow.

"How about I call Sushi Heaven and order California rolls?"

Kiki licked her lips. "Make sure you order the avocado, cucumber, and spicy crab."

"Now you're talking."

Kiki smiled deliciously. "And get the jumbo plate."

"Will do."

"And tell them to include extra wasabi."

"Anything else?"

"Do you really think that guy killed the whale?"

Roarsh rolled his eyes. "Who cares. We got 15,000 protesters showing up and all hell's gonna break loose. Besides, there are more important things right now."

"Like ordering sushi?"

"You got it," he said, reaching for his cell phone.

The drunk lying on the wooden bench across the holding cell finally passed out. Wearing faded jeans and a black t-shirt and in his early twenties, the man had been arrested after driving five miles in the wrong direction on Route 95 while miraculously not killing anyone. The other man in the cell had a shaved head, forearms like Popeye, and hands the size of frying pans. Large dark circles made his eyes look carved out, eerily hollow. He kept mumbling under his breath and staring angrily at the cement floor. He'd been apprehended earlier in the day for peddling fentanyl in Brewer.

Exhausted from the fitful sleep the night before, Caleb fought to keep his eyes open. Drifting off in the courthouse holding cell didn't seem like a good idea. They had charged Caleb under the Endangered Species Act which prohibited the "take" of a threatened or endangered species in US territorial waters. Caleb wondered how long he'd be held. He desperately wanted to leave the dim, fluorescent-lit cell and get fresh air. Windowless, the fetid room smelled like moldy socks and pee. An enclosure like this was Caleb's vision of hell.

Caleb cursed himself for the hundredth time as he sat without his belt and shoes. The impulse to take the *Mary G.* to Grand Heron had placed him in even hotter water, but the urge to flee had been overwhelming. The anger he felt at having his reputation and livelihood ruined had needed some physical outlet, and so he had simply chosen what was familiar and comforting, no matter how stupid.

When he was given his phone call, the one he yearned to make was to Pixie, but he didn't have her cell number, and since he needed an attorney, he'd called a former colleague of Mary's whose father practiced in Orono. He seemed to remember that he mainly specialized in getting University of Maine undergrads off the hook for DUI, petty drug offenses, and the occasional fraternity brawl, but he was the only criminal lawyer he knew. The guy still hadn't shown up.

The drunk sleeping on the bench began to snore. Caleb thought back to the night before, sitting under the stars with Pixie as if they were on the far side of the world, the only people on the planet. It was a fleeting moment of intimacy that made Caleb feel lonelier than ever. He wanted to live again. He wanted to be with Pixie. Hold her. Kiss her. Feel her against him. He closed his eyes for a moment, listening as the drunk's snoring grew louder.

Like the mumbling drug dealer, Caleb put his chin down and stared at the floor. His mind was numb. He tried to fight self-pity. He vowed that if he got out of this hellhole, he'd discover why Dirk Peters was trying to destroy him and make the slimy Brit pay. There had to be a reason. Peters believed in only one cause, his own, so there had to be more to the story – and Caleb, as he watched a carpenter ant scuttle across the cell floor, was determined to find out what it was.

The FedEx van pulled into the Stringer Cottage parking area in the late afternoon and a burly delivery man leapt out of the truck holding the package as far away from his nose as he could. He was relieved to be delivering whatever was in the box because it smelled like rotten eggs. The word fragile was scrawled across each side of the package, but the FedEx man knew better. People were crazy. They tried shipping anything. FedEx had strict rules. But hidden in packages were sometimes gerbils, hamsters, ferrets, mice, snakes, and lizards. Mostly, it was dimwits thinking the animal would survive the journey, but unquestionably, sometimes it was a creep taking perverse satisfaction in boxing an animal and shipping it to a certain death. Some of the stories he heard at the warehouse made him shake his head about his fellow man. He quickly walked up the pine needle covered path to the house wondering how this package ended up in his truck, but because it did, he was obliged to deliver it.

He tapped on the wooden framed screen door and an older man wearing green Dickies appeared. The FedEx driver held the package at arm's length as if he were handing over a baby with a full diaper. "A package for P. McGee," the delivery guy said, wrinkling his nose.

"Smells like hell," the older man said.

"Can't disagree, but it's yours now."

The old man reluctantly took the box and was about to carry it outside when a woman burst in from the kitchen. "What you got, Elrod?" she asked, before taking a double take as the stink struck with full force.

The old man grimaced. Without a word, the woman pointed outdoors.

As the delivery man left the house and started across the lawn, relieved to have ridden himself of the package, he heard the woman say with resignation and disgust, "Spencer Tate, you lyin', cheatin', sumbitch."

But at present, Tate was the least of Pixie's worries. She needed to bail Caleb out of jail, put on her sleuth hat, and figure out who put Peters up to raining hell on Caleb Gray. The sweet desire of the night before on Grand Heron seemed a dream that had been replaced by the nightmare of Caleb being led in cuffs up the town dock's rampway. The thought of Caleb in jail frayed her nerves. She could only imagine how much a man like that would hate to be locked up. Fortunately, Pixie understood how bail worked. Over the years, she'd received calls from dancers who'd fallen into Dallas' unsavory shadows and a couple of club bouncers who'd ended up in jail for one infraction or another. They knew Pixie had hit it big in real estate and had a generous heart and a large checkbook. In the seamy club world, she'd become known as the angel. When desperate exotic dancers came to her office, usually in tears, she'd helped. She settled with creditors, covered the cost of drug rehab, paid attorneys, and wrote the tuition checks for community college – all with a smile and a hug.

She left Elrod back at the Stringer Cottage to dispose of Spencer's "little" package. She was determined to find Dirk Peters, and Elrod had told her he'd heard that the Brit was holed up at Oceanview Motel. She would paste on a smile, apologize, and play to his vanities. That worked with most men, and would almost certainly sway a vain, egotistical idiot like Peters. The perfume and tight t-shirt wouldn't hurt either. Pixie hated the thought of what she was about to do.

The matronly desk clerk with silver hair piled on her head like a bath towel arched her eyebrows when Pixie asked with a coy smile which room was Dirk Peters'. Her request was met with stony silence. The woman, who wore a t-shirt with Jesus gazing toward Heaven above the words, *Disappointments, All of You,* started to frown, and it dawned on Pixie that the clerk wasn't inclined to give such information to someone who she'd never seen, much less a woman who looked like Pixie. Pixie read it loud and clear in the clerk's eyes: *The Oceanview isn't that kind of place, honey. Whatever you're up to, do it somewhere else. Not at this motel, not on my watch.*

Pixie's mind whirled. She drew a deep breath and pursed her lips. "I owe Mr. Peters money."

The woman raised her eyebrows and drew her head back, as if she were bracing for a sordid tale.

Pixie continued. "I was at the checkout line with a shopping cart full of groceries, when I realized I forgot my purse. 'Hell bells,' I said to myself. 'I done it again.' I can be downright forgetful. Here I was, in line, waiting to pay for everything, when I started to panic."

"And?" the clerk asked skeptically.

"Mr. Peters saved the day. He was behind me in line, a knight in shining armor, a king of kings, and paid for my groceries. I promised to pay him back. And here I am." Pixie smiled sweetly, thinking to herself, *I'll pay him back alright.*

Pixie dipped into her handbag and pulled out a wad of cash.

"Only to pay him back?" The woman stared suspiciously at the lump of bills.

Pixie turned up the wattage on her best Texas smile.

The clerk scratched her chin. "Well, alright. But I don't want any trouble. I'm not supposed to give out room numbers."

Pixie nodded solemnly, angelically.

Moments later, Pixie walked across the wet gravel parking lot under a gray sky, found Peters' room, and tapped lightly on the paint-flecked door, behind which she heard the sounds of a TV blaring. An annoyed voice called out, "Who is it?" and then she heard a chair knock over, a curse, and the sounds of footsteps. The door flung open and the guy who'd been sitting next to Peters at the bar, yelling "you killed Dirkster," stood before her, and when he set his bloodshot eyes on Pixie his irritation gave way to an appraising grin as if she was a lollipop that he wanted to lick.

"What a surprise. Horace Maddox at your service," the man said with a saccharine grin and rum-soaked breath. "You aren't carrying a bottle, are you?"

Pixie's heart sank when she realized it was Maddox. Boy, had he come down in the world. He'd been pointed out to her when she bought the island as the hombre who'd wanted to develop it for luxury homes. He hardly looked like the same guy. He'd lashed out at her after she'd smacked Dirk over the head with the bottle, and now she wondered if he'd play ball. She decided to play it light. "No, but if you need a love tap as well, you be sure to let me know," she replied. "Where's Dirk?"

"Oh, where's Dirk? Why would I tell you, Ms. Deep Pockets? You're playing nice now, but what happened a couple of years ago? Huh? You stole the island and ruined my life along with the rest of these bozos in Spring Harbor." His eyes narrowed. "I love seeing your little boyfriend in trouble, Mr. Caleb 'I'm going to be a convict' Gray . . . Besides, I need to protect my business partner, the Dirkster. Just you wait, soon you'll be begging to sell that island to me."

"Horace, I'm here to apologize to Dirk. And I'm just as sorry as I can be if I've harmed you in any way," she cooed. "What kind of business are you boys in anyway?"

"Ooooh, wouldn't you like to know," Maddox burped and suddenly leaned against the doorframe to steady himself. "So wouldn't that friend of yours, Mr. Jailbird, Caleb Gray."

Pixie's mind began to race. "Isn't there something I can do to convince you to share just a little teensy bit of your secret, Horace?"

Maddox raised his eyebrows and smirked. "What do you have in mind?"

"Not that, buster."

Maddox reached for the doorknob.

But before Maddox could slam the door in her face, Pixie reached into her handbag and pulled out a wad of one-hundred-dollar bills. She looked Maddox up and down. His t-shirt was stained and his khakis were ripped at the pockets. "You look like you could use some help."

Maddox's eyes hungrily fixated on the money locked in Pixie's dainty fist. "You think I'm desperate, don't you? For a few measly bucks I'd betray my amigo Dirkster."

"Oh, well," Pixie sighed. "Don't say I didn't try to make things up with you." She started shoving the money back into her handbag.

"Wait," Maddox said, his voice rising. "How much do you have in there?" He pointed at her handbag.

"Plenty. You tell me what's going on, and I'll make it worth your while."

Maddox scratched his chin. "$1,000 bucks."

Pixie turned to him. She felt herself moving into familiar territory. Over the years, she'd negotiated hundreds of deals, usually to her favor. "For the right information we can get into that ballpark."

Pixie watched Maddox's eyes start to sharpen and she knew she had him. "What's it going to be? I don't have time to stand here and grow old, Horace."

Pixie paused while Maddox stroked his stubble. Finally, he said, "Let's just say we're in the business of saving the world."

"Huh?"

Maddox paused. He pointed toward the sliver of Frenchman's Bay they could see through the trees across the street. "There's death everywhere, and we're going to stop it."

"You're superheroes, huh? Which one are you, Robin?"

"Laugh now. But just you wait. If you want more than that, I'll need to have cash in hand."

Pixie reached into her bag and handed Maddox five one-hundred-dollar bills. "There's more where those came from, but you need to spill some details. What 'death' are you talking about?"

"Lobsters are dying. Whales are being slaughtered. Fishermen like your buddy, Caleb Gray, are killing God's creatures so people can stuff their greedy mouths."

"What are you talking about?" Pixie was starting to wonder about Maddox's sanity. "People have to eat, Horace."

"Science," he said. "Ever heard of it? We are going to stop the killing through the wonders of science."

Pixie scoffed. "You don't much look like Einstein, Horace. Where's the test tubes?"

"You want more, I need to have more."

Pixie once again reached into her bag and pulled out five more hundreds. "OK now, Horace. I'm getting tired of your little games. Spill it. What are you talking about?"

Maddox reached for the money, but Pixie pulled it away. Maddox said, "I've got one word for you: bioengineering."

"You and Dirk are planning to bioengineer seafood?"

Maddox sneered. "We're investors. Human capital."

Pixie paused. "Usually investors have moola, Horace." She looked at his bloodshot eyes and unshaven face. "Businesses need brains and money." She shook her head doubtfully. "You and Dirk don't got either."

"I told you plenty, and you come back with insults. I'm not going to share any more secrets. The future of the planet is at stake. I've earned the rest of that money already."

Pixie's voice grew steely. "You're almost there, Horace. What are you and Dirk up to?"

"You think Dirkster shot that video of Gray for his home movie collection? Put two and two together, Ms. Deep Pockets. Or maybe you're the one who's no Einstein."

"I should have known. Dirk Peters is no activist." The words were barely out of her mouth when Maddox snatched the remaining money out of her hands. She shook her head. "I'm going to forget your bad manners. Who's behind this, Horace?"

"Like I said, I've told you enough."

132

Pixie put her hands on her hips. "You're destroyin' a good man."

"Gray? Who cares? Collateral damage."

"Anyone ever tell you you're a lizard?"

Maddox scrunched up his face and pretended to wipe fake tears from his cheek with a hundred-dollar bill. "It's a cruel world. Boo hoo. I've told you enough. Now vamoose before the Dirkster comes back. And just so you know, I'll deny I ever said one word to you."

The smell of gun oil clung to Peters' fingers. He'd purchased the used Glock from a toad-like man with a monk's fringe, bulging eyes, and hair sprouting from his ears at the hunting and fishing store a few miles outside of Spring Harbor. No questions asked.

Peters had never owned a gun before, but he'd fired blanks from a few weapons on sets. His favorite had been from *Bango and Dash* during a wild car chase. Peters had blasted away from the driver-side window with an AR-15 at the villains who were following. But now, as he handled the real thing, a Glock that fired real bullets, he had goosebumps all up and down his arm. He fantasized about wielding it if things got out of hand.

Going to purchase the gun was a relief from putting up with Maddox, who'd shown up at his motel room with no place to go. Maddox spent the afternoon sucking rum and coke and telling Dirk for the billionth time how he lost everything and how he was going to take over the town and squash the minions who'd ruined him. Ghastly. But how could Peters kick him out? Maddox held secrets that could ruin the whole operation and if betrayed, could send Peters spiraling into oblivion. Peters shivered. He'd thought about ways to deal with Maddox. If it was a movie, Peters would hire a hitman and have Maddox taken out. Or better yet, he'd do it himself with his Glock and quietly dump Maddox's body, weighted with cinder blocks from an abandoned construction site, into the sea where a frenzy of sharks would feed on his bloated carcass.

Instead, he pulled into the Oceanview parking lot, grabbed his newly purchased toy, and climbed out of his canary-yellow Malibu.

Peters found Maddox sprawled on one of the queen beds with his eyes half shut and the television blaring. He snapped off the TV and, affecting a demented smile, pulled the Glock out of a plastic bag and aimed the pistol at Maddox. Maddox's eyes shot open, and he shielded his face with a pillow.

"Don't do it!" Maddox cried. "I didn't tell her anything. Promise, Dirkster."

Peters lowered the gun and gave Maddox a quizzical look. "Tell who?"

"She wanted intel, and I told her to hit the road. You think I would betray you?"

"Who showed up, Maddox?" Peters asked with growing alarm.

"The woman who smashed you over the head."

"Pixie?"

Maddox belched. "That one."

"What did she bloody want?"

"Information."

"What did you tell her?"

"Nothing . . . *promise*."

Peters said coldly, "You bloody sold our secret, didn't you?"

"Honest . . . I didn't tell her anything."

Peters felt himself starting to panic.

"Come on, Dirkster. Would I do that?" Maddox pleaded.

"You'd sell your firstborn."

"Give me some credit. We're a team. Right?"

"What did you tell her?" Peters felt a wild urge to shoot Maddox. He raised the Glock. At the very least he would scare the blighter shitless and hope that he would keep his yap shut from now on.

"Come on, Dirkster. You wouldn't do that?" Maddox's eyes began to bulge.

"Try me."

"Okay. Okay. I told her about the miracles of bioengineering."

"What! Did you tell her about Utami?"

"Nada."

"The deal with Marley?"

"Nooo."

"You idiot." Peters fell into the lumpy leather chair by the window, let the Glock fall to the floor, and sunk his head into his hands. After a few seconds, he looked at Maddox. "You told her everything, didn't you?"

Maddox held his hand out, palm facing Peters. "Honest, Dirkster. I wouldn't blow the deal."

"You bloody fool."

"Look at the bright side."

"What's that?" Peters asked angrily, picking up the Glock and feeling the gun in his hand, still fighting the urge to use it.

"We're superheroes, Dirkster. Like the movies. We're gonna save the world and get rich doing it."

Maybe I will, Horace, Peters thought, but you're going to be lucky if you're still alive.

Chapter Seventeen—Franklin Washington

Franklin Washington despised Spencer Tate, but after retiring from the FBI, Washington, who grew up in a squalid tenement in Baltimore and fought his way out of poverty as a scholarship football player at William & Mary, found himself in one of the most lucrative security jobs in the world and wasn't ready to give it up. While Washington oversaw the League's security and fraud division and spent his days keeping players out of trouble and maintaining a close eye on thirty-two billionaire owners who lived by their own rules and often played in the murky sandbox of shadowy deals and huge profit, Pixie knew Franklin's biggest headache was none other than Spencer Tate. Two years earlier, Tate had been involved in trying to move the San Antonio Lone Stars to London and nearly found himself exposed for being in cahoots with the dirtiest owner in the League. Indeed, Washington had saved Spencer Tate more than once.

Fortunately, for Tate, Washington kept his mouth shut when he saved Tate's ass. Pixie recalled how Washington had cornered her in the Commissioner's box during the Super Bowl, and like a concerned father, had asked her why on earth she was dating Spencer Tate. At first Pixie was downright offended, but over time, came to realize the truth and began to strike up a friendship with the man nearly everyone but Pixie called "Papa Bear." Pixie liked the name Franklin, so that's what she called him.

After the conversation with Maddox, Pixie stood under threatening skies on the wharf overlooking Spring Harbor and the *Mary G.*, which was once more swathed in yellow impounding tape. She punched up Washington's number and heard the rumble of his voice. "You finally took my advice. I heard you're a single woman. Free and clear."

"No one's ever free and clear of Spencer," Pixie said with a sigh. "You ought to know that. The smell has a way of following you. Why haven't you made your break?"

Washington laughed. "I love football and the money isn't bad. Besides, I don't want to retire."

"A glutton for punishment."

Washington paused and got down to business. "Why the pleasure of a call, Ms. Pixie McGee?"

"I got a problem, Franklin," Pixie said, "and I need your help."

Pixie spent the next several minutes telling Washington about the series of events punctuated by Caleb's arrest and her conversation with Maddox.

"I saw *The New York Times*," Washington said when Pixie finished. He whistled. "I bet your lobsterman friend has every batshit environmental activist wanting his head."

"On a platter."

"With lemon and hot butter." Washington laughed at his own joke before turning serious. "What do you want me to do?"

"I need you to dig. I got to know what bioengineering company is behind all this, because someone's putting those two fools I told you about up to no good."

"There are bioengineering firms all over the planet."

"I know it. But I got faith in you, Franklin."

"A needle in a haystack . . . You said Peters is a movie actor?"

"More like *was*. His career hit the skids."

"Hmmm . . ."

Pixie felt a few drops of rain and moved under the overhang of a weather-beaten, cedar-shingled building that ran along the wharf. "A longshot?"

"Yup. But I'll see what I can come up with."

"My friend's life depends on it." Pixie heard distress in her voice.

Washington said, "Sounds like he's more than a friend. I hope he puts Spencer to shame."

"He does, Franklin. By a mile."

"Let me make some phone calls."

"Out of curiosity, did you hear about the little present I sent to Spencer?"

"I hear he returned the favor. That's why I was laughing when you talked about his smell."

"Is there anything you don't know?"

Washington gave an appreciative laugh before his voice turned serious. "Why a washed-up actor is trying to destroy your friend."

"Thank you, Franklin."

"I'll roll up my sleeves and get on it."

"I owe you."

"Not a thing."

Jonathan Tyler saw himself as a subtle Washington powerbroker. He avoided the kind of confrontation that made headlines and prided himself on being seen as the "pragmatic" Senator from northern California. He relished backroom deals and his constituents' perception that he was the politician who quietly got big things done and lived honorably among thieves. With a warm smile and dry wit, he knew how to plunge the knife into his opponents as if he were a skilled assassin. While other politicians blustered around Washington, Tyler, who wore wire-rimmed glasses and a simple haircut, drew a portrait of calm intelligence and accomplishment.

Yet even Tyler's patient demeanor was being tested at Johnny's Half Shell, a popular haunt near Capitol Hill, as he sat across from Oregon Representative Byron Hodge, the Chairman of the Natural Resources Subcommittee on Water, Wildlife, and Fisheries. Tyler had raised the topic of the Marine Institute of the Pacific's decision to advocate for a moratorium on harvesting lobsters and watched as Hodge slurped another oyster from a silver platter, which he'd plucked from a bed of crushed ice.

As a young man, Hodge had fished commercially for salmon off the Alaskan coast, and unlike Tyler, had the appearance of someone who'd grown up in a hard world – he had big, meaty hands, scarred from a decade of handling lines in frigid weather, and the blunt face of a boxer below a carpet of gray, bristly hair.

Tyler sipped a glass of Chateau Graville Lacoste and picked at his crouton-laden Caesar salad. "The institute made a courageous decision."

"You think?" Hodge shot back as he reached for another oyster.

"Francois drew a line in the sand and I, for one, think it's time that Congress took a similar ethical stand."

"I have no interest in passing legislation to put a billion-dollar industry out of business. It's ludicrous."

"What about protecting the environment? Is that foolhardy?"

"The data doesn't show sufficient cause to kill the industry no matter what Francois or anyone else says."

"Whales are dying, not to mention the environmental damage caused by traps and gear."

Hodge said, "You sound like a wannabe crusader, Jonathan. The lobster industry is the least of our worries. We have a war raging in Europe, the Middle East is blowing up, rising inflation is swallowing paychecks, and who knows what's going to happen after the elections in November. I can't help but wonder – why the sudden interest in the lobster industry?"

Tyler persisted. "My constituents demand it."

"Do they?"

"It's clear to me that the American people believe that safeguarding the environment is vital."

Hodge polished off another oyster and took a sip of lager from a sweating bottle. He leaned forward. "You're hanging your hat in the wrong place. A whale washes up on the New England coast tangled in fishing line and the environmental groups, not to mention the Marine Institute of the Pacific, start shaking their fists and screaming to shut down the lobster industry." His eyes narrowed. "That incident doesn't warrant putting a whole lotta people out of business and destroying the economy of the state of Maine. Besides, the lobstermen, at great cost, have already made modifications to their fishing gear and methods."

Tyler put his fork down. "Do you mean to tell me that your subcommittee is going to do nothing in the wake of the recent events up there?"

"My subcommittee has the responsibility to be rational. Every day some group wants something. Two years ago, it was a complete moratorium on harvesting menhaden off the coast of Virginia. Last year, a group lobbied to have the High Seas Driftnet Act lifted. Our responsibility is to be judicious, fair, and responsible."

"Given what I've seen, if you were being judicious, fair, and responsible, you'd be looking into shutting down the lobster industry. You simply aren't paying attention to what's going on," Tyler said.

Hodge sat back and wiped his mouth with his napkin. "I spent a decade fishing off the Alaskan coast. I'm not going to ruin working people's lives so Sandy Francois can grab a few headlines."

"You're on the wrong side of this issue, Byron," Tyler said sternly.

"It's possible I'm on the 'wrong' side of a lot of issues, Jonathan. But I don't think this is one of them."

"Whales are dying."

"Give me data."

"I've given you better. Did you even watch the video?"

Hodge shook his head and pursed his lips. "If I didn't know better, I'd say you were in some lobbyist's pocket."

Tyler raised his eyebrows, offended. "I'm an honest politician, Byron."

"An oxymoron."

"All I want is a healthier planet for my children."

Hodge sipped his beer and eyed another oyster before shifting back to Tyler. "I'm not buying it. If it's for the children, you sure as hell could find more pressing issues than what's going on in the lobstering industry."

"Maybe, but there are forces at play."

"I heard."

"Social media is going crazy."

"What else is new?"

"No. Really crazy. There's going to be a huge demonstration in the town where it happened."

Hodge slapped his napkin on the table and shook his head. "What does spearing a minke whale have to do with lobstering?"

"Everything. The guy speared the minke while he was hauling traps."

"You're saying I should shut down an industry due to one bad apple?"

"If you sit on your hands, I wouldn't want to be in your shoes, Byron."

"What are you suggesting?"

Tyler sensed Hodge's sudden unease and put his elbows on the table and leaned forward. "Do nothing and soon all those activists are going to be coming to Washington, and they'll be looking for you."

"It wouldn't be the first time."

Tyler smiled thinly and said as he rose from the table, "Maybe, but it might be the last."

The following morning, Roarsh snubbed his cigarette out on a dirty plate littered with chicken bones from the evening before and shoved the butt into an empty Red Bull can. Kiki was nowhere to be seen, probably still in bed after a night of partying. He casually picked up his phone and called Lexington Coach Lines, the largest charter bus company in New England. The man who answered sounded as if his voice had been shoved into a blender – hoarse and gravelly – and it became more irritated after Roarsh called him "dude" using his casual, caustic, surfer persona. Roark had grown up in Peoria.

"Come again?" the man asked, astonished after hearing Roarsh's request.

"I need 100 buses."

"To go where?"

"Spring Harbor, Maine."

"What the hell for?"

"To save the planet, dude."

"A protest?"

"Yup."

"When?"

"Early next week."

"You're kidding me, right? I haven't got a hundred buses."

"So, get them."

"It's not that easy. I can't just snap my fingers."

"You want Greenhaven's business?" Roarsh let his words sink in. "I can call someone else."

There was a pause. "Of course."

"Then find them."

"I'll need one hell of a deposit."

"Not a problem." Roarsh smiled. He relished working for Greenhaven. Unlike other environmental organizations that operated on threadbare budgets, Greenhaven had a significant war chest, funded by environmental extremists around the world. "Send me the invoice."

"What about details?"

"You'll get them."

"I'll need them."

"All in good time," Roarsh snapped, reaching for his pack of cigarettes. "Just get those buses."

Chapter Eighteen—Almira Babb

Ed Pratt's head was throbbing. He'd barely slept for the second night in a row because his phone was blowing up with texts and emails, not to mention calls from the media wanting to know how the town of Spring Harbor, Maine was going to handle the rumored explosion of protesters from around the country.

Ed heard light footsteps and spun around in his office chair. Almira Babb stood in the doorway, a tiny and spinsterish woman with gray hair pulled back in a bun and hawkish brown eyes penetrating through tortoise shell glasses. She'd grown up in Spring Harbor, and when her long-suffering husband died a year earlier, she'd gone back to using her maiden name and was more divisive than ever. She'd proved to be an ugly boil on the town's backside. She led the Chamber of Commerce like a dictator, with no tolerance for dissent and scant imagination, overseeing the aging town's slow demise as the younger generation fled Spring Harbor.

"We've got a big problem, Ed," she said. "I won't stand for the town to be threatened by a bunch of hooligans."

Ed rose and motioned for Babb to sit. She waved him off.

"You need to shut this down. Now," she demanded.

"How do you propose I do that?" Ed asked. "As much as I don't like the idea of protesters, it's a free country."

Babb pointed her bony finger at the Spring Harbor Police Chief. "Are you kidding me, Ed? Free? Free to do what? Trash the town, leave it in shambles, give it a terrible reputation?"

Ed's head pounded harder. "I'm coordinating with the county sheriff's office and state police. We'll do our best to contain the crowds."

"Has anyone spoken to the Governor?"

Ed shrugged. He knew the Governor, given the bad publicity surrounding her "trash episode," was unlikely to take a side, especially in an election year.

"The town's in an uproar. The selectmen are calling a special town meeting tonight. People are demanding answers. They don't want to hear, there'll be 'crowd control'. They want these anarchists stopped!"

Ed could feel the tips of his ears grow hot. He was tired, and especially tired of Babb telling him what he already knew. "You want me to stand on the side of the highway in Kittery with a sign that says, 'Go Away?' How about I build a wall around Spring Harbor, Almira? Or do you think a moat would work better?"

Babb stomped her foot and her voice became shrill. "Don't be cavalier, *Edward Pratt*. I've known you since you were waddling around in diapers. I won't have it."

"I'm going to do the best I can, Almira."

"Try telling that to the people tonight."

"I plan on it."

"If you don't have anything more constructive to say than what you just said to me, you better start looking for another job."

"A threat?"

"A warning."

"One and the same," Ed said. "Shame on you."

"Shame on me?" Babb's eyes thinned and she shook her fist at Pratt. "If you had locked Caleb up and thrown away the key from the start, this would never have happened."

"So now you're suggesting I suspend due process?"

"You tried to sweep the whale incident under the rug from the beginning. Made all these environmentalists think we don't care about whales and want to protect our own. You should have killed the chicken to scare the monkey."

"Innocent until proven guilty. Not a thing anymore?"

"Bah! What nonsense. If I were you, I'd start looking at want ads," Babb added coldly, turning to leave. "If you're lucky, maybe the Walmart in Bangor will need a security guard."

Caleb heard the rattle of the cell door. An officer appeared and motioned for him to get up. During the night, a few more men had been led into the crowded holding tank, and the cell smelled like an overflowing bin of moldy socks. Exhausted, Caleb lifted himself and was led through a corridor to the front desk, where a clerk, engulfed with stacks of paper on his desk, pointed across the room and said with a frown, "Your angel arrived."

Caleb swung his head and suddenly felt as if an oppressive weight had been lifted. Pixie broke into a smile and gave him a big wave. He turned to the clerk. "I can leave?"

Earlier in the day, Caleb had appeared before the court for arraignment joined by his attorney, an overweight man in his mid-sixties who cared nothing about him, lobstermen, or whales. He'd responded to the irritable judge's questions in a desultory manner before fleeing with only a brief word to Caleb. He hadn't inspired confidence, and yet here was Pixie and it appeared Caleb was a free man.

The clerk nodded and held out a plastic tray holding Caleb's wallet and phone. "Bail was paid. Don't leave the state and stay out of trouble."

Caleb moved swiftly toward Pixie, afraid the clerk was going to tell him it was all a mistake and toss him back into the holding tank. Caleb gave Pixie a swift hug and when he pulled away, Pixie pinched her nose with thumb and index finger, and said, "We need to get you a bath."

A few moments later, Caleb knelt by the Cadillac's rear door as the Berner rested in the back seat, a plastic cone around its neck to keep him from gnawing his stitches. The dog's tail slowly went *thump, thump* on the vinyl seat as Caleb scratched the Berner behind the ears. "Looks like our friend is on the mend."

"He's a trooper."

Caleb grimaced and turned. "How much did the vet bill cost?"

Pixie gave a knowing smile and said, "Not as much as bailing my friend Caleb out of jail."

"I broke the bank today."

"It was worth every penny."

"How much do I owe you?" Caleb asked.

"Nothin'."

Caleb shook his head and shrugged. As the relief of being freed set in, he was suddenly overwhelmed by the need for sleep. He looked at the dog. "What are we going to name our friend?"

Pixie's face lit up. "I was thinking 'Rocky'."

"Rocky?"

"Do you like it?"

"Sounds like the perfect name."

Pixie knelt and gave Rocky a big kiss on the forehead and a scratch behind the ears. "Welcome to the family, ole boy." She turned to Caleb. "Let's get you back to Spring Harbor." She pinched her nose again and said with a frown, "Seriously, you smell worse than the dog."

As they drove away from the courthouse and onto Old Bangor Road, Pixie first rolled down her window and then recounted her conversation with Maddox. When she finished, Caleb stared angrily out the passenger window, his wrists still red from being handcuffed, and said under his breath, "I knew those bastards were up to something."

When they arrived at the Stringer Cottage in the late afternoon, shadows were spreading across the patchy lawn and the bay was lit in golden hues. Elrod met them in front of the house. He was splattered in paint and behind him, a ladder stretched to the second-floor dormer. The front of the cottage was bathed in a soft, creamy pink with white trim, and despite the trouble they found themselves in, Caleb noticed Pixie's eyes sparkle when she saw Elrod's handiwork. When Caleb had heard Pixie wanted a pink house, he shuddered, but now he acknowledged it was a brilliant choice. The Stringer Cottage had never appeared so warm and inviting.

As Caleb held Rocky in his arms, Pixie said, "That's a beautiful paint job, Elrod."

"I had doubts," Elrod said, taking his baseball cap off and wiping his brow.

"But not now?"

"I guess it's okay." Elrod turned to the dog. The old man's craggy face broke into a smile. "Is this the hound?"

"Sure is," Pixie said.

"Got a name?"

"Rocky," Caleb said.

"He's a fine one."

"He's ours now," Caleb said. Rocky's hind quarters were shaved and a row of stitches ran along his hip.

Elrod's smile vanished. "Given all that's going on, too bad he won't be able to protect you."

"He's not a guard dog, Elrod," Pixie said.

"Clearly. I'm just saying you might need one," Elrod warned.

Caleb said, "Why's that?"

"The town's in an uproar. Rumor has it protesters are coming to tear Spring Harbor apart, especially you."

"Who says?" Pixie asked.

"Ed Pratt . . . he said there could be 15,000 of them activists."

"Hell," Caleb said, the color draining from his face. "When is this nightmare going to end?"

"And there's a special town meeting tonight. Almira Babb's on the warpath."

Caleb wasn't surprised. Babb was always after someone.

"I hate to say it, Caleb," Elrod said before pausing, "but you're enemy number one. People think you caused all this trouble by spearing that whale."

Caleb shook his head and set Rocky on the soft grass.

"They want blood."

Caleb noticed the smile disappear from Pixie's face. The joy from the new paint on the cottage had faded to concern.

"I'd stay away from the Town Hall tonight."

Caleb's fists grew into a ball. *This was his hometown. He hadn't done anything wrong. It was all a set up. No one was going to tell him what to do.* He stared hard at Elrod and Pixie and said, "What time is the meeting?"

Elrod shook his head as if to say, 'you're crazy'. "7 pm."

Caleb looked at Pixie. "I better shower. And I want clean underwear in case the mob tears me apart."

"You're going?" Pixie stared dumbfounded.

"That's right," Caleb said, his face hardening. "They can kill me, but they're not going to chase me out of Spring Harbor."

Peters held his head in his hands and fought the urge to shoot Maddox. The motel room was growing smaller and smaller, stuffier and stuffier, as late afternoon crept toward early evening. Dust motes hung in the air, illuminated by a sliver of light coming through the part in the curtains as Maddox sat on his bed and clipped his toenails – snip, snip, snip. After he realized that Peters wasn't going to shoot him, he had rifled through Peters' shower kit without asking, and now Peters was watching a pile of clippings rise on the bedspread. Peters considered every minute that he didn't fill Maddox full of lead a triumph of self-restraint.

Peters was about to question Maddox again, throttle him if necessary, to discover what he'd actually told Pixie, when Maddox – *snip, snip, snip* – casually said, "There's going to be a big meeting tonight, Dirkster. The whole friggin' town's going to be at the Town Hall."

"What?"

"Not what. When. People are in a panic. Furious. They think the protesters are gonna destroy the town." Maddox seemed to relish the thought.

Peters could feel his knees weakening. The thought of a local mob chasing him through the streets of Spring Harbor terrified him. "Why didn't you bloody tell me before now?"

Maddox shrugged and reached down to snip another toenail. "Cause you've been too busy accusing me of spilling the beans. As if I'd compromise our business deal. That's my way back on top." Maddox had a pleased, faraway look on his face.

Peters' mind spun. He felt the urge to call Marley and demand to leave Spring Harbor. It was dangerous for him to stay. He instinctively reached for the Glock that had been resting on his lap.

"What's the matter? You look scared, buddy boy. Like someone's about to steal your lunch money," Maddox said.

Peters was indignant. "Bloody right. I don't feel like being ripped apart by a pack of hyenas."

Maddox raised the toenail clippers at Peters and pointed. "Courage, Dirkster. Remember, you're a hero." He paused and carelessly swept the clippings off the frayed bedspread onto the carpet.

Peters scrunched his nose as Maddox took his thumb and forefinger and flicked a remaining toenail clipping off the bed.

Maddox went on. "We should go to the meeting."

Peters' eyes narrowed. "Are you insane?"

"Heroes stand up to bullies. They'll respect you."

"They'll beat me to a pulp."

Maddox reached for his rum bottle and took a slug. No one could say that Peters didn't enjoy his booze, but he was amazed at how much the man could drink. A hollow leg. "Naw. The one they want to pound on is Gray. They think he started all this. People are pissed at him. Sure, they think you're an activist snitch, for posting the video, Dirkster, but they want to boil Gray alive for giving you the opening."

"I'm not going." Peters folded his arms across his chest.

Maddox's eyes narrowed. "If you had it over again, would you be Bond?"

"What the bloody hell does that have to do with anything?"

"Don't be touchy. I'm just asking a question."

"It was an artistic decision."

"Wah, wah, wah. And how did that work out?" Maddox leapt off the bed and pointed his finger at Peters. "Come on Dirkster, a shred of honesty."

"Of course," Peters mumbled.

Maddox grabbed Peters by the shoulders and got in his face, their noses nearly touching. Maddox had the breath of a dragon. "This is one of those moments! Don't you get it?"

Peters could see the bloodshot veins in Maddox's eyes.

"You go to the meeting, and you'll be legendary. Activists around the world will see you as a god. You'll be Braveheart!"

"So, you're saying I'll be hanged, disemboweled, beheaded, and quartered?"

"Every director in Hollywood will be calling. Bond will be back on the table."

"You're a bloody fool."

Maddox leaned even closer. "Listen to me, Dirkster. You could have been Bond. Now you got a chance to be a real life 007. I'm telling you, you'll be one of the most famous activists in the world. You saved whales, destroyed the lobster industry. There'll be documentaries."

For an instant, Peters imagined himself sitting across from Spielberg as the famed director pushed a golden script across an elaborate mahogany table and showered Dirk Peters with praise. "You think?"

"I know, buddy boy. All you got to do is walk into that Town Hall and be a man."

Peters reached for the handle of the Glock. He pointed at Maddox. "If they touch one hair on my head."

"You're gonna be good."

"I'll—"

"Let's go!" Maddox jumped gleefully off the bed.

"Now?"

"We got to get a front row seat."

"Bloody hell. Why not be fashionably late?"

"Because, Dirk, the star of the show needs to be front and center."

Chapter Nineteen—Town Hall

The Spring Harbor Town Hall sat on a rise next to the Methodist Church. The parking lot overflowed, and cars and pickups were parked on strips of grass along Main Street under leafy oaks in the bloom of early summer and sap-dripping pines. A few gulls circled above while church bells tolled as if solemnly announcing a funeral. A handful of latecomers hurried to the Town Hall's entrance.

Inside the meeting hall, painted an off-white with thick, varnished floorboards, there wasn't an empty seat. People were forced to stand in the back, shuffling their feet as they waited expectantly to hear what the town was going to do to thwart the impending disaster. The town selectmen and Ed Pratt sat grimly in the front at a long rectangular wooden table facing the crowd. Almira Babb sat in the middle, pursing her bloodless lips.

Maddox and Peters failed to arrive early enough to find their front row seats. They sat four rows back near the aisle and were the subjects of angry stares and a few whispered threats. Maddox sat with his legs splayed and a smirk across his face, relishing the attention, while Peters sat next to him, his eyes darting back and forth as if he were waiting for some seething lunatic to bludgeon him. Foolishly, he'd allowed Maddox to convince him to leave the Glock in the motel room.

When Head Selectman Van Burnham stood, he rapped the cherrywood table with his gavel and called the meeting to order. He was built like a linebacker—square jaw, a thatch of gray hair, and thick arms from decades of building homes from Bar Harbor to Machias. He could stare down a bear, but he wasn't unkind.

"All rise," Burnham bellowed as he faced the flag and began to lead the Pledge of Allegiance.

Maddox stood and loudly recited the oath to deadly stares, while Peters, who didn't know the Pledge, put his hand over his heart and mumbled the words to *God Save the King*.

When everyone was seated, Burnham was about to speak when Babb rose from her chair, pointed at him and Ed Pratt, and said, "Let's cut to the chase. What's the town going to do to stop this?"

"It's not," Burnham said. A wave of disbelief swept through the Town Hall as murmurs turned into a flood of protest. Burnham banged the gavel several times to restore order.

When the hall finally quieted down, Babb asked, "What did you say?"

"We won't stop people lawfully protesting, Almira. This is America."

A man shouted, "What about our businesses? Our homes?" There were angry echoes of "That's right!"

"We won't stop people protesting, but we can try to contain it," Burnham said, his face grim. "Ed and I've been working on a plan with the state police to see that property is safeguarded and to ensure the protest will be peaceful."

A middle-aged woman in the rear of the hall shouted, "That's not what we want to hear, Van!"

"Maybe not, but there really isn't anything else we can do."

More angry voices began to ripple across the hall. A lobsterman, Cliff Pierce, stood up three rows away from Peters and Maddox. Pierce's face was weathered and his neck looked like cracked leather. He suddenly turned to Peters. "What are you doing here? You and Maddox have caused enough trouble."

Silence followed, and all eyes fell upon Dirk Peters. Peters started to slide down in his seat when Maddox stood up and said with intoxicated bravado, "He's caused trouble? Shoot the messenger, huh? Ha!"

At first, Pierce looked confused, but as Maddox proceeded, his face began to redden.

"You pillage the sea. Leave traps and gear all over the ocean floor. Kill whales. And most of all . . ." Maddox paused for effect, "made Spring Harbor a dump. Lobsters this. Lobsters that. If it weren't for you guys, Spring Harbor could be a glittering mecca instead of a shithole." Maddox swept his eyes across the hall. "I have a plan, but no one ever listens to me," he said, dripping with contempt. "Dirk here is a legend. Unlike you and the other idiots who haul traps, he's got conviction. He witnessed a whale speared by Caleb Gray and showed the world Spring Harbor's hypocrisy." Maddox paused again and declared, "Dirk Peters is a hero."

A man a few rows away shouted, "Shut up, Horace. You've always been too big for your britches."

Maddox gave him an unsteady middle finger. "You shut up!" Burnham yelled, "Order!" and pounded his gavel.

Ignoring Burnham and Maddox both, the same man turned to Peters. "Shame on you. What have you got to say for yourself?"

Peters tried to make himself as small as possible until Maddox whispered, "Braveheart. Bigger than Bond, Dirkster. Action!"

Peters suddenly felt as if the curtain was rising to a full house. He nervously swept his hand through his hair and set his jaw. He rose from his seat while noting the lopsided grin spreading across Maddox's face.

Peters stood for a moment in silence looking at the floor and raised his chin like Olivier delivering *Hamlet* to a West End audience. He said, "I witnessed a man harming one of God's greatest creatures." His voice building, Peters raised a finger. "While I understand that you may disagree, I chose to call out what I saw as a terrible wrong." He paused for effect. "Whales deserve to live as you and I do."

"Hear, hear," Maddox said, proudly. "Attaboy, Dirk!"

The man a few rows away turned and said, "Horseshit."

Burnham said, "Watch your language."

Peters continued, his voice growing steadier. "Friends, I merely speak the truth. When my activist friends come to town, they'll do so only in the name of environmental injustice . . . to speak against the harming of whales, the slaughtering of crustaceans, the environmental destruction caused by ignorance–"

"Ignorance?" Almira Babb questioned sharply, her voice cutting through the air.

"That's what my man said, Almira," Maddox shot back. It was no secret that Maddox detested Babb with every ounce of his bone and sinew. He blamed her foremost for his destruction.

"Be quiet, Horace," she barked. She gave a withering glance at Maddox before settling her eyes on Peters. "Who are you?" she asked accusingly. "And what do you want?"

"You've heard my name. And what do I want? Merely justice," Peters said, thrusting his chin forward.

Almira sneered. "Hmmm . . . justice? I think not." Through pursed lips she said, "You've caused great distress in Spring Harbor. You could have quietly brought the video to the authorities, but you wanted to go viral. I have no doubt that Caleb's actions demand scrutiny, but what's behind all this, Mr. Peters? Is it environmental justice or a ploy?"

Someone yelled from the other side of the hall, "That's right, what is this all about?" A murmur began to ripple across the room.

"I can assure you it's no ploy," Peters said. "If you're looking for someone to blame, you should be asking questions of Gray."

"Ask me what?" The entire audience turned at the words to see Caleb, flanked by Pixie and Elrod, in the back of the room.

Caleb stared back at the myriad of eyes now fixed on him. There was hardly a person in the hall he didn't know.

Rip Leland, with hollow cheeks and stubble on his chin, who'd been a clammer most of his working life, said, "Why'd you do it, Caleb? We got enough trouble with the state not to have one of us gaffing whales. I've known you all your life, and I thought you knew better."

"I didn't gaff the whale, Rip," Caleb said, shifting his eyes to Peters, who continued to stand. "I didn't do it. You have my word."

"For what that's worth," Maddox spat.

"Be quiet, Horace, or we'll throw you out," Babb warned. She pointed at Caleb. "What do you have to say for yourself? You've brought harm to Spring Harbor."

Caleb gestured toward Peters. "The video he made is a sham."

"Hardly," Peters said. He was trying to remain calm and to project the assurance of the moral high ground. He summoned his training and added, "the video tells the story."

A young woman, Brenda Burgess, who worked in the cafeteria at the high school, said to Caleb, "the man in the video was definitely you."

Cliff Pierce, who'd hauled traps for nearly fifty years, said, "It don't add up. I don't see Caleb gaffing a whale. I don't care what the video showed."

"A picture is worth a thousand words, Cliff," Burgess said.

"And words ain't always true," Pierce volleyed.

Babb took her glasses off, pointed them at Caleb, and shook her head. "Mary is looking down on you with shame," she said to stunned silence.

Caleb felt his neck burn. He stared at Babb in disbelief and disgust. He wanted to speak in his defense, but the fact that she had invoked the name of his dead wife had rendered him speechless. Ed Pratt looked at Babb as if to say, "you witch," and Burnham had hung his head.

Caleb felt a hand on his shoulder – it was Pixie – and then Elrod slowly pushed past him and said, "Almira, you've said some terrible things over the years, but that tops it. For all you who think Caleb brought trouble to the town, you're full of it. I've known Caleb and his family my whole life. You have too. They were good people, and he's a good man. Shame on you for believing that scoundrel," Elrod gestured toward Peters. "You're too busy wringing your hands and pointing a finger to realize Caleb ain't the culprit."

Babb leaned forward. "Very eloquent, Elrod. But not convincing. Say what you want, but this town's in big trouble, and we all know what started it."

Elrod shook his head. "This town's in trouble alright. But not because of Caleb."

"Peters didn't pick up that gaff, Elrod," Babb said.

"He's why we're having this meeting, but he ain't why the town's in trouble," Elrod responded.

"Why then?" Babb demanded.

"You, Almira. You've resisted every opportunity to help change the town. You've run the Chamber of Commerce into the ground and Spring Harbor with it. Everyone knows that. But everyone here is too scared to stand up to you."

"Bah! I've done nothing of the sort."

"You tell her, Elrod," Pixie said loudly.

Babb arched her eyebrows. "Who are you?"

"Pixie McGee, Your Highness."

"Ahh. The stripper who bought Millbridge Island."

"Call me what you want. But you should have the common sense to know that Caleb's not guilty and Dirk Peters is a lying fool."

"She hit the Dirkster over the head with a bottle! She should be arrested!" Maddox shouted.

Babb turned to Maddox doubtfully, then addressed Pixie. "The video, Ms. McGee?"

"A lie."

Caleb looked at Peters who was rolling his eyes at the accusation and striking a defiant and dramatic pose.

"I can't believe you're going to believe this washed-up actor over Caleb," Pixie continued, shaking her head. "In Texas, we call that a betrayal. Maybe in Maine you feed your young to the lions?" Pixie put her hands on her hips and glowered at Babb. "That would make sense given how few young people I see around here."

Babb made a motion as if she were waving away a mosquito. "You have no say in Spring Harbor."

"I pay my property tax same as everyone else."

"You're from away."

"Oh, so now you find it convenient to distrust people who ain't from here?" Pixie shot back.

"People lie. Videos do not."

Pixie pursed her lips and stared hard at Babb, her eyes narrowing. "If you believe that, you're a dang fool."

"This is about the town's plan, not a bickering session," Burnham interjected. "We can sort out blame later."

"The town needs to make a statement," Babb declared.

"What kind of statement?" Burnham asked.

"Denouncing the harming of whales. We need to assert that we believe in the sanctity of God's creatures, and that we share the protesters' concerns." She paused. "We denounce Caleb's actions."

A hushed silence fell upon the hall like a soft winter snow. Ed Pratt shook his head. "What's that going to accomplish, Almira, except to make a scapegoat out of Caleb? The protesters don't just care about whales. They want to put the lobster industry out of business. Destroy our way of life."

"Caleb deserves everything he's got coming," she shot back, giving Caleb a withering stare. "Everyone in here saw the video." She shifted. "There'll be no half measures. We have an army of activists marching toward this town. Resisting them will tell the world that we stand with Caleb Gray holding a gaff over a whale. It will be the death of the town. We'll be pariahs." She paused to let her words sink in. "But there's another way forward. Instead, we should join the protesters. We should show that we applaud the effort to clean up behaviors that are destructive to the environment. I propose a resolution. We make our friend Dirk Peters an honorary citizen of Spring Harbor for service to this community and welcome the protesters with open arms."

"We make the Englishman an honorary citizen?" Pratt asked, shocked.

"Exactly." She glanced at Peters. "We must see in our British friend a beacon of light that will allow us to clean out the bad apples within our community and present a fresh and shiny face to the world."

Upon hearing Babb, Peters broke into an uncertain smile as Caleb's stomach turned in disgust. Pixie said, "hell bells" under her breath and Elrod muttered, "damn fool."

"What's this going to accomplish?" Burnham asked.

"A peaceful demonstration. No property damage. Good publicity. Partners with our activist friends. And . . . maybe a boost to the town's economy if we can convince the protesters to enjoy our town instead of tear it apart."

"What about the lobstermen? Even if it's peaceful, that don't mean them protesters will leave us alone to do our jobs," Cliff Pierce said.

"It may not. But it buys time," Babb answered.

"You're saying all we got to do is paint that English fella as a saint and Caleb as a sinner and this whole thing will blow over?" Pierce questioned with a look of doubt stitched across his face. Babb coldly nodded as Peters tried to strike the pose of a man with a halo on his head and Maddox smirked. Caleb felt the air rush out of his lungs.

"Enough of this," the clammer, Rip Leland called out. "I want to hear from someone who actually knows Caleb."

"The boy's not perfect, but he's no liar," Pierce shouted, then pointed at Peters. "I'd trust Caleb over this scoundrel any day."

"That video doesn't add up," Leland said. "I've known Caleb and his family for years. I can't see him doing what Peters says."

The murmurs of dissent against Peters grew louder.

"I agree," a voice called out from the back of the hall. It was Janice Colby, who ran the bakery and was known for her straightforward demeanor. "We all know Caleb. He's been here his whole life, and we've trusted him. Do we really think he's capable of what's in that video?"

"The video doesn't lie," Babb countered.

"People do," Colby said. "Dirk Peters is an outsider. Caleb is one of us. We're going to throw him to the sharks for what? To save face?"

"It's not just about saving face," Babb replied, her tone icy. "It's about survival. The world is watching. To them, the video tells the story. They don't know Caleb except what they see on that video."

"And what happens when the world moves on and leaves us to clean up the mess?" Colby asked. "Caleb won't be the only one betrayed. This whole town will carry that shame."

"It's not about shame," Babb interjected. "It's about making sure this town has a future. The protests will happen regardless, but we need to minimize the damage."

"At what cost?" Colby asked pointedly. "If we sacrifice Caleb today, who will we sacrifice tomorrow? When does it stop?"

Caleb shook his head and peered angrily at Babb. He was about to respond to the chaos when Albion Wright, the owner of Spring Harbor Savings and Loan and half of Washington County, said, "So help me Caleb Gray, if those activists damage my properties . . . I've loaned money to nearly every lobsterman in this peninsula to buy boats, traps, gear, and whatever else is needed to fish, including you. With the help of that British fella," he scowled at Peters, "you've just delivered the lobster industry and this town on a silver platter to the state, and worse, to the federal government. It won't be long before the bureaucrats shut down lobstering because of you. When that happens," he paused and swept his eyes around the room, "my savings and loan will go bankrupt and every single one of you who makes your living from fishing and elsewhere will be out of work, and there'll only be one person to blame for everyone's misery. You, Caleb. If we don't do anything, we'll all be ruined."

Wright's speech temporarily quieted the crowd. It was as if everyone suddenly took a look over the precipice and didn't like what they were seeing.

Babb took advantage of the lull to call the question.

"All in favor of this resolution?" Babb asked, scanning the crowd. "I propose Dirk Peters be named an honorary citizen of Spring Harbor, Maine, and that we as a community collectively condemn the harming of whales in general and Caleb Gray's actions in particular."

Except for some low murmuring, the uneasy silence in the hall continued. Caleb could feel the tension build as he looked at the men and women he knew his whole life avert their eyes and stare at the floor. A few seconds passed when Babb asked, "What's it going to be?"

Alden Granderson, who owned the hardware store, said, "This isn't right" before Betty Brown, who owned a small clothing shop on Main Street and had a reputation for penny pinching, stood and forcefully said, "I'd like to make that motion."

"Shame on you, Betty," Elrod said.

"I second the motion," said another voice, from one of the Seavey brothers, who ran a lumber mill and had been quiet until now.

Burnham shook his head in disgust, his gavel heavy in his hand.

Ed Pratt said, "You'll regret this, Almira."

Burnham sighed audibly and called out, "All in favor?"

Caleb suddenly stood, his face tight with anger and pain. "I've had enough," he said loudly, silencing the room. He turned to Burnham. "Do what you want, Van. This town can decide without me." Without another word, he walked out, followed by Pixie.

A silence hung in the air as the door closed behind Caleb. Burnham sighed and rapped his gavel. "Okay, everyone. Let's vote on the resolution."

"You're out of your mind," Ed Pratt said, shaking his head at Babb.

Burnham held up his hand for silence. "Let's put it to a vote."

The townspeople's hands raised slowly, reluctantly. The resolution passed by a narrow margin. Spring Harbor had made its choice, though regret and unease hung heavy in the air.

Caleb felt the burning sensation in his neck as he looked across the harbor in the dusk. Lobster boats swung on moorings in the light breeze and a sloop with its sails furled and running lights glowing made a chugging sound as it headed out to sea. Elrod caught up to them and when they turned to face him, he just shook his head. Caleb heard Pixie say softly, "Oh, darlin'," and he met her tender gaze for a moment, but despite her presence, he'd never felt so alone, so cast out, so betrayed.

Franklin Washington had spent half the day with his assistant combing the information spit out by the League's security and fraud databases, AI engines, and Google searches. Washington's assistant, Sabrina, a former NSA analyst and Naval Academy graduate, peered into the glow of her computer screen digging for specialized bioengineering firms. Diet Coke cans and empty coffee cups littered the office. Washington had been surprised at the number of bioengineering startups flung across the globe from Tokyo to Oslo. There were nearly too many to count.

At one point, Sabrina pushed her chair away from the computer, sighed, and said, "Needle in a haystack. What now?"

Washington walked across his office, high atop Manhattan's darkening skyline, and peered at her computer screen. "Let's start where we began. How about California again?"

"We've done that."

"Like I said, Dirk Peters was living in LA."

Sabrina slid her chair back in front of the computer and punched her keyboard. A few seconds later, she said, "In California alone, there are nearly 4,500 firms."

"How about narrowing it?"

"Again?"

"How about new keywords?"

"Like what?"

Washington paused, folded his arms across his chest and said, "Go to patent and intellectual property filings for cellular seafood companies."

Sabrina grimaced. "Say that one more time?"

Washington repeated himself.

She tapped on her keyboard, waited momentarily for the results, and said, "I found several."

"Narrow it."

She tapped away. A few seconds later she said, "I can only find a couple."

"Who you got?"

"One is Meat Solutions. The other is Eco Food." She tapped her keyboard again. "Both are publicly traded companies. One is based in Eureka, the other in San Diego." She did a quick google scan. Moments later she added, "Lots of press coverage. They seem on the up and up."

159

Washington tapped his chin and sighed. "Okay. How about the same prompt and add venture capital and angel investors. Let's see if we got any names on the list."

Sabrina focused on the screen and typed in the additional prompt. Moments later she said, "Holy shit."

Washington leaned over her shoulder and said, "What do you have?"

"Oscar Leonid."

"Are you kidding me, woman?"

"Nope." She tapped quickly on her keyboard. "Look at that." She pointed at the screen. "There's a *New York Times* article about sustainable practices." The article, entitled *The Future is Mine,* featured a photo of the controversial billionaire sitting in the den of his palatial California home.

For a few minutes, they both read the article as Sabrina carefully scrolled the story. When they finished, Washington said, "He alluded to a bioengineering firm in southern California doing great work. On the verge of something big."

Sabrina turned her head. "Yup."

"He mentions a South African founder. But he doesn't give a name."

Washington turned away from the computer. "See what you can find about South Africans. Anything to do with tech and bioengineering startups."

Sabrina tapped her keyboard and peered into the screen. "Lots of names."

"How about add 'sustainable seafood practices'."

She typed again and waited. "Okay. I got one. Sebastian Marley." She typed again and paused. "Whew. Look at that." She pointed as Washington stared into the screen.

"Convicted. Served time," Sabrina said. "Looks like he and his cronies got snared in a tax evasion scheme using shell companies. He's hung around with some bad guys." She turned and stared quizzically at Washington. "Why would Marley be credible enough to get venture capital?"

"If he's our culprit, he's looking for a big payday. Why not make people think you've changed stripes and hop on the environmentalist bandwagon trying to create cellular seafood? A wolf in sheep's clothing."

Sabrina began to type furiously. A moment later, she said, "He lives in LA. Surprised he wasn't deported after serving time."

Washington shook his head. "Not much surprises me anymore. Money talks."

"You think he's the guy?"

Washington gave a slow smile and fist bumped his assistant. "It's our best shot anyway."

For one of the few times in her life, Pixie didn't know what to say. How do you cheer up a man after his entire town just turned its back on him? She understood pain and hardship better than most, but what had occurred a few minutes before in the stark Town Hall of a dying fishing town on the edge of nowhere made her furious and sad. She couldn't imagine how Caleb felt as they walked in the twilight with Elrod toward the Cadillac. Her life had taken several bizarre twists and turns, but nothing like what he was experiencing in that moment. As she watched this good man bowed by the weight of this sweeping rejection, she realized she never cared for anyone as much as she did Caleb Gray. Whether he wanted to be with her for the long haul or not, Pixie told herself she'd do anything for him. What Almira Babb had said about Mary was one of the cruelest things Pixie had heard, and she was no stranger to the world's cruelty. All she wanted was to sink her head into Caleb's chest and make him realize he wasn't alone and would never be if she had something to do with it.

Elrod opened the door to the car while Caleb waited silently with his hands on his hips carefully averting their eyes when Pixie's phone began to chime. She fought the urge to ignore it but then pulled her cell phone out of her handbag and noticed it was Franklin Washington. Her heart skipped a beat.

"I think we got our man," Washington told her moments later.

Pixie broke into a smile. "Where?"

"Los Angeles, Pix. He looks like a nasty little man." For the next few minutes, Washington gave her the backstory.

When he finished, Pixie said to Washington, "I'm catching the next flight to Tinseltown."

"You want me to join you?"

"I got it, Franklin. You're the best."

"Be careful and let me know if there's anything I can do. We'll keep digging around."

After Pixie ended the call, she said to Elrod and Caleb, "I'm going to California. It may be a wild goose chase, a lark, but it's all we got. I can't just sit around. I gotta do something. I have a lead, and if I can dig up some evidence, we might have Dirk Peters by the short hairs."

Caleb came to attention. "If you're going, I'm going."

"The judge said you can't leave the state," Pixie said.

"What more can they do to me? Besides, they didn't make me wear an ankle bracelet."

"True. But darlin'—"

"I'm going," Caleb interrupted.

Elrod walked around the car. "I'd like to go. I ain't ever been but always wanted to see Malibu."

"It's not a pleasure trip, Elrod. Besides, who's going to take care of our new friend Rocky?"

"I always wanted to spin around that town in the Cadillac."

Pixie smiled. "I promise, Elrod, after we clean up this mess, we're goin' west. Hotel California, Hollywood, sun and surf. We'll drive the Caddy and listen to George Strait and Patsy Cline."

Elrod broke into a grin. "I'm gonna look forward to that."

She paused and looked at Caleb. "But first we gotta get the dirt on Dirk Peters."

"What are we waiting for?" Caleb asked. "I appear to have worn out my welcome here."

While Maddox gleefully jabbered, Peters was aware of the icy stares as he stood waiting for the hall to empty so he could escape into the night. The town had granted honorary citizenship to him, but Peters knew it was a sham conferred by people frightened about losing their town and way of life. He was a marked man. *The Outlaw Dirk Peters.* While Maddox clearly relished the scorn, Peters felt bile rise in his throat. He wanted out of Spring Harbor before someone rearranged his handsome nose. If he got out of the Town Hall parking lot alive, he was going to call Marley and demand payment for services rendered. He'd done his job. He'd turned Spring Harbor, the lobster capital of the world, upside down, made the citizenry devour one of its own, and set in motion the largest environmental protest in memory. The hell he'd unleashed on Spring Harbor had momentum of its own. How could Marley deny his request?

After the hall had nearly emptied, Peters began to slink toward the exit. As he crept quickly toward the door, he heard, "Not so fast."

He turned as Almira Babb's index finger pointed at him like a wand. "I'd be careful, Mr. Peters," she warned. "Very careful. You may be an honorary citizen, but if I'm willing to destroy a man like Caleb Gray to save Spring Harbor, think of what I'll do to you."

Peters slowly shook his head under her withering stare before fleeing.

Moments later, under a lone streetlight in the dark shadows of the parking lot, Maddox said, "Don't you love it, Dirkster?"

"Love what?"

"The hate."

Peters grunted and looked fearfully into the darkness.

"There's some angry people out there." Maddox laughed and stared into the night. "You may be an honorary citizen, Mr. Bango and Dash, but you're not winning any popularity contests. But who cares? Think of it this way. You're the misunderstood hero. You're the lone voice in the friggin' wilderness. Captain Courageous—"

"Shut the hell up, Horace," Peters snapped. "Misunderstood my arse. I'm getting out of this town before they touch one hair on my bloody head."

Chapter Twenty—Honorary Citizen

Ed Pratt's anger was boiling when he picked up *The Bangor Times* and began to read the front-page story. Lou Farnham's words dripped with blood as Pratt angrily replayed the night before when the town of Spring Harbor turned its back on Caleb Gray.

Hollywood Star Dirk Peters Receives Honorary Citizenship While Protesters Descend Upon Spring Harbor

By Lou Farnham

Spring Harbor, Maine—In a night filled with drama and shock, the town of Spring Harbor bestowed honorary citizenship on Hollywood actor and environmental activist Dirk Peters, who has been recently hailed for his efforts to protect the world's oceans. The meeting, which was held at the Town Hall and attended by nearly every prominent figure in the small coastal community, took a dark turn as accusations reemerged against one of the town's own, lobsterman Caleb Gray.

Peters, known for his role in the blockbuster film, Bango and Dash, and his passion for marine conservation, was given the honorary title by Chamber of Commerce President Almira Babb, who had championed the move to join hands with environmentalists. The tide of activism has been growing in response to Peters' claims of unsustainable lobstering practices and allegations of an attack on a minke whale by Gray. According to Peters, Gray thrust a gaff into the minke, causing injury to the whale, a claim that Peters backed up with a video he posted on social media that has exploded in a hail of controversy.

Babb, sensing the impending storm of negative press and potential economic impact, introduced the resolution to honor Peters and, in her words, "demonstrate the town's commitment to preserving our precious natural resources." Her remarks were seen as a move to demonstrate harmony with the activists.

Critics of the resolution suggest that the town is acting out of fear rather than any moral principle. Proponents worry that failing to act would invite even more scrutiny from the activist groups authorities warned were organizing a massive protest in Spring Harbor. Spring Harbor now finds itself at the epicenter of a bitter divide. Gray's supporters argue that he's been sacrificed by a town more interested in currying favor with a Hollywood elite than standing by one of their own.

But for many in Spring Harbor, the decision to honor Peters and cast suspicion on Gray was inevitable. The environmental movement is coming to Spring Harbor whether the town wants it or not, and Peters' honorary citizenship might be the beginning of a new chapter—one in which tradition and livelihood clash with the ideals of celebrity activism. And while Caleb Gray's future hangs in the balance, the town is left grappling with the question of how far it will go to protect its reputation.

For Dirk Peters, this was a night of triumph. For Caleb Gray, some suggest it was a night of betrayal. And for Spring Harbor, it may be a night that will forever change its future.

Pratt swore under his breath, and in one fluid motion, tossed the paper into the trash. It was going to be a long day, and Pratt was in no mood to play nice. Almira Babb and the town had done a great wrong to Caleb, and Pratt was livid.

Pixie and Caleb fell asleep on the flight to LA. They'd driven most of the night to Boston in Elrod's pickup and wearily climbed aboard the Airbus A321. When the plane lifted above the Berkshires, Pixie felt Caleb's head drop on her shoulder and she found herself snuggling against him before falling asleep.

When the plane struck the tarmac at LAX, Pixie woke with a jolt and discovered Caleb staring pensively out the cabin window. "I need coffee," he said.

"Same here," Pixie answered sleepily. "Let's get us some caffeine and something in our bellies. then we can go find our friend, Marley."

"Sounds like a plan."

"Are you feeling any better?"

"I'm okay," Caleb said. He looked at her and said wearily, "I've never been to LA and something tells me I'm not going to like it. Let's find Marley and get out of here."

"Okay."

Caleb turned and again stared out of the window as the plane made its way to the gate. "You know, as disappointed as I am with my neighbors right now, Spring Harbor is home, and it's where I want to be."

Two hours later, Caleb pulled their rental car to the curb, and Pixie looked out the window at Marley's sprawling mid-century home perched on a bluff overlooking the Pacific. They could see a kidney shaped pool surrounded by a concrete terrace adorned with white-cushioned loungers and chairs. The sun glistened on the ocean in an oily haze and the air was still. Not a breath of wind.

Caleb and Pixie popped out of the car. Pixie smiled thinly at Caleb and said, "What do you think?"

"Let's go see if he's here."

Washington was only able to provide Marley's home address. If Marley oversaw a cellular seafood bioengineering firm, the name and location remained a mystery. Caleb and Pixie walked down steep stone steps wildly overgrown with creeping thyme, cotoneaster, and golden flowered bougainvillea. When they reached the door, Caleb pointed to a security sign. Pixie nodded and rang the doorbell.

They waited. There was no movement inside the house and Pixie pushed the doorbell again.

"No sign of our mystery man," Pixie sighed.

"We wait?" Caleb asked.

Pixie gave a sly grin. "You're forgettin' I sold real estate." She started heading to the side of the house.

"What are you up to?"

"I've snooped around a lot of houses and have the scars to prove it. Come on."

"What about an alarm system?"

"Most homeowners don't want to be bothered. They don't turn them on."

"I illegally left Maine and now I'm going to end up in a California jail for trespassing."

"Come on," she said. "Easy peasy. We'll just take us a little look around."

Caleb raised an eyebrow but said nothing. If he were going to prison, at least the weather would be better out here. He'd heard tales of prisoners being able to see their breath in their cells back in Maine.

They peered into windows and finally fought their way through bushes to the patio. Pixie stuck a finger into the pool and said, "Like bathwater. How about a swim?"

Caleb nervously looked around. Pixie was starting to freak him out. "How about we go back to the car and wait?"

"Oh, come on. Let's have us some fun." She walked over to the sliders and tried to open them. No luck. Then she started walking back to a small garden shed engulfed in a clump of bushes next to the house and Caleb reluctantly followed. When Pixie tugged the door open, they saw that the shed was filled with a few brightly colored flowerpots, garden equipment, and pool cleaning supplies. Pixie stuck her head in and said to herself, loud enough for Caleb to hear, "*I wonder . . .*"

She began rummaging around and, a few moments later, proclaimed triumphantly, "I knew it."

Pixie emerged holding a key with a huge smile on her face. "Never fails. It was sitting under one of the flowerpots. People always put keys under something thinking no one will look. Dumber than dumb."

"We aren't going inside, are we?"

"Why not?" Pixie asked, beaming. "We got a key. You're in a heap of trouble. What's a little more? We got to find out a few things about our friend, Marley. And the best way to do that is to go into this skunk's house and see what smells." She put her hands on her hips and frowned. "If you're a fraidy cat, you can go sit in the car."

Caleb shook his head. "The hell with that."

She smiled. "I thought you'd see the light. I got a hunch our friend Marley will share a few of his secrets with us." She turned to the sliding terrace doors. "Let's see if this key does the trick."

Pixie slid the key into the lock and frowned. She struggled for a moment and said, "Dang."

Caleb said, "Let me try."

She handed him the key and he slid it into the lock and jiggled it. He struggled for a moment and jiggled it again when suddenly, the key turned. Caleb said, "Presto, though I'm probably going to regret this."

A moment later, they were inside the house. To Caleb, it was eerily silent. He'd expected to hear the wail of security alarms. Yet nothing. The living room: a light hardwood floor, an off-white sectional couch, stuffed accent chairs. A television sat in the corner next to built-in bookshelves adorned with leather-bound classics that looked like they'd never been cracked. A few abstract pastels and oils hung on the wall and an empty pizza box and dirty highball glass sat on a sleek walnut coffee table.

Pixie studied the living room for a moment and went down a hallway past a bedroom and bath to the kitchen. She turned to Caleb, who'd followed, and pointed at the sink. "Full of dishes." She eyed an overflowing trash can. "And stinky garbage." She opened the refrigerator. It was nearly empty. "Our man eats takeout and lives alone."

Caleb nodded. Pixie exited the kitchen and Caleb followed. They went into a small wood-paneled den off a dining room that overlooked the Pacific. There was a mahogany desk with a few files scattered on top and a safe tucked in the corner. Caleb picked up one of the files and began rifling through it.

"Anything interesting?" Pixie asked.

"Homeowners' insurance."

"How about that one?" She pointed to a thin file. Caleb dropped the one in his hand, reached for it, and flipped it open. He skimmed through it. "Nothing."

Caleb grabbed another file as Pixie started to open desk drawers. After a few seconds, Caleb placed the file on the desk. "Still nothing."

Pixie looked up. "Same here." She turned to the safe in the corner. "I'm darn good at breaking into houses, but I'm no safe cracker."

Caleb shrugged. "That's not in a lobsterman's job description either."

"A dry well." Pixie shook her head.

They turned to leave when they stopped in their tracks. They heard what sounded like someone talking on a cell phone, and a quick glance out the window revealed a man walking down the stone steps to the house. "Looks like we got a friend," Pixie whispered.

"Let's go." Caleb grabbed Pixie's hand and started for the terrace when keys began to rattle, and the front door flung open.

168

Caleb spotted a closet in the hallway and pulled Pixie behind him into a tiny, musty space and jammed next to a vacuum sweeper and a broom. Once their heartbeats calmed, they could hear Marley walking through the house to the living room yammering away on the phone.

"Yes. Yes. Yes. We've been working on it, Jonathan," Marley said in a clipped South African accent, his voice rising and falling. "I understand the stakes. The meat will be smashing. Succulent. A few more tweaks here and there and it will taste like the real thing . . . Yes, I know you've got a lot invested. I know we've got the industry where we want it thanks to that fool lobsterman. I can't say that Peters inspired much faith, but what he was able to accomplish in so short a time is nothing short of miraculous." Marley fell silent. A few moments later he broke in defensively, "I realize time is of the essence. Like I said, we've got the best team of scientists in the world."

Pixie and Caleb held their breath as Marley walked down the hallway past the closet. His voice grew louder, betraying his irritation. "How long?" Marley repeated. "Like I've said, 'soon'. We're working hard, Jonathan. I've got the whole bloody team focused on the solution . . . I promise you we're near a breakthrough. A big, big, smashing breakthrough. Revolutionary. It will be marvelous. But we need a tad more time. I assure you, every five-star restaurant in New York and Paris will be serving Utami lobster and you'll be a happy, happy, rich man."

When the call ended, Marley rattled around for a moment and shouted, "Bloody hell! Screw off!" They heard a bang and then Marley began to yelp. "*Ow, ow, ow, ow.* My bloody hand. Idiot!"

Caleb and Pixie heard a stream of curses from the kitchen and a cabinet opened and a bottle uncorked. Soon Marley paddled past them muttering to himself in bitter tones as he moved toward the living room.

In the darkness, Pixie tapped Caleb on the shoulder. The closet was growing oppressive from the smell of cleaning solution, mothballs, and dust. Caleb nodded and slowly opened the door. He could see the entrance to the living room at the far end of the hallway and Marley slumped, with his back turned, looking miserably out to sea holding his drink.

Caleb gestured to Pixie, and as they were about to stealthily slide out of the closet, Marley made a sudden movement, turned away from the large picture windows and sat down on the couch. He put his feet up on the coffee table, took a gulp, and tapped his cell. A male voice answered on speaker seconds later. "Sebastian?"

"Who else would it be?"

"I know what you're going to ask," the man said.

"Well?" Marley asked testily.

"We're getting there. I keep telling you that. We can't flip a switch and have cellular lobster taste like it was caught off the coast of Maine. It's not that easy."

"You've been saying that for months."

The man pushed back. "Because it's true. You're the one who's been making promises to everyone."

"You bloody told me we'd have it by now. The meat still tastes like plastic."

"What can I tell you? It's going to take more time than we thought."

"I haven't got bloody time! I have investors breathing down my neck. I've got Jonathan Tyler calling me nearly every day demanding updates. I've got the situation in Maine totally primed for people to demand a replacement for lobster, *yet . . . yet . . .* we have lobster meat that tastes like shit! Do something!"

There was silence. Pixie and Caleb shared a quick, meaningful glance in the light cast by the crack in the door.

"Did you bloody hear me?"

"You set unrealistic expectations, Sebastian. I warned you. This is the price you pay when you try to make scientific advancement conform to your own timetable."

"I don't need a bloody lecture. You're forgetting you work for me. You're on a short leash with me right now."

"You and I know that if I walk, you're dead meat." He gave a short laugh. "No pun intended. Besides, I know too much. You can't afford another divorce."

Marley jumped off the couch and started pacing. "How long before the meat won't taste like brass polish?"

"Like I told you, science doesn't have a timetable."

"That's not what I want to hear."

"Look, Sebastian, we're working on it. This is a new genetic territory. If you want me to guess, I'd say a few more months."

"Months?" Marley shook his lumpy fist, walked to the large picture window, and rested his forehead against the glass.

"That's what I said."

"Unacceptable," Marley muttered.

"Tell these people the truth. It's going to be a little longer. What's the big deal?"

"What's the big deal? Are you joking me?"

"No."

Marley pulled away from the window and started to shout. "We're in a race to get our product on the market! We're about to throttle the commercial lobster industry and put it out of business. But . . . we have NO product yet. And you're telling me 'what's the bloody big deal?' Tell that to Oscar Leonid and Jonathan Tyler."

"What can I tell you, Sebastian? I can't get blood from a stone. We need a few more months."

Marley snarled. "I want you working round the clock."

"It's not the Manhattan Project, Sebastian."

"Do it!"

"Employees are already complaining about their pay. There is no way they are going to accept longer hours too."

"Get it bloody done," Marley grunted and abruptly ended the call.

Marley took a huge pull on his drink and began to pace around the living room. Back and forth, back and forth, talking to himself in miserable, angry tones until he yanked open the sliders and walked to the edge of the patio and stared out at the Pacific.

"Let's go," Caleb whispered. Then he and Pixie crept out of the closet and dashed to the front door.

Less than a minute later, Caleb pulled the rental car away from the curb and sped past Marley's silver Porsche back toward the freeway.

"Whew, that was close," Pixie said, brushing dust off her jeans.

"Your buddy Washington came up big."

"He always does," Pixie said, breaking into a slow smile as they drove along the ocean past palatial homes perched on the cliffs above the beach. "Franklin's as good as gold."

Washington answered his phone on the first ring. He stood on the tarmac at Teterboro Airport waiting for the habitually late Spencer Tate and the Commissioner's entourage of lawyers. Washington and League officials were headed to Europe under a cloak of secrecy. In his relentless thirst for publicity and power, Tate had dreamed up an audacious plan to hold the League Championship in London. Washington immediately recognized Pixie's twang and said, "Tell me."

Five minutes later, Washington whistled and said, "Jonathan Tyler. Oscar Leonid. You're playing with fire, Pix."

"Yup," she said.

Washington shook his head as Tate's limousine pulled up a few yards from the plane. Tate climbed out of the limo with the Brazilian diplomat's daughter on his arm. In her mid-twenties, she wore diamond earrings, a black, scooped-neck t-shirt, white, pleated, wide-cropped poplin pants, and had a Vida half-moon bag slung over her shoulder. Washington rolled his eyes. He detested Tate. Any sane man would take Pix in a heartbeat. Earthy, sparkling, and a survivor.

"I'll have my assistant get on it, Pix. No worries," Washington said, turning his back to Tate and the South American cutie as he spoke. "I gotta go. Gotta catch a flight."

"Where you going, Franklin?"

Washington frowned. The last thing he wanted to do was to mention Tate's name. "No place."

"Don't tell me you're going to Port Arthur?"

Franklin laughed, then said, "I heard Spencer sicced his lawyer on you."

"He wants the diamond back and more."

"Don't you worry about Mr. Commissioner. If he pushes you too hard, I'll remind him of a few skeletons he's got in the closet."

"I don't want you gettin' fired, Franklin."

"The last person he'd fire is me. I know where all the bodies are buried."

Pixie laughed.

"I got Spencer, but you watch yourself, Pix."

"I will," Pixie said.

"I don't want anyone hurting you."

"I know it. You're the best."

"Be safe, woman."

An hour and a half later, Washington's assistant, Sabrina, called Pixie as she and Caleb leaned against the railing on the Malibu Pier watching a handful of sunburnt, liver-spotted old men fish. "I had to dig hard," Sabrina said. "But I found info."

Pixie gave Caleb a thumbs up.

"Utami is listed anonymously as a private LLC. The names of the owners aren't disclosed on the incorporation documents . . . but . . . after some searching, I found a few old job postings on the *Journal of Science* website for a bioengineering seafood startup in Southern California and a Gmail address. I traced it and discovered that it sourced from Costa Rica. At that point, I decided to have a little fun. I hacked it."

"Franklin said you were awesome. What did you find?" Pixie asked, watching one of the fishermen pull his rod back and fling a short cast.

"Utami has two physical locations. One in Costa Rica and another right under your nose in Burbank."

"Anything else?"

"The company is shrouded in mystery. It was a bear to find its headquarters. But I zoomed in on Google Earth and it looks like Utami sits in an old television studio facility. I dug some more and hacked into the security system. Super easy. Just let me know if you want to snoop around. I'm sure they must have a security guard, but I can shut down the surveillance system."

"How'd you learn to do all this, honey?"

Sabrina laughed. "Let's say they teach a special skill set at the NSA."

"Okay then. Say no more, darlin'," Pixie said. "We'll keep you posted."

"Give me the green light, and I'll put the security system to sleep."

"Amen. Can you text me the address?"

"You got it."

At twilight, Pixie and Caleb drove by the old aircraft hangar-style studio in a sea of concrete lots and rundown warehouses. Pixie could imagine the old television shows being shot here and glittering stars, the ones her mother used to watch on their old TV set when Pixie was an itty-bitty thing, drive into the lot in shiny convertibles underneath the bright, ever-present Southern California sun. Pixie remembered the old reruns on *TV Land* like *I Love Lucy* and *Bewitched*, and sitting on a torn, stained, plaid couch watching her mother give a rare hacking laugh between pulls on her cigarette.

"What do you think, Caleb Gray? Should we look around? My new best friend Sabrina can make them go dark."

Caleb gave a hesitant look. "I had no idea we're tangling with one of the richest men in the world and also Senator Jonathan Tyler." As he spoke, Caleb stared at Pixie intently. "When I testified in Washington during the fight about whales, Tyler was one of the senators on the committee. I remember his questions. He acted like he wanted to be your best friend while he slipped a knife into your back."

"Most of these rich, powerful men are snakes. It took me a while, but I think I finally figured it out. I have Spencer to thank for that."

Caleb nodded. "You know, even if we get into the building, we still have no proof that Utami set me up and Peters manipulated the video. I can't imagine breaking into the lab is going to get me out of this mess." He paused. "And if we get caught, not only is it going to make it even messier, but I'm going to be dragging you down with me."

"What's a little more trouble?" Pixie smiled thinly. "We've made a pretty good team so far. Let's just poke around and see what we find."

Caleb took a deep breath. "OK, first, you're amazing. Secondly, my father used to tell me in for a penny in for a pound. We might as well see this thing to the end."

Pixie texted Sabrina to kill the surveillance system. It was past midnight on the East Coast, but if she could manage that, maybe they'd find a way in.

Soon a return text pinged. "*Done.*"

They parked the car in a deserted, trash-strewn lot. They walked in the shadows trying to avoid a couple of dim streetlights in case Sabrina couldn't disconnect all of the cameras. Pixie realized their chances of entering the building were slim. There'd be no keys hidden under flowerpots, but she'd learned that sometimes if you trust fate, you get rewarded.

When they neared the former studio, they slipped down a side alley. Caleb and Pixie walked silently around the building. It was obvious that Utami was operating on the downlow. No fancy corporate sign and a dingy building with the appearance of being abandoned. Perfect for flying under the radar. Suddenly, a man materialized from the darkness. Pixie's heart began to pound and her mouth went dry. The man appeared to be moving toward them purposefully, but then he stopped and lit a cigarette. He leaned against the building and took a drag, then started scrolling on his phone. A few yards away, Pixie spotted a doorway with a lone light above it. Caleb crouched and grabbed Pixie's hand to do the same, but Pixie broke away and started walking directly toward the man. She felt her pulse throb and the blood rush from her lips. It was like walking on stage when she danced. She'd improvise the moves.

"Is this Utami?" Pixie asked in the sweetest voice she could muster. Startled, the man shoved his phone in his pocket and stepped toward her. "Cause I'm looking for Sebastian Marley. He told me to meet him here. He said he'd be waiting to show me around."

The man dropped his cigarette and snuffed it out with his shoe. "Sebastian was supposed to meet you?"

"And my friend." She pointed to Caleb who slowly emerged from the darkness. She let her voice drop. "I guess he stood us up."

The man squinted as Caleb walked toward him. "This is above my paygrade," the guy said. Pixie noticed he was wearing a white lab coat with the name Jonas on a plastic card clipped to the pocket. He added, "I'm a lab technician. No one tells me much."

"Sebastian told us he'd give us a tour."

"No one gets a tour," the man grunted. "This place is off limits."

"Even to investors?" Pixie asked, her voice sharpening.

The man took a step back. He stammered, "He said he'd meet you here?"

"That's what I said. Get the wax out of your ears."

He shuffled his feet for a moment. "It's late. Marley never comes in this time of night."

Pixie could see that he was a man used to obeying orders, so she pushed. "We flew in from New York, fresh from Wall Street. My friend and I," she pointed at Caleb, "we're potential investors in this little operation, and we don't want to be seen in broad daylight, getting our photo snapped, drawing lots of attention." She pointed at his name tag. "When Sebastian finds out you told us to hit the road, he's going to be one angry hombre."

"I didn't tell you to hit the road," the lab technician said, backtracking. "I said Marley is never here this time of night."

"We came for a tour. Someone better give us one or we'll be unhappy campers."

Flustered, the man repeated, "Marley said he'd meet you here?"

"That's right. You got five seconds to find someone to give us our tour or we walk."

"Okay. Okay. It's just that I'm the only person here tonight except for Lester."

"Who's Lester?"

"He's the security guard."

"Where is he?" Pixie asked.

"He's on break. He goes every night for a burger."

"So, it's just you. You, my friend, so lead on." Seeing that the man was wavering, Pixie added, "I promise you we'll make sure you're in good with your boss tomorrow."

The lab technician reluctantly gestured for Pixie and Caleb to follow. Caleb broke into a half smile and lightly pinched Pixie's elbow. Her face lit up. She turned and grinned. "I haven't had such fun in years," she whispered.

Once they entered the building and were walking down a narrow corridor, Pixie was struck by how the studio had been partially divided into a series of stark offices and conference rooms. It all appeared temporary. No pictures on the wall, corporate slogans, or sign that anyone working at Utami was there to stay. When they came to a small foyer area, she noticed a security camera on the ceiling and thanked her lucky stars for Franklin Washington and Sabrina. Caleb looked up at the camera and gave Pixie a quick nod.

"I need you to sign in here," the lab technician said, pointing to a clipboard, trying to hide his discomfort. His routine had been disrupted, and he probably still wasn't certain he was doing the right thing. He didn't even get to finish his smoke. Pixie breathed a sigh of relief that he didn't ask for ID.

Pixie watched Caleb as he signed *Horace Maddox* in small script and gave a bogus New York address. Pixie signed her name *Taylor Swift* in nearly illegible swerves and jotted down Spencer Tate's swanky midtown location. The lab technician nodded after they finished and said, "Okay, what do you want to see?"

Caleb said without hesitation, "The labs."

The guy shook his head. "I could get into a lot of trouble."

"Listen," Caleb said. "My partner and I are not going to invest in a lab that we haven't seen. I'm sure you can understand that, can't you? How are we to know we aren't being conned?"

They walked down a long corridor and entered a large, brightly lit laboratory with black soapstone slab tables, computers, whirring machines, electronic microscopes, test tubes, industrial sinks, and sterilized glass-covered petri dishes with pink lumps that looked like silly putty, and enough blinking lights to illuminate Times Square.

"This is the main lab," Jonas said. "It's where everything comes together."

"This is how you guys bioengineer the meat?" Caleb asked, sniffing the air.

Pixie smelled something, too. Formaldehyde. She scrunched her nose.

At the question, Jonas' expression relaxed. He seemed to drop his guard and transform into 'science guy'. "It's a tricky process, but we're making great progress. When we get the formula right, the plan is to produce 130 million pounds of lobster meat a year."

Caleb took a step back in shock. "That's what Maine lobstermen produce annually."

"That's the goal. It's audacious, but that's Marley."

"Are you going to produce it all here?" Pixie asked incredulously.

Jonas shook his head. He was now enjoying being the expert and seemed to forget his earlier caution. He was overcome by self-importance. "Way too expensive. My supervisor told me the operation will move offshore to Costa Rica. Much cheaper. And I overheard Marley boasting about tax incentives."

"What's holding production up?" Caleb asked.

The lab technician looked cautiously at them. He hesitated before pointing to one of the large rectangular petri dishes.

"Theoretically, we should already be producing edible meat that tastes as good as the real thing."

"But?" Caleb asked.

"We've run into some genetic kinks."

"Is that why it stinks?" Pixie asked, scrunching her nose again.

"That's the problem. Smell and taste. The meat has the same density and consistency, but it isn't edible yet."

Jonas motioned for them to follow him into another part of the lab. He pointed to a cage holding two rats who began to quiver when they spotted him.

"*Rats*?" Pixie asked, scrunching her nose again.

"You know the saying 'a canary in a coal mine'. Well, Utami has the rat test." He paused. "Whenever we think we've made a breakthrough, we see if our friends Hickory and Dickory will eat the lobster meat."

"And . . .?" Pixie asked.

The lab technician shook his head. "They won't touch it. Every time they see me, they start to shake."

"So, rats won't even eat Utami lobster," Caleb said.

"Cell-based cultured seafood, really any meat produced in a lab, is a tricky proposition. It's incredibly complex. You got to get the DNA right. DNA determines the species and characteristics of the meat, texture, and taste. It's like a fingerprint. We have almost all the pieces in place, but if you don't have them all in perfect symmetry," Jonas paused and looked away.

"But you feel like you're on the verge?" Pixie asked, glancing at Hickory and Dickory who'd scampered to a corner of the cage.

The lab technician nodded. "While it isn't fast enough for Marley, we're making progress. The extra capital might be just what we need to make it work."

"What's the rush?" Pixie asked.

Jonas held his breath, and finally said, "Market forces."

"Explain?" Caleb asked.

"There are other companies working on this. Who knows how far along they are?"

"A race," Pixie said. "And Marley needs us to help him to the finish line, is that it?"

"Yup. All over the world there are bioengineering firms trying to figure out how to make cellular seafood. Salmon, Sea Bass, Mahi

Mahi, Stone Crab, Lobster, Cod, Halibut, Swordfish, Tuna. Name the fish, and there are scientists right now trying to genetically engineer it. It doesn't take a rocket scientist to figure out what this will mean. Billions of dollars in profit. People will be able to buy lab-produced seafood that tastes like the real thing at a fraction of the cost." He paused. "For investors, it's going to be a sweet deal as long as we can get the genetic footprint right."

"You mentioned before something about market forces. Were you just referring to the competition?" Caleb asked.

Jonas hesitated. "Well, I did hear something that might be interesting to you as investors. It's not on the up and up, but it might make a whole lotta money for people."

Pixie realized the lab technician was relishing his new role as the source of information for a captive audience. He was taking advantage of his temporary self-importance.

"I heard something else. The whole thing with the lobsterman and whale in Maine was sketchy."

"How so?" Caleb asked, as his heart started to pound.

"I heard a rumor that actor was hired to create a shitstorm. Marley wants to get all the environmentalists crazy about the lobster industry and how bad those guys are."

"Where did you hear that?" Pixie asked, delighted to have her suspicions confirmed. Peters was on Utami's payroll. *Activist my ass*, she thought, as she and Caleb shared a quick glance.

"That guy Peters that's been on the news shows was in here a couple of weeks ago with Marley. Lester, the security guard, told me he overheard some of their conversation."

"What else did you hear?" Caleb asked.

"That's it," Jonas said, shrugging.

Pixie sighed. She'd heard enough, so she pulled out her cellphone.

"Hey, what are you doing?" the guy protested.

"Takin' a few pictures. You don't mind, do you?" Pixie started snapping shots of the lab.

"Hey. You can't do that!"

"Say 'cheese'." Pixie took a picture of Jonas, whose face was turning crimson.

"I'll lose my job."

Pixie gave a sweet smile and Caleb tugged at her elbow. The guy tried to snatch the phone out of her hand, but Caleb grabbed his arm and waved his index finger in front of his face.

"We'll be going," Pixie said, and she and Caleb darted out of the lab.

They started laughing like school children as they sprinted down the dark alley, and when they reached the car, Pixie looked at Caleb over the hood and said, "I'm havin' a ball," in between breaths.

Caleb grinned. "Did you see his face when you started taking photos?"

Pixie laughed. "But what about when you grabbed his arm and wagged your finger?"

"Well done, Taylor Swift," Caleb said, reaching his fist over the hood toward Pixie.

"You did pretty well yourself, Horace," Pixie said as she fist bumped him.

"I still don't think we have enough to prove anything about Peters," Caleb said, suddenly frowning.

"I know it," Pixie said. "All we got is what they call 'hearsay'. We need the ole smokin' gun."

Ten minutes later, Lester waddled into the building with a fresh ketchup stain on his uniform collar sucking a monstrous soda from a straw. The technician was slumped in a chair staring at the floor.

"What happened?" Lester asked, sensing something was wrong.

Jonas looked up and nervously told him what had occurred.

Lester immediately grabbed the sign-in sheet, squinted, and grunted. "Taylor Swift?" He tossed the clipboard on the table and swore. "You moron."

As they merged into a nighttime snarl of slow-moving freeway traffic, Caleb's mind raced. He kept thinking about the Senate hearing a few years before, and Jonathan Tyler's questions delivered in a calm, professorial tone, but unlike the other senators, who were bombastic and preened for cameras with the hope of a sound bite on the evening news before they raced recklessly to create the next controversy, Tyler's questions struck like harpoons. Tyler's persistent questioning and intricate grasp of the lobster industry made Caleb believe something personal was at stake. Now he knew for certain that Tyler had an agenda beyond the environmental concerns of safeguarding whales. The problem was going to be proving it.

Caleb thought about what Marley had said while he and Pixie were breathing dust bunnies in Marley's broom closet. Tell that to Oscar Leonid and Jonathan Tyler. Leonid enjoyed his controversial reputation. He was brash, egotistical, unpredictable, and opinionated. He invested millions in futuristic enterprises, so it was no surprise that he'd invest in cellular seafood. Unless he was involved in a conspiracy to destroy the lobster industry, there'd be no conflict of interest, only bad judgment in hooking his star to Sebastian Marley and Utami. Tyler, however, was another story. His investment would be an egregious act. Tyler had crafted an image of the environmental warrior and honest politician who fought the "bad" guys. Given what he'd heard so far, Caleb now felt certain that Tyler's crusade about whales had been for profit. Caleb was in the crosshairs of political malfeasance.

Caleb knew in his heart the lobster industry was on borrowed time. Global warming, increased scrutiny of fishing methods, rising costs, and a desire for young people to find other, easier ways to make a living cast a shadow on what was once a thriving industry. But Caleb believed in fair play. If natural market forces moved people to consume cellular lobster, so be it. But the idea of Marley and Tyler colluding to destroy a way of life by cheating and lying made him livid. He was now even more determined to fight back.

Caleb drove in silence. He recalled the Marine Institute of the Pacific's very public and damaging allegation that lobstering had contributed to the depletion of endangered whales. The announcement struck the lobstering industry like a hammer and pushed two of the largest supermarket chains in the country to ban lobster sales. Now Caleb heard that Healthy Farms had followed, another major blow to the industry. When Caleb testified in Washington, he'd seen the institute's director, Sandy Francois, hobnobbing before the hearing. Then during the proceedings, Caleb noticed that she couldn't take her eyes off Tyler. He remembered thinking how odd that was, but, of course, his main concern at that time was parrying the barbed questions. The recollection suddenly struck him like lightning. Without hesitation, Caleb swerved between cars into the right lane and took an exit ramp off the freeway.

"Who are you, Mario Andretti?" Pixie asked, gripping the door handle. "I thought we were trying to catch the redeye?"

"We're headed to Hacienda Bay."

"What for?"

"To see Sandy Francois, the Director of the Marine Institute of the Pacific. My hunch is that she and Jonathan Tyler share a lot more than a desire to save whales. Sorry, something just clicked in my head."

"Bring it on. I'm havin' a blast." Pixie quickly pulled out her phone and set a course with her GPS.

Chapter Twenty-One—Hacienda Bay

Halfway through the five-hour drive north they stopped at a truck stop outside of Bakersfield. Caleb took a gulp of coffee, stabbed a fry with his fork, and chewed it carefully while Pixie nibbled on a grilled cheese. It was Caleb's second cup of coffee, an attempt to fight off the exhaustion trying to overtake him. Pixie yawned and sipped her glass of iced tea. "How you doing?"

"Considering I haven't slept in a bed in three days, okay."

"You want me to drive?"

"You're as tired as I am."

Pixie reached across the table and gently took Caleb's hand. The gesture brought comfort, helped his mind slow down. "Let's get a hotel room. Sandy Francois can wait. We need sleep and to get cleaned up. I smell worse than Utami lobster."

Caleb smiled, rubbed his eyes, and slowly shook his head. "For someone who wanted nothing to do with anyone, I've strayed pretty far, haven't I? One morning I'm hauling traps off Pond Island, the next my name is smeared all over the news. From anonymous to pariah in a blink of an eye."

Pixie took a careful bite from her sandwich, her warm, understanding eyes resting on Caleb.

"Never in a million years could I have imagined that I would be a fugitive at a truck stop in the California desert." He shook his head and rested his fork on his plate.

"It's sort of romantic though, isn't it? You're part fugitive, part detective. Sort of like a movie," she said, still holding Caleb's hand.

Caleb smiled briefly. "If I'm in a movie, I should have held out for a different role. Are you sure you're still up for this? I can get you to a flight home."

"And miss the fun?"

Caleb paused, nodded, and said, "We need to find out the connection between Tyler and Utami, not to mention if Sandy Francois figures into all of this. We know one thing for sure, Peters and Tyler are on Utami's payroll."

"The theory here is that Tyler and Francois are friends with benefits?"

"It adds up."

Pixie paused. "How about I ask my friend Sabrina?"

"You think Tyler and Francois would be dumb enough to leave a trail?"

"Animals in heat are reckless." Pixie slowly released her hand from his and took a sip of iced tea. "I'll text Franklin to get on it right away."

"What next?"

"We said something about gettin' cleaned up."

Caleb sniffed his shirt and grimaced.

Forty minutes later, Pixie turned off the water, slid the curtain back, and reached for a towel. The soap and hot water had only made her sleepier. She wondered if Caleb was waiting for her, ready to pull her close. He'd showered first and slipped by her with a towel strapped across his narrow waist as she went into the bathroom to undress. Despite her exhaustion, she ached to fold into him.

When she popped her head out of the steamy bathroom, she sighed. Caleb was asleep, curled on the far side of the king bed. 'Well, that's progress,' she thought. As trucks roared by the hotel, she dropped her towel and reached into her traveling bag for fresh underwear and a t-shirt. After drying her hair, she fell into bed and huddled next to Caleb, soon falling asleep in a dreamless void.

"*Nothing*," Sabrina texted as Pixie and Caleb stood outside Café Valencia in Hacienda Bay at ten thirty the next morning. "*If they're messing around, they must be using burners.*"

Pixie showed Caleb the text. He took a sip of coffee from a large paper cup and frowned. Caleb wasn't ready to abandon his hunch that Tyler and Francois' united assault on commercial lobstering derived from a different sort of union, and that the two were in bed with Marley as well. He took a deep breath and peered once more around. Upscale and ultra expensive, Hacienda Bay seemed a fantasy land. Ritzy shops and restaurants, quaint mission revival architecture, and the idle wealthy milling about aimlessly. Caleb wondered if any of these people had an idea what it felt like to put your life on the line and head out to sea in frigid weather on an early winter morning to haul traps. How simple it had been for Sandy Francois to declare a war on lobstermen, safe in a world of wealth and power. She had used her pulpit as a weapon to try to destroy a way of life.

Caleb studied Pixie for a moment as she texted Sabrina. When he'd awakened, she was curled next to him with her foot touching his, her hair spread out on the pillow. She smelled sweet, like citrus. He'd felt a stir. He ached to trace her jaw with his fingertips and kiss her, but a bolt of fear hit him. He quietly climbed out of bed, dressed, and went to the lobby to grab coffee and check his messages.

His phone had been a minefield. Voicemails from his attorney, a couple of texts from Ed Pratt, Lou Farnham from *The Bangor Times* wanting comment, an officious email from the district court outlining the conditions of his bail. Caleb hadn't answered any of them.

He finished his coffee and tossed the cup into a litter can. "Nothing, huh?"

"Not a trace. You still think they're hooking up? Part of a grand conspiracy?"

Caleb set his eyes on Pixie. "My gut tells me 'yes.'"

"Let's go. We got nothing to lose. Let's pay your lady friend a visit."

Set on a cliff overlooking Hacienda Bay, the Marine Institute of the Pacific loomed above pounding surf, kelp beds, and frolicking sea otters. By partnering with organizations such as Greenhaven, it had become an environmental watchdog under Francois' leadership, helping Francois become a global star to environmental activists and conservationists. Some of Francois' initiatives weren't misguided, Caleb admitted to himself. But the lobster moratorium was an overreach. It was fine with Caleb if she wanted the institute to be world renowned, but she needed to do her homework before condemning a whole fishery – there were other fisheries that were far less regulated than the lobster industry after all – and if she indeed was in bed with Tyler in more ways than one, then her actions had moved beyond mere hypocrisy.

When Pixie and Caleb entered the institute's lobby, decorated with murals of marine life and a large granite sculpture of a sea lion sitting near the entrance, workers were setting up tables and staff were securing gold and silver balloons to the light sconces dotting the walls. A young woman with long red hair and a face flush with freckles, looking like she walked out of an Orvis catalogue, hurried over and told them the facility was closed. "We're getting ready for a gala tonight," she said apologetically. "I'm sorry, but we'll be open tomorrow."

Pixie asked, "A gala?"

"It's our annual summer kickoff."

"Fancy?"

The woman smiled. "Black tie."

"Oohlala. Who's the big soiree for?"

"Two hundred and fifty supporters who care deeply about the institute."

"What's on the menu?" Pixie asked.

"A delicious vegan menu," she said proudly. "We don't want to contribute to greenhouse emissions. Certainly no red meat, poultry, or fish. The institute is carbon neutral. One of our director's significant achievements."

"Among many," Caleb said dryly.

Pixie asked, "No lobster?" in as innocent a voice as she could muster.

The woman recoiled. "Lobster? Haven't you heard?"

Caleb played along. "Heard what?"

"About the institute's ban on the industry? It's been wildly successful, a necessary step to save whales. Sandy took a courageous stand and now supermarket chains and other responsible food producers have banned the sale of lobster."

"I wonder what will happen to those lobstermen?" Pixie asked.

The woman shook her head. She was a warrior, Caleb thought. "Whales are endangered because of lobstermen. Sometimes these decisions are difficult. It's a small price to pay."

"Where'd you grow up, honey?" Pixie asked.

The woman smiled. "La Jolla. But I went to boarding school in New England. Have you heard of Groton? And Berkley for marine sciences. I've always been environmentally conscious. I did internships for a variety of organizations during college, including one with Senator Tyler."

"Tyler?" Caleb asked.

"He's been a champion of the institute. He's a trustee."

Caleb and Pixie exchanged a quick glance. The connection between Tyler and Francois suddenly grew stronger. For a moment, Caleb thought about how different his world was from the young woman standing next to him. Internships? During high school, he hauled traps with his father, mowed lawns, and washed dishes at Ebb Tide. To pay for college, he cleaned oil burners, roofed houses, stocked shelves at an Orono supermarket, and toiled as a short order cook at an all-night diner. His father expected him to work hard, get dirty, and pay his way. Caleb grew disheartened at the thought of the growing divide in the country between the haves and have-nots. The woman with freckles splashed across her face had no way to identify with people like Caleb. She lived in the same rarified air as Francois, Tyler, and Pixie's old boyfriend, for that matter. To her, the institute's moratorium on lobstering was a significant act of courage and achievement. Whatever empathy she had for workers took a back seat to her crusade for the environment.

"You worked for Tyler?" Caleb asked finally.

"For a magical summer," she gushed. "The man will be president."

"Will he be here tonight?" Caleb questioned.

"Of course. He's going to be the featured speaker."

Caleb glanced again at Pixie.

Pixie said, "What time does this shindig start?"

For an instant, a cloud passed across the woman's face. She said hesitantly, "6 pm. It's invitation only though."

Pixie nodded. "Well, good luck. Sounds like a big to-do."

The woman seemed relieved as Pixie and Caleb turned to leave.

When they stepped outside, Caleb could see Pixie's mind spinning. "What are you thinking?" he asked.

Pixie paused. "When was the last time you wore a tuxedo?"

Caleb looked confused. "Senior prom. It was purple. Worst thing you ever saw."

Pixie smiled. "You won't be wearing a purple tux tonight. We're crashing the party, darlin'. I wanna see if you're right about sparks flying between Tyler and Francois."

Pixie looked spectacular in a satin charmeuse one-shoulder gown. Her blonde hair fell to her shoulders and shone in the evening light. With her flawless skin and carefully painted lipstick, she was dazzling, like a glittering movie star about to step onto a red carpet. In the line of beautiful people entering the institute, heads turned. Caleb was the object of some attention himself. An older woman wearing exquisite teardrop earrings and holding a Chanel clutch rested her eyes on Caleb. With silver hair pulled into a bun, she said in a grand voice, "Haven't we met before? Santa Fe? The Sierra Club event in April?"

Caleb replied, "I don't think so."

The woman was insistent. "I'm sure. I never forget a face."

Caleb shrugged.

The woman said, "If not, you have a doppelganger."

Pixie took Caleb's hand, gave her a sly grin, and said, "I don't think I could handle two."

"Oh, I could," the woman said as her husband arched his eyebrows and gently tugged her toward the institute entrance.

When Pixie and Caleb stepped inside and neared the table littered with name tags, Pixie whispered, "Let me do the talkin'."

Caleb said, "Absolutely. I feel like an idiot and my collar itches."

Caleb nervously scratched his neck as they slowly navigated their way through the maze of people at the lobby's entrance. His face grew warm as they moved closer to the two female staff members handing out name tags and checking names off the guest list. Caleb grew more uneasy. He didn't like crashing a party. He didn't like wearing black tie and finding himself in a sea of dazzling people in a place far from home. He longed for Maine and to be on Grand Heron watching the sunset with a cold beer in his hand. As he glanced around the institute's foyer, he realized how inconsequential his whole existence was compared to these men and women who could make or destroy lives through their financial and political might. And the most sobering part of it all is that they wouldn't even meet those that they destroyed. How could he possibly fight their collective will?

As they neared the table, Caleb's nerves were completely on edge. He was bone tired from worry. All he wanted was a little peace and quiet, a return to routine and anonymity. When their turn finally arrived, a staff member smiled and said, "Your names?"

"Mr. and Mrs. Gray," Pixie said without hesitation.

Pixie's words struck a chord in Caleb that made all his fretting dissipate. *Mr. and Mrs. Gray.* For a moment, Caleb studied her. She was gorgeous and sparkling and real. *So, so real.* Her gown showed every exquisite curve, and Caleb felt a burning desire despite the intense anxiety which made his neck stiff and his heart pound.

Despite his troubles, it hit him – wildly, almost absurdly – that being with Pixie was exhilarating. She wasn't just fun; she was a force. Here they were, scheming to crash a party they had no business attending, and Pixie carried herself as if she owned the institute, radiating the confidence of its most generous benefactor. Caleb felt as though he were ready to live again. He smiled to himself as the woman behind the table began hunting for his and Pixie's name tags, while the other woman ran her index finger down the guest list. Pixie had the right attitude. He resolved to try to see this as an adventure.

"I'm sorry, I don't see your names," the woman said, looking up.

The other said, "Or name tags."

"That's strange," Pixie said, feigning confusion. "Jonathan said he added us to the list."

"Jonathan?" one of the women asked.

"Yessiree. Jonathan."

"Jonathan who?" asked the same woman who was eyeing them skeptically.

"Why, Jonathan Tyler. Who else?"

The women glanced at each other. One of them said, "The Senator put you on the list?"

"That's what he told me he was going to do."

"Do you know when?"

"Last week when we were having dinner."

The woman looked confused. "I don't know what to say. Your names aren't on the list. Surely, he wouldn't have forgotten something like that."

"He asked us to give a gift to the institute," Pixie said with a puzzled turn of her head. "*A large gift*. But maybe he decided the institute has all the funds it needs," she added sarcastically.

Caleb could see the growing concern on the staff members' faces. People waiting to get their name tags were growing impatient. Caleb knew the high and mighty weren't accustomed to waiting.

"Why don't you step aside for a moment while we get this sorted out," the other woman said, hoping to avoid a scene.

"Sorted out?" Pixie asked. "We flew in from Jackson Hole today at Jonathan's request, and now you're telling me we need to sort this out?" Pixie turned to Caleb in a huff. "Let's go."

Pixie grabbed Caleb's arm and turned. Distressed, the staff member holding the guest list said, "Wait. It must be a misunderstanding. Your names again, and we'll make tags for you."

A few minutes later, after quickly pulling their name tags off, Pixie and Caleb exchanged grins and then fought their way to one of the crowded terrace bars through a sea of people already clutching drinks. Uniformed servers deftly moved amidst the crowd offering vegan spinach artichoke cups, mushroom duxelles crostini, carrots in a blanket, and spicy vegetarian wonton bites, along with crystal flutes filled with champagne. Rolling waves crashed on the rocks below. The air held a chill, and Caleb watched a scarred trawler limp into the harbor. Maybe fishing for albacore, Caleb thought.

It didn't surprise Caleb that everyone seemed to know one another. The crowd conversed with ease, comfortable in their surroundings and wearing perfectly fitted evening dress. Caleb was about to ask Pixie what she'd like to drink, when he felt a tap on his shoulder and turned. A statuesque brunette with smoky eyes wearing a string of pearls on a long, exquisite neck, brazenly asked, "Who are you?"

Caleb stepped back.

"My god, you're beautiful," she said.

Caleb started to stammer when Pixie snapped, "He's taken."

The woman smiled and said, "Oh, well. Lucky you."

"Yes, I am. Now you can move on to some other hombre." Pixie stared the woman down.

"Now who's jealous?" Caleb asked after the woman slipped into the crowd.

"I thought we were trying to get you out of trouble."

"We are."

"Well, that one's a carnivore. She would eat you up and spit you out. Maybe I'm old fashioned, but I don't like women who are forward."

"You were a dancer."

"I needed money, darlin', but I didn't lose my moral compass. And I never tried to steal another woman's man."

Caleb managed a grin. He enjoyed seeing Pixie territorial. "Thanks for the warning. I'll watch myself amidst the cougars."

"If I'm going to be Mrs. Caleb Gray this evening, you better behave. Hear?"

Seconds later, Caleb spotted Jonathan Tyler step onto the terrace like a movie star. Caleb thought about all the scorn heaped upon him and realized that he had clenched his fists. He nudged Pixie, and they watched as Tyler was mobbed by well-wishers. Tyler wore his formal wear impeccably. His hair was perfectly combed, and he wore glasses, which gave him a contemplative, studious appearance, as if he spent his days teaching undergrads at Harvard. Caleb could see Tyler enjoyed the attention. He glowed in the early evening light as a waiter handed him a glass of champagne. There'd be no schlepping to the bar for the Senator. Even from a distance, it was obvious how much Tyler enjoyed being the center of attention and having people fawn over him.

Caleb realized Tyler was alone. No Mrs. Tyler on his arm. He could also see that despite attracting a crowd, Tyler seemed to be distracted, furtively peering over shoulders, searching for someone. Caleb wondered if Tyler was looking for Francois, and when he saw an attractive woman in her mid-forties cut through the crowd in a tight-fitting gown holding a glass of red wine, he knew. She positively beamed as Tyler raised his head in recognition and stepped through the adoring well-wishers to give the woman a hug and a delicate kiss on the cheek. When they moved away from each other, Caleb noticed that they held hands for a lingering instant before they fell into easy conversation.

Pixie whispered, "Did you see that?"

"Sure did."

"Rabbits. They can't wait to peel their clothes off."

Caleb felt a growing rage. These people, Peters, Marley, Tyler, and now Francois, as if they didn't have enough already, had come together to obliterate the commercial lobster industry and destroy him. He was feeling the urge to confront them right then when Tyler turned his head and caught Caleb's eye. Tyler's expression took on a quizzical and troubled appearance, and Caleb wondered if he recognized him or was just trying to place Caleb's face. Tyler blinked and whispered in Francois' ear. Seconds later, the senator was cutting through the crowd toward Caleb, his eyes flickering with recognition.

Caleb took a deep breath. His every instinct told him to grab Tyler's skinny neck and fling him over the terrace railing but instead he steeled himself for the encounter. When he arrived, Tyler said with false charm, "Haven't we met?" Tyler studied him and stuck out his hand. Caleb reluctantly shook it.

"I don't think so," Caleb said.

Tyler turned to Pixie. His face lit up. "Senator Jonathan Tyler." Caleb noted that there was nothing false about the charm now.

"Senator," Pixie drawled in barely concealed contempt.

Tyler gave an uneasy smile and turned back to Caleb. "Did we meet in Washington?"

Caleb shrugged, finding solace in Tyler's unease. "I'm not placing you."

"A lobbyist?"

"No."

"What do you do?"

Caleb said vaguely, "A little of this, a little of that."

"Have you supported the institute before?"

Pixie said, "I have. For years."

Tyler turned his full attention on Pixie. "I definitely wouldn't have forgotten your face," he said with what Caleb felt was an overly long glance at her cleavage. It was clear that Tyler's time in the midst of the treachery and deceit of politics had honed his instincts. Caleb could tell that he wasn't going to let this go.

"Strange, I've never seen you here." Tyler's eyes began to flash with distrust. He glanced at Caleb's missing nametag, glared, and said, "What's your name?"

Unsmiling, Caleb stared hard at Tyler and snapped, "John Doe."

Tyler broke into a thin smile and with a lower voice said to Caleb, "One of the things I pride myself upon is that I don't forget a face. A politician's gift."

"Another in a long line of gifts," Caleb replied. "How fortunate you are."

Tyler said with a hint of menace, "You have the advantage of me now, but I'll remember where we met, and then we'll pick up the conversation from there, Mr. John Doe."

"I look forward to it, Senator."

"Like I said, I never forget a face," Tyler snapped before slowly moving away toward Francois, who was chatting with an animated group of donors.

When Tyler was out of earshot, Pixie arched her eyebrows and whispered, "John Doe?"

Caleb shrugged. "It was the only thing I could think of."

"Well, you sure didn't do anything to throw him off your scent. It won't be long before the good Senator figures out who you are." Pixie grabbed Caleb's hand and said, "We need to make hay while the sun shines."

They navigated their way through the throng of people, and after discovering a corridor leading to a string of offices and a conference room, they drifted away from the crowd and ducked down the narrow hallway. They passed office doors, a few open, some shut tight, until they came to the end of the carpeted corridor and found Francois' office suite. The nameplate on the lightly stained wooden door made no mistake: Dr. Sandy Francois, Executive Director

"Fancy, huh?" Pixie asked.

"I bet it's locked tight."

"I might just take you up on that." She reached for the handle and the door opened easily.

"So much for security."

"Francois probably figures with a bunch of millionaires here tonight, who's gonna steal anything? Either that, or she left it open so she could meet Tyler here for a little fun."

With that unpleasant image kicking around Caleb's mind, they slipped into the office suite and closed the door behind them. In front of them sat Francois' administrative assistant's desk. On the desk sat a large, curved screen computer and a neat stack of files.

Caleb noticed that Francois' office door was cracked. He pushed it open and found a spacious room with large windows facing Hacienda Bay. A cherry wood conference table sat in the corner, stuffed chairs made up a sitting area, and Japanese prints adorned the walls. Built-in bookshelves held scientific periodicals, a small, delicately carved wooden sculpture of a seal, and a handful of sterling silver-framed photos of Francois around the world: on an Arctic research ship, standing at the base of Machu Picchu, and with a group of people, including Tyler, in front of the Lincoln Memorial. A closed laptop sat on a messy, sprawling desk.

While Caleb started to feel the same unsettled feeling he had at Marley's house, without hesitating, Pixie began to rifle through drawers. Caleb couldn't help imagining a security guard bursting through the door and the mayhem to follow.

After a minute of sifting through Francois' desk, Pixie looked up, shook her head, and said to Caleb, "Nothing, darlin'. All she's got are pens, pencils, paperclips, mouthwash, Motrin, mints, and tampons."

"It was a longshot."

She nodded and began to eye the laptop on top of Francois' desk.

"What are you thinking?" Caleb asked.

Pixie smiled slyly. "You think ole Sandy would notice if her laptop walked off into the sunset?"

"In a heartbeat."

Pixie reached behind the desk and unplugged the charger.

"What are you doing?" Caleb asked, his pulse starting to pound.

"What do you think?"

"Are you kidding? Let's get out of here. We wouldn't be able to open it anyway."

"Just leave that to Pixie, Caleb Gray," Pixie said, her face determined. "We're not leaving without something to show for our efforts."

Tyler looked away for a moment before settling his eyes on Francois. It was a rare moment where they'd found themselves alone as the party swirled around them. Soon, dinner seating would begin and Tyler would have to slip back into the role of Senator from California.

"Let it go, Jonathan," Francois said, sipping wine.

"I've seen him before."

"You keep saying that."

Tyler shook his head and for an instant closed his eyes. "Somewhere," he mumbled.

"Forget about it."

"I can't."

"Why not?"

"He doesn't belong here. John Doe my ass."

"Maybe he doesn't like your politics?"

Tyler arched his eyebrows. "I meet plenty of people who don't like my politics. Hell, that doesn't even register with me anymore. No, this guy raises all my red flags."

"Maybe you're jealous? He's awfully good looking in that rugged, outdoorsy, hunky kind of way," Francois teased.

Tyler sighed and stared off at the Pacific. In the distance, a purse seiner was making its way into the harbor at dusk. He squinted as he watched the boat. Suddenly his head snapped back as if he had taken a strong jab to the face. "Shit!"

"What?"

"He's the lobsterman."

"What lobsterman?"

"The one who testified at the senate hearing a couple of years ago. The one Peters set up."

Francois' jaw dropped. "It couldn't be. How the hell could he get in here?"

"I swear my life on it." Anger mixed with uncertainty swept across Tyler's face.

"What could he possibly be doing?"

"I don't know. But I don't like it. This could be very bad."

Francois started to blanch. "You think he knows?"

Tyler gripped his wine glass and tried to regain his composure. "Maybe. Maybe not. But we better find out."

Fifteen minutes later, as guests slowly took their seats for dinner, Sandy Francois entered her office. There'd been no sign of Caleb Gray or the woman who accompanied him. The institute's two security guards had come up empty.

Tyler's realization had set off alarms, and Francois' mind raced with uncertainty. She checked her office. Nothing seemed out of place. She tried to calm herself and took a deep breath. She was about to breathe a sigh of relief when her heart stopped. Her laptop was gone. Vanished. She wanted to scream but instead put her head in her hands and whispered, "*Oh no. Oh shit.*"

In a sleepy voice, Sabrina said, "Press and hold the shift key and click on the power icon."

"Easy peasy," Pixie said, her face flush with concentration. She'd changed into jeans and a t-shirt and Caleb had shed his tux as they waited at the gate in SFO for the last redeye to Boston.

"Okay. This is where it gets tricky . . . Listen carefully."

A few minutes later, Sabrina said with satisfaction, "Can you see the cursor moving?"

"Sure can," Pixie said with a smile as passengers began to line up to board the flight.

"I've got it from here. After I download everything, turn the laptop off and dump it in the trash."

"Got it."

"When you get to Boston, I'll call you. No text messages or email. Let's not make the same mistakes we're hoping they made."

"Fingers crossed."

Five minutes later, Sabrina said, "All set. Get rid of it. Safe travels."

Tyler had entered Francois' house in the darkness through the back entrance to avoid the suspicious eyes of neighbors. Tyler and Francois rarely met at her home, which sat on a small cul-de-sac perched above Hacienda Bay. They preferred hotels where they would arrive separately to keep their affair away from prying eyes.

Tyler said angrily, sitting in one of the plush chairs in Francois' living room, "Tell me again what you downloaded?"

Francois sat on the couch, put her head down, shook it, and slowly looked up with bloodshot eyes. "The videos."

"But we agreed to delete them, Sandy. That was the deal."

"Well, I liked to watch us. It's hot."

"What else?"

"There's nothing about Utami. I swear."

Tyler rose out of his chair and started pacing. "Let's get this straight. We agreed to delete the videos. But you kept them."

In a clipped voice, on the verge of tears, Francois said, "Yes."

"And now Gray has your laptop."

"Maybe someone else stole it?"

"Wake up, Sandy." Tyler paused and took his glasses off and pointed them at her as if he were a prosecuting attorney. "Is the laptop password protected?"

"Of course."

"Encrypted?"

"No." She shook her head. "It's not like I have state secrets, Jonathan."

"Is there anything else? Are you telling the truth?"

Francois started to cry. "The offshore account."

Tyler's eyes narrowed. "What about it? "

"I kept records."

"On the laptop?" he asked, his voice rising.

Francois looked up, tears streaming down her cheeks. "Yes."

Tyler sat on the couch and grabbed Francois by the shoulders, staring incredulously at her. "It won't take two seconds to figure out you've been siphoning gifts from the institute, and I've been diverting campaign funds. Do you understand that?"

Francois started sobbing.

"What else?"

"Nothing. I swear."

"Tell me you didn't use your birthdate or something moronically simple as a password."

Francois shook her head as her face flushed with anger. "It's a complicated password, Jonathan. I'm not stupid."

Tyler said in a low voice, "If they get into that computer, I'm ruined. We both are. Understand?"

Francois attempted to steady her voice. "It's a complicated password."

"Are you sure there's nothing about Utami? Think, Sandy."

She closed her eyes for an instant and sighed. "Nothing," she finally said.

"No documents or references to Marley or me in your email?"

"I told you, I'm not a moron."

"If they hack the computer, all they have is the two of us humping like dogs and a trail of stolen money."

Francois looked away to hide her tears.

After a moment, Tyler said with angry resignation, "Whatever possessed you to keep those bank records and videos?"

Francois turned and mumbled, "I don't know."

Chapter Twenty-Two—Bluff

Pixie and Caleb sipped coffee purchased from a coffee shop by their gate. As the sun rose over Boston Harbor, the soft summer light lay translucent on the still water. Morning travelers walked steadily by pulling their suitcases along.

Pixie checked her phone. No word from Sabrina. She was tempted to call, but it was barely 7am. They had kept Sabrina up late enough the night before. Let the poor woman sleep, Pixie thought.

Caleb gripped his knapsack. "Let's get out of here."

Pixie nodded.

Caleb said, "If she hasn't already, soon Francois will discover that her laptop is missing, and there's going to be hell to pay."

"I'm not so sure Francois is gonna call the police."

"The police might not be our only worry. People who've already broken the law generally won't have any problem breaking a few more. And I would be surprised if Tyler hasn't remembered who I am yet."

Pixie nodded and checked her phone again.

When they exited the terminal and were headed for the parking garage, Pixie's cell started to chime. She took a deep breath and answered. "What did you find?"

"I saw more of Sandy Francois and Jonathan Tyler than I ever imagined – or wanted, for that matter," Sabrina said. "Kinky, to say the least."

"So," Pixie responded, "not the kind of home movies you'd show to your momma?"

"Let's just say they taught me a thing or two."

Pixie laughed. "The videos alone could ruin Tyler and put Francois in deep doo doo with her bosses. If you didn't find anything else, at least we got that."

Sabrina paused. "I did find something else."

Pixie looked at Caleb, raised her eyebrows, and pointed at the phone.

"I found financial records about the institute, strategic plans, board minutes, scientific papers, and official stuff. Her internet history is relatively benign. But . . . our friend Sandy has a joint offshore account with Senator Tyler. It looks like they've been moving money, but I can't find the source of the funds. Having an offshore account is usually a red flag but not always. It'll take a lot of digging to find out if it's dirty money." Sabrina paused. "And it's amazing how stupid people are with their computers. I found a photo, too. It was a snapshot of Francois and Tyler, a few other people, and here's the kicker, of Marley. Looks like they were in Central America. I did some analysis, and it's Costa Rica for sure."

"Everyone's tied to Utami?"

"Yup. But we can't prove that. It's only a photo."

"Guilt by association?"

"It depends on what you're after."

"Justice."

"I get it, but a photo won't stand up in court. And like I said, it might take a lot of digging to find out about the money source for their Cayman account."

"But we got bargaining chips."

"It depends. Does Tyler's wife know about the fun he and Francois have been having? Do she and Tyler have an agreement, an open marriage? Francois is a different matter. Embarrassing for sure. But she's divorced. No kids. She could write off the videos. Lots of people have out-of-the-mainstream sexual habits. The photo with Marley is flimsy evidence, but if you put the video and photo of Marley together with the Cayman account, you could scare the shit out of them."

"What are you suggesting?"

"The videos are good, but the photo and offshore account records are even better, for your purposes, anyway." Sabrina paused. "If there's an obscure photo of Marley in her hard drive, what else did she save? She probably doesn't even remember she downloaded a photo of the three of them. And if she didn't remember that, what else might be there? Why not play on it? Scare the crap out of them. Bluff. They have too much to lose. Send them the photo, mention the offshore account, and tell them it's just a sample of what you found. I made sure she can't get access to her drives on another device. If they don't play ball, threaten to share the pictures linking them to Utami, the Cayman account, and the sex videos with the media. That will get their attention."

"Oh, honey. Diabolical."

Sabrina said, "You have the upper hand if you play it right. If they already know the laptop is gone, they're probably going insane. Just play on their fears. You'll be taking your tactics from the Agency playbook, not that you heard that from me."

Roarsh rubbed his eyes and lit a cigarette. A half empty coffee cup sat next to his computer as the morning light filtered into the office. He began to scan his email when his face lit up and he murmured, "Holy shit."

Kiki was sitting at her desk sipping Red Bull and checking text messages. She asked, "Whatcha got?"

Roarsh eyed the email again and banged his fist on the desk in amazement. "You won't believe this."

"What?"

"It's sick."

Kiki looked annoyed. Roarsh knew she hated when he played coy with information. "Tell me, will you?"

Roarsh rose quickly from his desk and said, "This is huge." He pointed at the screen. Kiki came over and peered at the email from one of Greenhaven's senior operational staff. As she read, her jaw dropped.

"30,000?" she asked, astonished.

"That's way bigger than North Dakota."

"How are we going to coordinate all those people?"

"We're not. There's no way."

"They're on their own?"

Roarsh smiled. "Yup. It's going to be chaos.

"Crazy."

Roarsh pointed at the screen. "This is wild."

"Out of control."

"It's perfect," Roarsh said, his cigarette bobbing up and down between his lips. "Serves those asshole whale and lobster killers right."

Caleb breathed a sigh of relief when he crossed the Piscataquis River Bridge and crossed into Maine. He and Pixie pulled off onto the Kittery exit and found a diner about a half mile from the Trading Post. Over thin coffee and soggy eggs, they lowered their voices and discussed the next step. They'd agreed during the ride north from

Boston that they'd email Francois a link to one of the videos, where handcuffs had been in play, a screenshot of the offshore account routing number, and the photo of Tyler and Francois with Marley. There'd be no threats, only evidence. *The first thing you do is make them squirm,* Sabrina had said.

Caleb held up his phone and said to Pixie, "Here's what the email says . . . ***Thought you'd enjoy this. More to come.***"

"I like it. Short and sweet."

"Do people really get into that?" Caleb asked.

"What?"

"Handcuffs."

"Whatever floats their boat."

Caleb shook his head. "Shall I?" He put his finger over the 'send' button.

Pixie grinned and said, "Let's see how Francois likes this position."

Pixie held up her coffee cup as a toast and they clinked coffee mugs. "What do you think their next move will be?"

"If it were me, I'd wave the white flag. But I'm not like these people, that's for sure," Caleb replied.

"We should be ready for them to come in, guns ablazin'."

"No doubt, but I'm still holding out hope for surrender," Caleb said as he pushed around runny eggs with his fork.

Chapter Twenty-Three—Thirty Thousand

Francois had spent a sleepless night after Tyler had left for his drive home to Pacific Heights. He'd departed in smoldering silence. Coolly analytical by nature, Francois had resigned herself to the worst and believed she could withstand it. The videos would be embarrassing, and she'd be portrayed in a terrible light, but scandals had become commonplace, and people survived them. Divorced and childless, she met a powerful man and slept with him. Sure, the videos were weird, and publicly explosive, but lots of people captured their erotic kink watching themselves.

The challenge would be to prove she hadn't stolen funds from the institute or associated herself with Utami. She would say it was all a misunderstanding. She wanted to believe that the institute's trustees valued her contributions too highly to demand her resignation and would want to avoid accusations that would hurt the organization's reputation, particularly around a longtime and highly respected director. But Francois wasn't sure. She needed to be prepared to fight back. She would remind them that the Marine Institute of the Pacific would be nothing without Sandy Francois. She'd raised millions of dollars, taken the institute from a scrawny scientific organization to international renown. They needed to be reminded that she would be nearly impossible to replace.

A sense of calm swept over her as the morning sunlight filtered through her bedroom curtains. She told herself that she could withstand the accusations and scorn. She took a deep breath, reached for her phone, and opened her email. Her heart started to race when she scrolled down from the video link. Her jaw hardened as she stared at the photo that had been cut and pasted and the offshore account routing number. In a spark of anger, she banged her fist into the mattress, cursed, and felt a sudden hollow in the pit of her stomach. She could have sworn she'd left no trail about Utami. Yet, there was Marley and Tyler standing next to her. What else had she forgotten? All the night's rationalizations gave way to panic. Her life as she knew it could very well be over.

Ed Pratt was beside himself. He knew Spring Harbor was in deep trouble when the state police colonel himself had called Pratt and shared the latest bad news. "Thirty thousand," he'd said. Then he added, dryly, "We need to be prepared for the possibility that they may not behave."

Almira Babb's stunt had failed. Making Dirk Peters an honorary citizen of Spring Harbor had fallen flatter than a halibut. All she had done was divide the town, betray Caleb, and show the protesters that the town was running scared. Pratt had tried to reach out to Caleb, but his texts had gone unanswered. He was furiously working with Van Burnham and state agencies to fend off the coming storm. The town's maintenance crew had begun erecting barriers.

It was no surprise the Governor had made no comment. There'd been talk about calling out the National Guard but pleas fell on deaf ears in Augusta. The protest would take place in a few days and Pratt wanted to climb under a rock. His phone was incessantly chiming, buzzing, and vibrating with calls, texts, and emails. Adding to the misery, he had to try to keep Dirk Peters from getting his head bashed in, while fighting the urge to do it himself. Pratt knew that if one hair was ruffled on Peters' head, he'd be a martyr for Greenhaven and thousands of protesters. If that happened, Pratt knew that Spring Harbor would sure as hell be toast.

Tyler nearly exploded when Francois called him on his government issued phone. He quickly exited his palatial Pacific Heights home while his wife was getting the kids ready for school and took the call outside. Francois knew better. They'd always used burners, but she'd been hysterical, so he listened in disbelief as the woman who'd always shown steely composure and self-assuredness explained through sobs and sniffles what had occurred. Tyler was a political animal. He was accustomed to eyeing an issue from all angles. He knew the videos would destroy his marriage and suddenly realized he didn't care. In the age of presidential scandal and the citizenry's low expectations for politicians' personal conduct, he didn't think the videos alone would crush his hopes for the Oval Office. Surely, the videos would be a damaging broadside, but he might survive the political storm. Stealing campaign donations and his association with Utami, however, had far more crushing, legal implications. The FBI would be all over him. He would be censured in Congress, indicted, and possibly convicted of influence peddling and fraud. Plus, who knew what Francois would say under threat of prosecution. There'd be appeals, hundreds of thousands of dollars spent on legal fees, disbarment, jail time, and, in the end, a ruined political career, his presidential ambitions down the toilet.

When Tyler ended the call after demanding Francois pull herself together, he swore and slowly walked back into the house. Two hours later, on his way to catch a flight to Washington, he was still calculating his next steps when his burner phone rattled. It was Marley. The South African began nervously telling him what had happened two nights before at Utami. A lab technician had allowed a man and woman posing as investors into the lab. They'd asked questions and fled after the woman snapped photos. Marley told Tyler he called a security agency specializing in corporate espionage to ascertain the identity of the couple, but while they were there, the cameras had inexplicably shut down.

"Are you kidding me?" Tyler asked. "Why didn't you call me earlier?"

"The lab tech and security guard just fessed up."

"Did he answer their questions?"

Marley paused. "He was vague. He said he doesn't remember what he told them. I'm not sure, but I suspect he may have leaked some things we don't want out there."

"Goddammit," Tyler said. He added disgustedly, "Don't bother to run the ID check."

"Why not?"

"Because I know who they are."

"How could you possibly?"

"He's the lobsterman in Maine."

"Gray?"

"That one."

"The woman?"

"A blonde?"

"Yes."

"I don't know her name, but I know they're onto us, Sebastian. You better get your shit together. As a matter of fact, we both need to get our shit together."

Marley's voice rose an octave. "There's no way you can be traced, Mate."

"Oh, yes there is."

Tyler proceeded to tell Marley the story from the night before and the threat of "more to come." He skipped the part about the video sexcapades.

"What now?" Marley asked, clearly shaken.

"I've been sitting here trying to figure out next steps. We may need to play ball."

Marley took a deep breath seemingly trying to regain his composure. "I know a man," he began cautiously. And for the next few minutes explained his relationship to a former South African Defense Force veteran and mercenary living in Texas. Nervously, Marley finally asked, "What do you think?"

"Don't bullshit me, Sebastian. Is this guy real? I thought hitmen only existed in the movies," Tyler asked skeptically.

"Honest, Jonathan."

"Then if we have to contact him, keep my name out of it. Understand?"

"Got it."

"And Sebastian . . ."

"Yes?"

"Does Peters know about me?"

Marley swallowed. "No."

"Are you sure?"

"Certain."

"You better not be lying, Sebastian."

There was silence.

"If you end up making that call, put Peters on the list. I'm not going down because of that worm. Hear me?"

"I hear you, Jonathan. But if I make the call, I'm going to need some help with the finances. Guys like that don't work cheap."

"You'll get it," Tyler snapped.

"What's the first play?"

"I don't know, but I don't want to go nuclear until I don't see any other option. And," Tyler hissed, "if you do have to contact him, don't screw it up."

Dirk Peters clung to his motel room like pine sap to a shoe. The honorary citizen of Spring Harbor had awakened the next morning to find the Malibu sitting on concrete blocks and stuffed with rotting bait fish. Peters didn't give a bloody hell about the Malibu, except he now had no escape route, and he couldn't help but consider what humiliations he might suffer should the townspeople's wrath need another outlet. For all intents and purposes, he was an inmate of the Oceanview Motel.

Peters had fired off a string of texts to Marley demanding to leave Spring Harbor. He'd done his work, stirred up nearly every crazed activist on the planet, set environmentalist sharks loose upon the town in an ugly feeding frenzy, and all but ensured Utami's future. What else did the South African want? Peters wanted his money and to return to Southern California to a newly invigorated acting career before he ended up in hospital with broken legs.

His desperation grew the longer Marley failed to reply. The only silver lining was Peters hadn't laid eyes upon Maddox since the rental car was trashed. When Maddox had seen the Malibu packed with festering herring, he kept saying, "You gotta love it, Dirkster. Feel the hate. You're big time again!" Then poof, Maddox had disappeared.

Finally, his phone chimed. He nervously looked at the caller ID. The call read Greenhaven International. When he answered, a man introduced himself as Roarsh. He said he was the Assistant Director of North American Operations and was "stoked" to tell Peters the Brit had been chosen as the protest's featured speaker.

"You're kidding me?" Peters asked.

"I'm not. You're totally a hero, dude."

Peters felt his heart begin to pump and ran his hand through his hair. He couldn't believe it. The final steppingstone. Back to top billing. "Is this bloody real?" he asked.

"It's real, man. Can I count on you?"

Peters took a deep breath. His star had risen. Clear sky, sunny days. Blockbuster movies ahead. "Of course."

"This demonstration is going to be wild."

"How many?" Peters asked, feeling suddenly giddy from a rising tide of vanity and narcissism.

"Thirty."

"Thirty?" Peters' voice betrayed his disappointment.

"Thousand, dude. Thirty thousand."

"Thirty thousand?" Peters' jaw dropped.

"You're a rock star. Details to come."

After the call ended, Peters sat on the edge of the unmade bed and stared at himself in the mirror. He slowly began to grin, his bleached teeth glimmering. Dirk Peters was back on top.

Elrod came out of the Stringer Cottage squinting from the glare of the late-afternoon sun. He met Caleb and Pixie on the front lawn, their legs wobbly from the exhausting events of the last several days. Pixie patted him on the shoulder and asked, "How's the pooch?"

"On the mend."

"Bless his heart."

"California?" Elrod asked.

"Interesting to say the least," Pixie answered.

Elrod turned to Caleb. "Ed's hunting for you."

"What for?"

"He said he needs to talk."

"There's nothing left to discuss."

Elrod shrugged and said, "You better go into town and find him. He's up to his gills in trouble. He's been sticking his neck out for you."

"We're exhausted, Elrod. Besides, I'm not sure I want to be in town these days."

"Suit yourself, but it seems to me that you could do better by a man who's put his job on the line for you."

"Okay. I'm going," Caleb said, shaking his head. "No rest for the wicked."

Pixie said, "I'm going to." She turned to Elrod and pointed at Caleb. "To keep him out of trouble."

Caleb was about to walk back to the truck when Elrod said, "I hope someday Almira Babb burns in hell."

Pixie's mouth opened in surprise at the usually taciturn, mild-mannered Mainer's ire.

"She sure deserves it," Elrod added.

Caleb and Pixie found Ed Pratt in his office in the Spring Harbor Municipal Building with a phone pushed to his ear and a look of frustration stitched across his face. After a few minutes of heated discussion with a bureaucrat in Augusta, Ed put the phone down, motioned for Pixie and Caleb to sit, and said, "I've got more bad news for you, Caleb."

Caleb said, "What else is new?"

"This is," Ed said, leaning forward. "The Coast Guard moved your boat to Lubec."

"What the hell for?" Caleb asked.

"A few crazies have threatened to sink the *Mary G.* and burn your home down."

"Is that all? Why not come for me with a noose and be done with it?"

"When the protesters arrive, we'll have a state trooper watch the house." Ed paused and took a deep breath. "But about that noose."

Caleb shook his head.

Ed said, "There've been a few death threats. Most likely not credible, but I needed to tell you." Pratt lowered his voice, "I'm sorry, Caleb, but this has turned uglier than I ever imagined."

"I suppose you're going to tell me to go hide somewhere."

"I thought about it. But I knew you wouldn't take my advice."

"I'm not leaving. I haven't done anything wrong."

"It doesn't matter. Right or wrong, you've been cancelled."

"Ready, fire, aim," Pixie said.

"We'll have Deputy Collins stick with you during the protests."

"Collins?" Caleb asked. "The kid isn't even shaving. What can he do?"

"I figured you'd say that."

"What else have you figured, Ed?"

"In a few days, thousands of protesters are going to descend upon Spring Harbor filled with self-righteousness. Mobs have their own momentum, Caleb. There's no telling what might happen, particularly if they're being riled into a froth by bad actors. Short of the National Guard – which for God knows what reason has not been called up – circling the town with bayonets, there's not much we can do but weather the storm as best we can."

Caleb put his head down for a few seconds, then looked up and said, "Pixie and I just got back from California."

Ed's jaw dropped. He covered his ears. "Don't tell me you left the state. I don't want to know anything about it."

"We may be able to help," Caleb said.

Ed pulled his hands away from his ears. After a moment he leaned back in his chair and said with resignation, "Okay, I'm listening."

"This is real, Ed," Caleb said.

"Bring it on."

Fifteen minutes later, Caleb and Pixie finished sharing the story of Marley, Tyler, and Francois. There was a long pause as they waited for Pratt to react. Pratt took a deep breath and tapped his fingers on the desk. "So let me get this straight. You left the state illegally, broke into a house, lied to gain entrance into a corporate facility, crashed a party, stole and hacked a computer, and are now attempting to extort Jonathan Tyler, a potential nominee for President of the United States?"

"All in a days' work, darlin'," Pixie said proudly.

"How do you expect an officer of the law to use any of this?" Ed asked, exasperated. "I can't believe you're admitting to even one of those things."

Caleb said, "They're dirty, Ed."

"You have a photo with Tyler, his girlfriend, and the guy from Utami. A bank account in Grand Cayman. Not all offshore accounts are illegal. For now, it doesn't prove a thing. At least not yet. Sex tapes? 'More to come?' You think you have big problems? Wait until Tyler sends the FBI to your door."

"I'm telling you. They're dirty. This whole ordeal is a setup."

"Maybe so, but you haven't proved anything yet. Not from the law's perspective. Just innuendo and circumstance."

"It's a conspiracy, Ed."

"It may be. But nothing you've told me is going to save the town from protesters . . . or for the moment, you, Caleb."

"What more do you need?"

Ed sighed and took on a softer look. "I get it. Believe me. I'd be grasping at straws if I were in your shoes."

"These aren't straws."

"Look. You both need to get out of town. Go somewhere and hole up in a quiet place until the storm passes."

Caleb said, "Not happening. I'm not going to run like I'm guilty of something."

"Can't you talk sense into him?" Ed asked Pixie.

Pixie shrugged. "You and I both know he ain't going to change his mind. You just do your best to keep him safe."

They left Ed's office and were climbing into the pickup truck when Caleb's phone dinged. It was a simple text from an unknown number. He stared at his cell for a few moments, then finally said, "Tyler wants to meet with me."

"When?"

"Tonight."

"Where?"

"Ellsworth."

Caleb handed the phone to Pixie. The text read:

We can work this out. Ellsworth-Hancock Airport tonight at 10pm. J.T.

Caleb pursed his lips in concentration. "You don't think it's a trap, do you?"

"Only one thing's for sure. He's not flying to Maine for a vacation."

"What do you think we should do?"

Pixie smiled. "Let's see what the good Senator wants. I suspect a deal or a threat."

Caleb clenched his jaw. "Or both."

Chapter Twenty-Four—The Senator

The Cessna Citation sat by the private aviation building with its engines silent and its rampway down. The plane's cabin was dimly lit as Pixie and Caleb walked across the night-shrouded tarmac. When they neared the airstair to the plane, Caleb took a deep breath.

When Pixie and Caleb entered the cabin, the pilots were nowhere to be seen. Tyler was alone, and he didn't take the trouble to rise from his chair. Instead, he coldly motioned for them to sit. There were no pleasantries, no handshakes. A whiskey sat on a tray next to Tyler's seat, but he didn't offer Pixie or Caleb a drink. He had dark circles under his eyes and the haggard look of someone who hadn't slept. Caleb could relate. Certainly, he didn't resemble the debonair Senator they saw at the Marine Institute of the Pacific.

"You were supposed to come alone," Tyler growled.

Caleb glared at him. "She's with me. If you don't like it, we'll leave."

Tyler shook his head and said to Caleb and Pixie, "Turn off your phones and put them on the table."

Pixie smiled and said, "What, we haven't earned your trust?"

"I trust that you're trying to destroy me," he said. "You want to hear what I have to say, you switch off your cells."

Caleb glanced at Pixie. He powered down his phone. Pixie followed and they set their phones on the built-in faux cherry wood table in front of them.

"What about you?" Caleb snapped.

"My plane, my rules."

"We leave," Caleb said.

"No, you won't," Tyler said, lowering his voice and leaning back in his leather seat. "You won't leave, Mr. John Doe. You think your life is unraveling now, just walk out that door and see what happens."

"You act like you're holding all the cards, which is strange," Pixie said. "I was under the impression we had a few to play ourselves. King, queen, handcuff, bedpost, Cayman account with your lady friend, Marley photo, is a right smart hand."

Tyler ignored her. He was a man used to getting his way. He acted as if he were in a corner booth at Ebbitt's Grill bullying a rival politician. "Here's the deal. You delete the videos and forget everything else you stole from Sandy Francois' computer, and your life becomes much simpler."

"How's that?" Caleb asked.

"I'll get people in high places to call off the dogs. The charges against you will be dropped. You'll be a free man." He paused. "And you won't have to worry about money ever again."

Caleb sat back in his chair. "What's that supposed to mean?"

"You'll get a cut in Utami. It will be more lucrative than anything you'll ever haul out of the Gulf of Maine, that's for sure. Understand? All you have to do is destroy whatever you found in Francois' laptop and keep your mouths shut."

"So, I sell out lobstermen?"

Tyler's eyes hardened, and he looked at Caleb in disbelief. "Don't you understand what I'm offering?"

"I think I do. You want us to sell out and then to kiss your ass the rest of our lives for a few crumbs, which might not even come our way once we have no leverage."

Tyler looked at Pixie and said, "Tell him he's a fool to pass on this offer. I'm a United States Senator and a man of my word."

Pixie said, "I only see one dang fool, and he's sitting across from me if you think we're going to buy that 'man of my word' garbage."

Tyler's face reddened. "Take the deal."

"Or?" Caleb asked.

"You think you're in a world of hurt now. You wouldn't want it to get out that I'm not the only one accused of stealing money. How about that you siphoned off thousands of dollars from the Lobstermen's Alliance? Stole from hard-working people? Talk about betrayal. Or cheated on that beloved wife of yours? Believe me, for the right price, I can find a woman who'd be happy to tell everyone you screwed around behind your wife's back."

Caleb's ears grew hot. "You prick."

Tyler turned to Pixie and pointed his finger. "And you, Ms. McGee. I know things about you that you don't even know about yourself. Running a prostitution ring when you were a stripper. Filing false business returns to pad your real estate profits. The IRS will be hounding you for the rest of your life. More recently, I hear you've been stealing priceless jewelry from Spencer Tate. I spoke with Spencer this afternoon. He dropped everything to take my call. He'd enjoy making your life miserable. I'm certain I could add to both lists, given time and imagination."

Tyler paused and sipped his drink. His sharp teeth flashed and his eyes narrowed. He hissed, "Take the deal. A good life is a handshake away. No more problems. No more heartache." He turned to Caleb. "You can walk down that gangway a wealthy man."

He was met with stony silence.

"What's it going to be?" Tyler finally asked.

Caleb glanced at Pixie. Her eyes were hard as steel.

Pixie said, "Handcuffs, Mr. Senator? Whips and leather? How about that video where Ms. Francois makes you wear a bra and panties and call her 'daddy?'"

"You're playing with fire."

"Maybe so," Pixie said suddenly standing. "But I learned long ago that you don't make a deal with a rattler. My mamma said it always comes back to bite you."

"I tell you what," Tyler rejoined. "Why don't you sleep on my offer. Neither of us goes nuclear until we've had a chance to cool down. Surely, that's an acceptable compromise for the present?"

Pixie and Caleb looked at one another and then Caleb turned to Tyler and gave him a curt nod before rising to leave.

When they left, Tyler angrily finished off his whiskey and reached for the burner phone in his Berluti briefcase made of gorgeous Venezia leather. He dialed Marley. After a few rings, the South African answered.

"Contact your man," Tyler ordered.

"Are you sure, Jonathan?"

"Yes. Get it done now. And like I said, don't screw it up."

Pixie and Caleb drove back to Spring Harbor in silence trying to make sense of the conversation with Tyler. Pixie and Caleb had no doubt that Tyler would try to destroy them. They had bluffed with 'more to come,' and Tyler had volleyed with a promise to ruin them with a litany of falsehoods. He was not a man used to being at a disadvantage, and he would come after them with everything he could summon to destroy their credibility. After the giddiness of their exploits in California, Caleb now felt his world getting more desperate and complicated with every turn.

As they neared Spring Harbor, Caleb suddenly realized how bad he felt. He didn't want to be alone. He didn't think it was safe for Pixie to be by herself. Mainly, he just wanted to climb in bed with her and feel her next to him and in the morning wake up from this nightmare. He crossed the bridge to Millbridge Island and pulled into the parking area by the Stringer Cottage. Pixie gazed at him, her eyes beckoning for him to stay.

"You want to bunk here tonight?" she asked softly.

"More than anything. But first I better go check my house," he said. "I'll come back. In the meantime, ask Elrod to stay over and tell him to lock the doors."

Pixie reached out and put her hand gently on his cheek. "You okay, darlin'?"

"Not really."

"Me neither."

"How'd we get into this mess?"

Pixie shook her head and slowly took her hand away.

Caleb said, "I better get going. It's been a long day."

"Honey."

Caleb looked at her.

She leaned over and kissed him. Her warm lips lightly touched his and before he could say anything, she slid out of the pickup. Caleb watched her in his headlights until she disappeared up the path to the cottage.

Ten minutes later, he sat stunned in Elrod's pickup staring at his house. Every window in his one-story Cape had been shattered. *Whale Killer* had been spray painted in blood-red paint across his front door. Greenhaven had arrived.

Chapter Twenty-Five—Vacationland

Ron Dane, aka "Gold Finger," lived a few miles north of Ozona, Texas and raised quarter horses on his 500-acre spread. He'd made his way to America after surviving a decade of skirmishes in war-torn parts of Africa and Asia. An army veteran, he'd left South Africa and never looked back. He had happily traded careers. Contract killer paid far more handsomely than soldier of fortune, and generally, no one was shooting back. He picked his jobs carefully, with targets across the globe. The last "hit" was a Swiss banker named Max, who'd threatened to extort money from a German arms dealer doing dirty business with the mullahs in Tehran. To his family's dismay, Max was struck by a commuter train in Geneva. Nobody could figure out why he was wandering near the tracks on an early winter morning. Intoxicated? Depressed? Suicidal? His grieving family buried him with many unanswered questions.

Dane prided himself on leaving behind no clues. His resume included a disfavored Russian oligarch hiding in Mexico, an enemy of a Saudi Prince residing in London, and a French socialite who'd discovered his wife and her Italian lover had cheated him of millions.

Marley contacted him cryptically through a Romanian dark site called Wild Phantom, a chat room for anonymous mail. As a young man, Dane had done "work" for Marley's father, who'd made a small fortune during apartheid and squandered it making unwise bets during the Mandela years. Dane never liked Marley's father, but he was willing to take the old man's money. As for the son, Dane found him not merely an elitist but a conniving opportunist.

Marley's proposition was clear. At first Dane didn't like it, as three separate targets presented logistical difficulties. Then he heard the word 'Maine'. The temperature in Ozona was a scalding 102 degrees, too hot for Dane's liking. He would relish a bit of temperate weather. What put him over the edge, however, wasn't the cool breezes of the North Atlantic.

Dane craved lobster. And he vowed to devour as much of the crustacean as possible during his "trip" to Vacationland.

On a fine spring morning, one hundred Lexington Coach Line buses sat idling in neat rows spewing diesel fumes in a massive parking lot a few miles north of Gillette Stadium in Foxborough, twenty miles outside of Boston. For the bus company owners, it had been a mad scramble to assemble the fleet of coaches that would carry the first wave of protesters on the seven-hour journey to Spring Harbor. Greenhaven was following its usual playbook, ensuring the first group of activists arrived together to begin overwhelming the authorities.

Soon after, thousands more activists would crash the town, journeying from distant places around the globe, salivating at the opportunity to wreak havoc on people so unenlightened that they were still harpooning whales.

Roarsh shifted his weight and held up his phone. "People should be coming soon."

Kiki gazed at the buses and shook her head in disbelief. "This is surreal."

"I thought nothing would ever be as big as Fargo."

"Me neither."

Roarsh turned to her. "What was the name of the lobster dude again who killed the whale?"

"Gray."

"I bet that dude is hiding in a cave somewhere."

"That's certainly where I would be."

"Maybe someone will harpoon him."

"That would be awesome," Kiki said, lighting a cigarette.

"That town is dead meat."

Kiki laughed and took a drag. "Lobster meat that is."

Roarsh smiled. "We're going to boil that place like a lobster, that's for sure."

"I'm hungry," Kiki whined.

Roarsh laughed. "Sushi?"

Dane made the decision to fly to Portland instead of Bangor. He took a one-way early morning Southwest flight from Midland to Dallas Love Field and paid cash after taking a taxi to DFW. On Delta, Dane flew under an alias to Portland with a stop in Atlanta. He rented a nondescript Nissan sedan and after landing soon pulled onto Route 95.

A few years before, he'd read about a place in a town he couldn't pronounce that boasted the best lobster rolls in the world. "A must experience," the article said. Red's Eats in Wiscasset was about an hour north of Portland and four hours south of Spring Harbor. After waiting in line for thirty minutes, Dane plunked down at a picnic table overlooking the Sheepscot River on a beautiful summer afternoon and ate two huge lobster rolls, a large order of onion rings, and then topped off his meal with blueberry cake.

Fully satisfied, he went across the street to a bakery that was about to close and bought a large cup of coffee and then continued driving north on Route One past inlets and coves, with a few sweeping views of the Atlantic. When he hit Bucksport, the sun was setting and the car's GPS told him to drive west. After about twenty minutes on side roads, he pulled onto a dirt track and found a double wide trailer tucked into the woods.

A man with a ruddy face, thick beard, and ponytail met him and said to Dane, "Follow me." He was part of a secret paramilitary network of extremists called the Sword and Shield. Dane had used them twice before.

Dane went behind the trailer to a shed where the man motioned for him to come inside and pulled out a silver briefcase. He popped it open. Inside was a disassembled military grade sniper's rifle, made to army specifications. The rifle fired a high velocity, .223 round. The scope was ten-power. The man smiled and said, "You can't miss with this baby." He paused. "Here's the poison." He carefully handed Dane a small misting bottle of Ricin sealed in a plastic bag.

In response, Dane nodded and handed him an envelope stuffed with bills, and said, "You never met me."

Twenty minutes later, as the sun set and darkness pooled across Route One, Dane sat tired and frustrated, unable to turn as coach bus after coach bus plowed north. It reminded him of an invasion.

Marley had said the protest was going to be big. Dane could care less. All he wanted was a place to sleep, to scope out Spring Harbor the next day, and to finish the job. Then, on the way back, he would stop at the lobster shack he spotted near Belfast and order a twin lobster dinner and a celebratory IPA. The "job" would cost Marley and his "friend" a cool half million. A hefty deposit had already been made and the rest of the money would be wired to Dane's Nevis Island account when the job was done.

After the last bus finally passed, Dane continued north on Route One until he passed Whiting and quietly checked into the only motel where he'd been able to find a vacancy within a forty-mile radius of Spring Harbor. Before going to sleep, he assembled the rifle and sighted the scope. The barrel was slightly shorter than he would have preferred, but it made the weapon easier to conceal. He checked the muzzle suppressor and fitted it on the barrel. All in all, he couldn't complain. As always, luck played a role in any job, but he was confident in his abilities. He prided himself on his professionalism, and so far had managed to avoid leaving behind any messes that could implicate him.

Caleb had spent most of the morning nailing plywood over his shattered windows and installing deadbolts on his house. He called Ed Pratt and told him about the vandalism, and Ed had sent Deputy Collins to investigate. After phoning Ed, Caleb called Pixie and Elrod to explain what had occurred. When Collins arrived, he circled around the home shaking his head and muttering, took some notes on a pad of paper, and left. So much for the police keeping an eye on his home, Caleb thought.

Caleb was taking no chances. After discovering the vandalism the night before, he retrieved his 12-gauge shotgun from the basement closet, loaded it with bird shot, and tucked the Remington Fieldmaster under his arm. He had no plans to leave. His mind turned to Tyler and Francois. Releasing the videos and other information could deal a blow, but potentially not enough to end things in his favor in Spring Harbor. The photo of Tyler, Francois, and Marley? Too easy to explain away, a mere coincidence in the eyes of most. The Cayman account? Ed Pratt was right. Not every offshore account was dirty. Caleb's grip tightened on the shotgun as he considered his options. Should he strike first? Could he afford to? Caleb wondered what Pixie thought and needed to call her. He wanted to hear her voice. He realized how much he needed her, but he wasn't about to ask her to come over. It wasn't safe. Officer Collins had said earlier the first group of protesters had arrived the evening before, set up a tent city on the high school football field and town green, and were already beginning to raise hell.

After securing the plywood boards, Caleb went behind his house and noticed something strange. The way the sun was playing off his extra trap stock looked odd. When Caleb took a closer glance, he began to seethe. Someone had taken wire cutters and destroyed almost all the traps, easily a few thousand dollars' worth of damage.

He was a proud man, a sixth-generation Mainer, and it was time to take a stand.

Even though he recognized that the horde of protesters might provide excellent cover for him, Dane wanted no part of what he witnessed in Spring Harbor. The roads were clogged and the town was besieged with activists holding signs, chanting, and shouting insults at the state troopers trying to keep them from breaking through the wooden barriers set up along the waterfront. But despite the chaos, he watched a handful of activists drift into the few shops that were open.

Dane kept a distance from the police and made sure to blend into the crowd. Dane rarely asked questions or cared about the circumstances around a "hit," but he felt sympathy for the townspeople. The protest was beginning, and he could smell the protesters' desire to torch Spring Harbor. On another day, Dane would have enjoyed sitting on the deck at one of the few restaurants, admiring the ocean view while he savored a lobster and drank a beer. But he had a job to do. And after scoping out the town, he began to assemble a plan. Marley had asked him to take out the actor who narrated the video in addition to Gray and McGee. Probably Peters knew too much. Three "kills" weren't going to be easy, but Dane had dealt with complications before. A few years earlier, he'd assassinated a Bahraini prince and two associates in Tenerife. The job had been dodgy, but Dane had pulled it off.

He'd committed the photographs of the targets to memory and developed what he felt was the most sensible plan. He was told that McGee and Gray would likely be together, so he decided to stake out her place on Millbridge Island as it was isolated and so he could avoid the likelihood of witnesses. If they showed up together, he could take care of them in private, and then finish off the actor, who was likely to be in the midst of protesters, with the small misting bottle of ricin he purchased from the Sword and Shield guy.

Afterwards, Dane would slip back down the coast for a glorious twin lobster dinner.

Chapter Twenty-Six—Hitman

Dirk Peters soaked up the attention of the crowd. Like a modern-day Braveheart, he drifted among the protesters, basking in the adulation. He glowed when a chant struck up as if he starred for Manchester United. *"Dirk, Dirk, Dirk."* After being threatened by angry townspeople, Peters felt liberated and emboldened among the mob of Greenhaven supporters. It was the beginning of a golden road back to stardom. The following day, he would deliver his environmental rant to the thousands of activists with as much flair as possible, do interviews with the media hordes who had descended upon the town, and rub elbows with celebrity activists before returning to LA where he would collect a tidy sum from Utami and watch his acting career rise like a phoenix.

Adding to Peters' good mood and rising fortune, he hadn't seen Maddox since the Malibu was stuffed with rotting fish. He seemed to have disappeared.

Peters sauntered among the crowd of sycophants when a young woman with a button nose wearing a halter top and cut-off jeans fell into his arms, hugged him, and buried her head in his chest. As they gently swayed, Peters felt her shapely curves against him as she murmured, "Dirk Peters, I can't believe it's really you."

The day was getting better and better, and, at that moment, Peters thought of himself as the luckiest bloke on the planet. He knew for sure he wouldn't be sleeping alone on this night. It was just like old times. He'd have plenty of adoring ladies to choose from.

A few hours later, Dane stole a weathered kayak from a spit of sand above the tide line and paddled across the narrow gut separating Millbridge Island from the peninsula. He kept his head low beneath a baseball cap, sunglasses shielded the sharp glint of his eyes, and binoculars hung loosely around his neck. If anyone questioned him, he'd play the part of the dedicated birder, out in search of Bald Eagles, or perhaps a rare Roseate Tern.

The kayak cut silently through the water until he reached the shore, where he hauled it into a stand of spruce and shed his disguise. The binoculars hit the forest floor with a dull thud. Dane unlatched the silver briefcase at his side and started assembling the rifle with the kind of efficiency that came from years of practice. Fully outfitted, he moved through the shadows of the mossy woods with practiced stealth.

The tree line opened to an overgrown dirt track, and there it was – the Stringer Cottage, secluded and quiet. *Perfect*, he thought. Dane knelt and crept forward, his eyes fixed on the house. He found a good stand between several pines where he adjusted the scope and scanned the windows for movement. If he was lucky, two clean shots and he would be back in the kayak in minutes.

Caleb was already making his way toward the Stringer Cottage. Pixie hadn't answered her phone. He couldn't get Elrod to pick up either, which wasn't unusual since he wasn't used to having a cell and so often strayed away from wherever he had placed it. Caleb didn't want to leave his house unattended, but he'd become increasingly uneasy about Pixie and now dread prickled at him as he drove the narrow road. He'd left his house, unable to shake the feeling that something was wrong. While his mind was filled with thoughts about Tyler's threats and the damage the protesters had already inflicted on his property, something told him that he needed to get to Pixie fast. The closer he got to Millbridge Island, the more he had a premonition of disaster. By the time he drove across the Millbridge Island bridge, he was overwhelmed with a sick feeling in the pit of his stomach. Something was terribly wrong. Intuition told him to park the truck behind a stand of trees, out of sight of the cottage. Retrieving the shotgun from behind the seat, he checked the Remington and moved swiftly, his boots crunching softly on the pine needle path to the house. That's when to his horror, he heard a scream and rifle shot.

Elrod was in his shed, leaning over the carburetor of his old Evinrude outboard, a smear of grease across his weathered face. He'd been on the lookout for shenanigans since Pixie had arrived the evening before, so he took systematic breaks to walk around the property. So far, everything was quiet, unlike the chaos unfolding in town, which had left him unsettled. From what Caleb had reported about the meeting the night before with Tyler and the vandalism that had taken place at Caleb's house, Elrod feared what might come next. From what he heard about the protesters, they'd arrived in droves and overrun the town. Elrod had never heard of anything like it. No matter what Almira Babb promised, no good could come from turning on your friends and neighbors. It seemed to Elrod that you were either a community that bonded when times were tough or you weren't much of a community at all.

Elrod had left Pixie in the house and made sure he'd locked the door before he began working on the old outboard. He worried about her and Caleb. He felt protective of both, as if their budding romance was something that he needed to kindle. As Elrod cleaned the fuel line, he kept peering through the shed window. He'd been listening for the sound of approaching cars, but so far hadn't heard anything. Nevertheless, something told him to put the fuel line down and do another patrol of the area. He instinctively picked up the wrench that was lying on the bench and was headed toward the door when he heard what sounded like the yelp of a wounded coyote and a gunshot.

Pixie swore under her breath when she realized her phone had died. She plugged the cell into the wall behind her nightstand and scolded herself for being careless. With all her heart, she'd hoped Caleb would stay the night before so she could hold him and protect him from the wolves that were howling at his door. When Pixie thought back on her self-pity after her breakup with Spencer, she realized how paltry her loss was compared to what Caleb had surrendered when Mary died. That a man who'd already lost so much should be put through what Caleb was experiencing was downright criminal. She knew Caleb had lost faith in the world. She resolved that she was going to do everything in her power to help him live again. Despite the sunlight pouring through the window, she fought a sadness in her heart that what she had resolved would never come to be. How could it when protesters had already begun to tear Caleb's world apart by damaging his house and a senator was hellbent on his destruction? It seemed almost impossible that she and Caleb would ever have a chance to find peace together. It was almost comical, she mused. She'd walked out of Spencer's life seeking an oasis of tranquility on Millbridge Island, and found she walked into the most tumultuous time in her life since she'd left Port Arthur. She was in love, but she was also feeling increasingly vulnerable, especially now that she was without Caleb. She hoped he would hurry back because she was starting to get spooked.

Pixie walked to the window and looked at Frenchman's Bay, sparkling under a bright summer sun. A lobster boat chugged toward a cluster of small islands rising from afar above the tideline. A few gulls swooped back and forth. She suddenly felt tears welling. She hated to cry. She scolded herself and wiped away a tear as she stood silently by the window wondering what was next.

Dane smiled when he spotted the woman standing by the upstairs window. An easy shot. He wondered if he should wait to see if the man was with her. Then he could take both down, which would be much safer. He pondered his options and decided to take the sure thing, then hunt for Caleb and Peters.

He'd settled into position behind a clump of fir trees, the rifle steady in his hands. The windows of the cottage gleamed faintly in the sunlight. He'd scanned each one methodically, adjusting the scope to account for distance. Dane began to sight his rifle and followed the woman as she moved in full view around the bedroom. He kept a bead on her as she drifted closer to the window. He breathed slowly and placed his finger on the trigger. This was the moment of truth when he would take a life. Dane reminded himself it wasn't personal. Only business. He was about to pull the trigger when she disappeared from view. Dane exhaled and relaxed his grip while he waited patiently for her to come back in front of the window. He calmed his breathing, took his eye momentarily off the scope, and relaxed his neck muscles. He paused to reassess the situation. Should he be more patient and see if the opportunity to take two of the targets presented itself? This was what happened when you agreed to multiple kills. You found yourself second guessing.

When he put his eye back to the scope, there she was peering through the plate glass, looking for all the world as if she were longing for someone. The expression on her face seemed melancholy, almost as if she knew what was about to come. She was beautiful. What a shame, Dane thought, but he had a job to do. It was time. *Enough.* The lobsterman would have to wait.

Dane carefully sighted the rifle, took a deep breath, then, right before he pulled the trigger, he felt a sharp pain in his shoulder. An involuntary yell escaped him as the pains quickly multiplied. Suddenly his neck, arms, and face were on fire. As the muffled echo of the rifle's suppressor diminished, he became aware of an angry, maddening, buzzing sound. Panic set in as the yellow jackets swarmed, their venom searing his skin like fire. The rifle clattered to the ground as he thrashed and slapped at his body. The deadly focus of a second ago had been replaced by pure, primal fear.

After hearing the scream and gunshot, Caleb raised his shotgun and ran along the path to the house. He feared the worst and hoped he wasn't too late. The thought of losing Pixie tore at him, and he vowed that if they survived, he'd never let her go. Mary had been the love of his life, but Pixie had been his savior. The thought of losing her was too much as he raced to the Stringer Cottage.

Elrod moved in the direction he thought the scream and sound of the rifle firing had come from. Soon he saw the spastic movements of a large man in a baseball cap writhing and swatting at himself. Elrod's eyes darted to the rifle on the ground. Without hesitation, Elrod crept closer, wrench in hand. Soon he realized why the man's movements were erratic. He was trying to fend off a swarm of yellow jackets. The damn fool had sat down on a yellow jacket nest Elrod had avoided for years. He didn't notice Elrod until it was too late. The wrench connected with a sickening *thunk*, and the man crumpled to the forest floor.

Caleb bolted up the path, his heart racing, trying to tamp down the panic he felt. The thought of losing Pixie too was unthinkable. He felt his mouth go dry and his pulse hammer as he cut across the patchy lawn to the house. He realized there was a possibility that the person who fired the shot might have him in his crosshairs, but if he had already taken Pixie, Caleb didn't care at all.

Caleb tore open the back door into the kitchen, saw that nothing was disturbed, then took the narrow stairway two steps at a time. When he peered wildly into the bedroom, he discovered a shattered window, a bullet hole in the wall, a patch of blood on the pine floor, and Pixie sprawled awkwardly on the floor. His dread gave way to relief when he saw her start to sit up. He dropped down beside her, folded her in his arms, and said, "stay down."

As Caleb looked more closely, he noticed a glass shard had cut her forehead.

"That sumbitch," Pixie swore, touching the cut on her head. "Another inch." Caleb tried to keep from shaking. He knelt and put his hand out. Pixie took it carefully and placed his warm palm on her cheek.

"What just happened, darlin'?" she asked, bewildered.

When Dane regained consciousness, he found himself bound to an Adirondack chair. His limbs were heavy, his head was pounding, and his skin burned where the yellow jackets had stung him. His face and neck felt horribly swollen. Each breath was a struggle, his throat tight with the swelling, the air coming in short, panicked gasps. Across from him, a wiry, grease-streaked man held Dane's rifle directly at his chest. A woman – Pixie – stood with her arms crossed, her eyes cold and calculating. The other target, Caleb, had a shotgun slung casually over his shoulder, though his stance was anything but relaxed.

"I think he's coming out of it," Caleb said. "Don't murder him until he talks, Pixie."

"He missed me by that dang much," she said angrily, holding her forefinger and thumb an inch apart. "If it weren't for those bees, he would've ruined my hairdo."

Dane groaned, his lips cracked and swollen. "What the bloody hell happened? Did someone hit me in the head?" he rasped, his words thick and slurred. His eyes darted to the three of them, then to the rifle, and back again.

Elrod shrugged, the rifle steady in his hands. "You sat on a yellow jacket nest. The wrench was my way of saying hello."

Pixie took a step forward, her voice sharp. "Who sent you? And don't even think about lying."

Dane didn't answer, his focus shifting to the tightness in his chest. He sucked in a shallow breath, then another, but it wasn't enough. The burning in his throat was worse now, and the panic crept in faster than he could control it.

Elrod dangled a bottle of Benadryl in front of him. "You look like you could maybe use some of this."

Dane's eyes locked on it, desperate. He tried to swallow but gagged on the effort. "I need – give me–" His voice broke into a wheeze.

"You need to start talking," Caleb said. "Now."

Dane shook his head weakly, sweat starting to bead on his forehead. He coughed, the sound wet and raw, and tried again to speak. "Please," he rasped, his chest hitching with the effort. "I . . . can't . . ."

Pixie tilted her head, her gaze icy. "You know what happens next, right, darlin'? Your throat's going to close all the way. Breathing's already getting harder, ain't it?"

Dane's breathing quickened. The chair creaked under him as he squirmed, tugging at his bindings. "Help–" he choked, barely audible.

Pixie didn't move. "First, you'll get dizzy. That swelling's going to keep spreading until your airways are completely blocked. Then you'll pass out. And if you're lucky, you won't feel the rest."

Caleb leaned on the shotgun, his eyes cold. "What she's saying is, you don't have much time."

Dane's lips moved, but the words didn't come. His eyes flew from the bottle in Elrod's hand, then at Caleb's emotionless face. They really weren't going to help him.

Pixie crouched to his level, her tone calm, almost clinical. "You're probably wonderin' if you'll make it. That's the thing about anaphylaxis. Once it starts, it don't stop on its own. You need something to counteract it. Fast. Like that Benadryl. Or maybe an EpiPen. You got one of those stashed somewhere?"

Dane's head lolled forward. He gasped, his body trembling, and forced out a strangled word: "Please."

"You've got something to say?" Elrod asked, his voice a low rumble.

Dane's breathing was a wet rattle now, his body shuddering with every gasp. The tension in his face broke, replaced with raw fear. "I'll . . . talk . . ." he croaked. "Just . . . *please* . . ."

Caleb straightened, nodding toward Pixie, who snatched the Benadryl from Elrod and stepped forward. She held it just out of Dane's reach. "One word out of place, and this stays in my pocket."

"You need to spill it or we'll call the police chief. He'd be real interested in knowing you were sitting outside the cottage with a sniper rifle and missed Pixie by an inch." Caleb said.

Dane's chest heaved. His voice was barely a whisper. "A bloke named Marley . . . sent me . . . .."

Pixie filled a cap full of Benadryl and said, "Good start. Open wide." Dane gulped the medicine. "Now keep going," Pixie added.

Once his breathing was more under control, he continued. "Marley ordered a hit on you and Caleb . . . and that actor, Peters. Marley didn't give a reason, and I didn't ask. It's business. Nothing personal."

"Did you have any contact with Senator Tyler?"

Dane's eyes narrowed with confusion and surprise. "I don't know anything about Tyler."

"How much was the bounty?" Caleb asked.

"A half million."

"Now I'm downright offended," Pixie said. "I'm worth a heap more than that by myself."

"Listen, you let me go, and I'll disappear into thin air." He paused, still struggling to regulate his breathing. "You'll never see me again. Promise."

"Why wouldn't we turn you in?" Caleb asked.

Pixie stepped closer to Dane, her arms still crossed but her voice steady and sharp. "You know what your boss is up to, right? Marley and his crew want to burn the commercial lobster industry to the ground."

Dane blinked through his swollen eyes. "What are you talking about?"

Caleb leaned on his shotgun, his gaze cold. "Marley's not just gunning for me and Pixie. He's trying to destroy the commercial lobster industry by creating cellular lobster to replace it. No more independent fishermen. No more natural lobster. The death of a whole way of life for working people up and down the coast of Maine."

Dane said nothing, but his lips pressed into a thin line. Finally, he said, "I like lobster. Real lobster."

"Then you oughta hate Marley," Elrod said, his grip tightening on the wrench he hadn't put down. "He's killing the only thing keeping places like this alive. People don't come up here for fast food and chain hotels. They come for the sea, the lobster boats, the real Maine."

Pixie leaned down, her eyes level with his. "You're just another hired gun in a long line who thinks a fat paycheck is worth destroying everything. But here's the kicker – you're not going to win. Not you, not Marley, not Tyler, not anyone else they hire. Because we're not going anywhere."

Caleb stared hard. "And let me tell you something else – lobster's personal around here. You mess with that, you're not just fighting me, Elrod, and Pixie. You're fighting everyone from Kittery to Machiasport."

Dane's breathing was still ragged, but he gave a slight nod. "I didn't sign up for this lobster war. You know what's bloody funny? I wasn't even going to take the contract from Marley until he told me the job was in Maine. I figured I could squeeze in a few lobster rolls and maybe eat a lobster or two while I was here, so I took it. You think Marley cares about me? Hell no. I never liked the bloke. If you let me go, I'll help you."

Caleb gave Dane an appraising look. Finally, he said, "Here's the deal. You help us take Marley and Tyler down, and we'll figure something out."

After a moment, Dane nodded. "But first I'll need to hear the plan."

Pixie cleared her throat. "My department, boys. Now listen up."

All three men turned to her. She had a glint in her eye.

Chapter Twenty-Seven—A Simple Arrangement

It was a simple arrangement. If Dane did what Pixie demanded, he would be allowed to slip away into the underworld. In her life, she'd cut deals with all sorts of folks, but this was the first time she shook hands with a contract killer.

When darkness finally arrived and the northern sky revealed a sea of stars, Dane and Caleb waited in Dane's rental car in the Oceanview Motel parking lot. A few spaces away, Pixie and Elrod hunkered down in the cab of Elrod's pickup keeping an eye on the South African. Caleb sat in the Nissan's back seat with his shotgun in case Dane decided to renege. He made it very clear to Dane that he had no qualms about shooting him in the ass with birdshot and calling Ed Pratt if he strayed from the plan.

Spring Harbor was a tangle of cars and protesters. Every inch of open space seemed to be taken with tents or activists sitting on camp chairs and partying in the glow of cooking fires. A loudspeaker boomed from the waterfront as a protestor ranted about whale-killing lobstermen to bloodthirsty cheers.

The four waited for over an hour until they saw two shadowy figures emerging. It was Peters and a woman headed toward his motel room. She was hanging all over the Brit and walking unsteadily. Pixie relished the thought of what was going to happen next.

Dane climbed out of his car in the darkness with his baseball cap pulled low and strode toward the unsuspecting Peters. In a flash, he had Peters' arm twisted behind his back, casually guiding him from behind toward the car. The woman at first stood paralyzed, then fled in the night back toward town. With a swift move, Dane shoved Peters against the Nissan, tied his hands behind his back, pulled a laundry bag over his head, tightened the drawstring, and pushed the bewildered Brit into the back seat next to Caleb.

After navigating their two vehicles through a maze of traffic on the choked narrow two-lane roads – something Spring Harbor had never seen – Dane, his bound captive, along with Caleb, Pixie, and Elrod finally arrived at the Stringer Cottage. Dane forced Peters through the house and into a pine chair in the freshly painted living room. Peters gasped, "I'm bloody suffocating," as Dane shined a blinding flashlight beam in his face and yanked away the laundry bag. Bug-eyed with fear, Peters gulped for air.

"I'm going to give you two choices," Dane said, cradling his empty rifle and standing behind the table with the flashlight pointed in Peters' eyes.

"What's this all about?" Peters quavered. "Don't you know who I am?"

"Oh, I know, mate," Dane replied. "You can tell me what I want to know, or I'll end your miserable life and make Sebastian Marley a happy man."

"Marley?" Peters stammered. "Tell me this is a joke. Where am I?"

"No joke. You've got two problems. First, you've got a fleet of angry lobstermen who'll be out of a job if you continue to lie about what happened on that boat. Secondly, Marley hired me to kill you. For some reason, he must not want you around anymore, mate. I've already been paid for your death and would be happy to carry it out. If that's what you want, all you need to do is keep quiet."

"You're kidding, right?" Sweat poured from Peters' temples.

"Not at all. Lying will be fatal. You either confess about what you did to set up the lobsterman and everything you know about Utami and Marley's plan, or you don't see sunrise tomorrow. Do you understand?"

"Yes," Peters replied shakily.

"Good. Now sing."

Peters did – describing his first meeting with Marley at the Wilshire, the tour of Utami labs, the fake whale attack video, the promised payout, and a prominent senator's involvement. It all came spilling out, all traces of bravado gone. When Peters finished, Dane said, "If you ever mention meeting me, I'll hunt you down. Understand? I don't exist. Forget you ever saw me. If you speak a peep, you're a dead man. In fact, if in the future you do anything I find offensive, I'm going to come for you hard because I don't like you, or Brits in general really. Remember, I've already been paid for your hit."

Peters gulped and nodded. "Can I please go now?" he squeaked.

"Not so fast."

"I told you everything you wanted to know."

"For your sake, I hope that's true."

"Please, I beg you. Let me go."

"That's not up to me." Dane kept the blinding flashlight beam trained on Peters' face and slipped the laundry bag over his head. Peters started to protest. Dane picked up the rifle that he'd set aside moments earlier and tossed it to Caleb as he entered the room. Then he slipped into the night. While he'd miss out on his full payout, he was a free man. He had a good feeling that Marley wasn't going to be in position to demand a refund.

When the laundry bag was removed a second time, Peters looked confused – stunned, really, by the specter of Caleb, Pixie, and Elrod peering down at him.

"Howdy, Dirkster," Pixie said, a smile curling her lips.

"What the bloody hell?"

She picked up the phone from the table. "This'll be the best movie you ever made. Wait till your friends at Utami see this. Quite a performance, really."

Peters blinked, his mouth twitching. "You, you–"

Caleb grabbed Peters' chin, lifting his face. "Watch your mouth. I'm sure she's got a bottle here somewhere. And you better hope Marley and Tyler take the bait and call off the dogs. If they don't, I have other plans for you."

Elrod pointed a gnarly finger at Peters. "And they ain't rosy."

Peters asked, surprised, "Tyler?"

"That's right," Caleb said. "The good senator from California."

Peters closed his eyes and lowered his head. It occurred to Caleb that he had never seen a man look so dejected. Pixie settled on the couch by the fireplace, typing away on her phone. "How's this?" she finally asked Caleb.

"We've got a dandy video of Dirk Peters. We need to talk—now. This is your one chance to make things right. Enjoy the link. p.s. Turns out your friend with the rifle is a big fan of lobster, and he likes his real."

Caleb nodded. "Send it."

"Sent."

"Let's see how long it takes Tyler to call."

"I'm guessing fast. Like slop through a pig," Pixie said.

Elrod smiled. "My father used to say that. Only he would say 'slop through a hog'."

Pixie grinned as her phone began to chime.

"Hello, Senator," she cooed.

"He's clearly under duress," Tyler spat, his voice dripping with venom.

"Perhaps, but I don't think you're going to be able to prove that. It's why I only framed Peters' face. And we got very chummy with your hitman friend. We struck a deal, actually."

"What kind of deal?"

"If you don't make things right, he's coming for you."

"Do you realize you're threatening a United States Senator?"

"Is that what you are? I thought you were a snake. I guess sometimes there's not much difference between the two."

"I could have you locked up for life."

"No, Senator, you can't. You need to start singing an entirely different tune. If you don't, we release Dirk's video, your star turn in 'Senator Sexcapades', the photo of you and Francois cozying up to Marley, and the Cayman account for what you and Francois stole and then see how long it will take the Feds to connect the dots. You put your hand in the cookie jar, and you got caught, Senator. And now it's time to face the music."

Silence. Finally, Tyler barked, "Where's Peters?"

"He's right here in my living room," Pixie replied, "enjoying my hospitality."

Pixie looked up to take in the most woebegone face she could remember seeing.

"What do you want?" Tyler finally asked.

"It's simple, Senator."

"Spit it out."

"First, you get the police and everyone else off Caleb's back. We want the charges dropped. And we want Greenhaven out of Spring Harbor by tomorrow. Got it?"

"What else?" Tyler asked.

"Tomorrow morning, Sandy Francois releases a statement clearing the lobstermen of killing whales. You put a bug in the media's ear that the whale attack video was fake. Utami files Chapter 11. And Sebastian Marley? He goes back to whatever rock he crawled out from."

"Is that all?" Tyler's voice was tinged with sarcasm.

"Oh, dear me no. Here's the kicker – you hand in your resignation as a U.S. Senator and swear off public office for good."

"Are you kidding me? That's outrageous!"

"Is it? Considering the alternative? Utami, influence peddling, an offshore account, a contract killer, and some juicy footage that'll haunt the internet forever. Seems a small price to save your reputation and keep you out of jail. You don't strike me as a man who would thrive in prison, Senator."

Tyler fell silent for a long moment. "Is that it?" he asked in a voice filled with resignation.

Pixie glanced at Caleb and Elrod, giving them a thumbs-up. "That's it."

"And Peters?"

"Oh, if he talks, he's a dead man. Our new contract killer friend will see to that. He said he ain't got any patience for Brits, much less sniveling ones."

"The videos?"

"Unlike you, Mr. Senator, we live by our word. They'll never see the light of day unless you decide to do something stupid."

Pixie ended the call and looked up.

Caleb and Elrod grinned. "Where'd you learn to talk like that?" Elrod asked.

"A trailer park in Port Arthur, Texas."

Elrod beamed. "It sure bred a dandy."

"What about him?" Caleb asked, pointing at Peters, sagging in the chair.

"Let him go," Pixie said. "He won't cause trouble, will you, Dirkster? Remember your friend Dane is out there, and he didn't seem to take much of a shine to you, did he, darlin'?"

Peters stared at the floor in ruined silence.

Chapter Twenty-Eight—Reckoning

Later that evening, Elrod stood beneath the harsh glare of a single light above the front door of Almira Babb's imposing home. The house loomed over Spring Harbor like a sentinel, its windows dark, save for the faint glow of one upstairs room. Below, the town spread out in the shadow of the hill, with protesters' campfires flickering like restless embers, and farther out, the faint, cold lights of Bar Harbor glimmered on the horizon.

After the chaos of the night – after Peters had fled the car and pushed his way through the volatile crowd – Elrod felt the weight of this moment settle on him. He rarely got riled, but he had a score to settle. He clenched his fists, braced himself, and banged hard on Babb's door. The hollow thud echoed in the stillness. A light flicked on in an upstairs window, a sudden glow spilling out onto the lawn.

When the door finally creaked open, Almira Babb stood there, wrapped in a robe, her feet snug in fur-lined slippers. Her lips curved into a thin, expectant smile.

"So," she said, her voice like a blade drawn from its sheath, "you haven't finished your say, Elrod?"

"Why'd you do it, Almira?" his eyes boring into hers.

"You know perfectly well why. To save the town," she said coolly, her hand lifting to gesture toward the fires below. "From them." Her disdain crackled in the air like a live wire.

"And what did it get you?" Elrod demanded.

"We'll never know, will we? Who knows what would have happened if we didn't act as we did? The town could be burning right now. The Babbs and the Tibbetts' names are etched into Spring Harbor's history. You should've been thinking like I did, of the town and not of one man. I'll be damned if I was going to let a pack of hooligans destroy what our ancestors spent their lives building."

"You know Caleb would never gaff a whale," Elrod said, his tone steady despite his anger.

"Do I?" Babb replied, her bloodless lips barely shifting.

"It's time for you to go," Elrod stated matter-of-factly.

"Why's that, Elrod?" Babb gave a contemptuous smile. She pulled her robe tighter, her lips pressing into an even thinner line.

"You've run this town into a ditch. Everybody knows it, but they're too scared to say it."

Babb's eyes narrowed into daggers. Finally, she exhaled sharply. "But you aren't?"

"Nope."

Babb spat, "It'll take more than you showing up at my front stoop to chase me off."

"Do everyone a favor, Almira, and disappear."

"Not a chance."

"There's a storm coming, and it's aiming at you. I mean it. Get out while you still have whatever shred of respectability you got."

"Go away, Elrod."

"You'll see, Almira. People ain't going to put up with you much longer once they know Caleb's an innocent man."

Babb waved her hand. "Bah!"

"That's right. You'll get yours."

"Go away," she barked before starting to close the door. But just before it shut, she paused and fixed Elrod with an icy glare. "You'll find me a dangerous opponent, Elrod. I can make your life miserable, you know."

"Just try, you old witch," Elrod said to the closing door.

Elrod stood in the uneasy quiet that followed, his breath coming hard and fast. Finally, he turned away from the house and walked toward his truck. He'd waited for years to tell Almira Babb off, and he had to admit, it felt good.

In the early morning light, Sandy Francois stared incredulously at the computer screen and wiped away a tear. She hadn't bothered to put on makeup and her auburn hair hung limp from neglect. The thought of pushing send made her stomach turn. Maybe it was a small price to pay for her sins, but she knew as soon as she sent the press release, her credibility as an environmental warrior would be destroyed.

Sitting in her office overlooking Hacienda Bay, she thought of all she had and all she was about to lose. She took a deep breath, cursed, and struck the computer key.

FOR IMMEDIATE RELEASE

Contact: Sandy Francois, Executive Director
Marine Institute of the Pacific
Email: press@mipacific.org

Marine Institute of the Pacific Updates Position on Lobster Industry and Whale Conservation

Hacienda Bay, CA -- The Marine Institute of the Pacific today issued a formal statement revising its earlier position regarding the lobster industry's impact on endangered whales. After extensive review, the institute acknowledges that its previous advocacy for an outright ban on lobstering did not account for the proactive measures already in place. The institute has agreed to work collaboratively with commercial lobstermen to find common ground and develop solutions that safeguard both the sustainability of the lobstering industry and the protection of endangered whales. This partnership aims to foster innovative practices that minimize entanglement risks while supporting the livelihoods of those who depend on the fishery . . ..

Jonathan Tyler's Chief of Staff shook his head in disbelief when Tyler showed him his press release. "Are you kidding?"
Tyler snapped, "Send it."
"I don't understand?"
"Now."
The news struck Washington like a January nor'easter.

Jonathan Tyler, Rising Star in Washington, Abruptly Resigns from Senate

By Sophia Sing
Senior Correspondent Washington, D.C.

In a shocking announcement that has left both colleagues and supporters reeling, Senator Jonathan Tyler, a prominent senator from Northern California and a power player in Washington, abruptly resigned from his position Thursday afternoon. The move, which Tyler attributed to a desire to "spend more time with my wife and children and return to private law practice," has sent waves through the political landscape, where Tyler has long been regarded as a rising star and a potential presidential candidate.

The senator offered no further explanation, leaving unanswered questions about the timing of his resignation . . . .

Dirk Peters sat in the dingy bus station waiting for a ride to nowhere. He nervously glanced around, scanning the crowd for the assassin. Part of the deal with Gray and McGee had been to admit to doctoring the whale video. With the memory of that big man with the gun and the flashlight flashing across his mind, he stared at the wording on his **X** account and swallowed. He closed his eyes and imagined his new life. He knew it would be even worse than the tawdry one he'd been living. "Bloody hell," he muttered under his breath and punched send.

A few seconds later, as he contemplated the ruin that was his life, he awoke from his reverie to a voice angrily shouting, "Hey, buddy, are you that guy on TV who sells the drops?"

Ron Dane sat on the deck overlooking Penobscot Bay. Despite his injuries and capitulation, he wasn't about to flee Maine without eating lobster. With face, arms, and neck peppered with welts, a painful knot swelling atop his head, sunglasses precariously perched on his nose, and a baseball cap tugged low, he turned to the young waitress and ordered the twin lobster dinner. In hindsight, Dane was glad that he hadn't followed through on the hit on the woman and the lobsterman. They were good people.

Dane felt a stab of anger as he thought about Marley's attempt to destroy a way of life. He sipped his beer and took in the stunning view. The sky was a sharp blue and above, an osprey circled. Sails unfurled, a ketch tacked toward open sea. Dane decided it would be prudent to disappear for a few months, maybe into the jungles of Laos or possibly into the African bush. But first, he'd enjoy his lobsters with hot melted butter and a squirt of lemon and consider paying Sebastian Marley a "friendly" visit.

Horace Maddox stood bleary-eyed on the empty, trash-strewn green, watching two Spring Harbor town workers clean up the aftermath of the protest. Piles of garbage, broken signs, and a few cracked windows had been the extent of the carnage. Maddox muttered under his booze-ridden breath, kicking at an empty beer can. While searching aimlessly and fruitlessly for Peters, he'd spent the last two days drinking cheap rum and mingling with the protesters, but now even they were gone.

"Dirkster! Where are you, buddy boy?" he yelled drunkenly.

In his hand, he gripped the Glock he'd snatched from Peters' motel room during the protests. He knew it was a stupid thing to be carrying around, but he hoped that it would cause Peters to come looking for him. He waved it half-heartedly in the air, with the dim hope that Peters might see the weapon from wherever he'd disappeared and come trotting back like a dog looking for his bone.

In a fit of frustration, Maddox stamped his foot and flung the gun toward the ground. "Damn you, Dirkster!" he cried. The moment the Glock hit the turf, a *pop* split the air.

It took Maddox a second to register what had happened. The first clue was the warmth spreading across his foot. The second was the sudden, searing pain shooting up his leg.

"Jesus!" he howled, hopping on one foot and grabbing at his shoe, now oozing red.

Across the green, the two town workers paused to stare. They'd done their best to ignore Maddox, but the sound of a pistol firing got their attention.

"Did he just . . .?" one asked, pointing.

"Yup," the other replied, nodding. "The frigging moron shot himself."

"It hurts! Help me!" Maddox cried, teetering on one foot, waving his arms. "I'm bleeding to death!"

The first worker squinted at him, unimpressed. "Pretty sure you're gonna survive, Horace. I told you to put away that gun."

"Well, Horace, I've gotta hand it to you. This time you 'literally' shot yourself in the foot," the other worker said with a hint of a smile.

"It *hurts*! Call an ambulance!" Maddox wailed, now on the ground clutching his foot.

But both workers simply shook their heads in tandem.

"Spring Harbor's finest, ladies and gentlemen," the second worker said to no one in particular, tossing a bottle into a trash bag with a theatrical flourish.

"Someone better call Peters," the first added, laughing, "so he can get it on video."

Maddox's hopping slowed as he winced, pain and anger mingling in equal measure. He'd thought about the injustice of his life, and cried out, "We had a deal, Dirkster! A hundred grand! And now I'm dying."

The first worker turned to his buddy, "Jackass."

"Should we call an ambulance?"

"Naw."

"You think it'll kill him?"

"Hopefully," the first worker said and slowly turned to spear a plastic bag.

Spencer Tate sat in Ferrar's exclusive private dining room, his classic Patek Philippe watch catching the soft, golden light as he flicked his wrist impatiently. His date – the Brazilian bombshell he'd taken to London – was late. Unforgivably late. Spencer scowled at the empty chair across the table.

Standing nearby, Marcel watched with a long-practiced composure masking the glee he secretly felt. His pencil-thin mustache twitched slightly as he adjusted the starched linen napkin on his forearm.

"Will Monsieur Tate be dining alone this evening?" Marcel inquired, his tone oozing feigned concern.

Spencer shot him a sharp look. "What does it *look* like?" he asked, gesturing at the empty seat.

Marcel inclined his head, the mustache now betraying a faint smirk. "*Très bien, monsieur.* Perhaps I might suggest a few menu items?"

Spencer folded his arms and reclined in his chair, his scowl fixed in place. "You may," he said.

Marcel leaned forward, lowering his voice conspiratorially. "For a man of your exquisite taste, may I recommend an unparalleled dining experience?"

"Get on with it," Spencer snapped.

"Very well." Marcel gestured with a flourish. "For wine, a Chateau D'Yquem from the storied year of 1918. We have just one bottle remaining."

Spencer's eyes widened, his indignation bubbling up like cheap champagne. "Are you insane?"

"Monsieur," Marcel said, his expression one of pure innocence. "Only the finest for someone of your stature."

Spencer opened his mouth to protest, but Marcel cut him off with theatrical flair.

"And to accompany, might I suggest the Almas?"

Lubec lay far astern as the *Mary G.* cut through a light wake. Pixie sat near the stern on a crate, tilting her face into the sun. Though the day was clear, the air held a chill, and the rare beauty from Port Arthur pulled her baggy wool sweater tight. With his hind leg in a splint and a row of stitches still visible, Rocky slept on a makeshift bed of blankets next to the warmth of the engine box, his head resting on his paws, while Caleb, a free man, gripped the wheel, keeping course for Grand Heron. The last few nights had been the most intense Pixie had experienced. Caleb had been gentle and loving, and for the first time, she felt more than she'd ever felt for a man and all the sweeter for the wait and for the enormous relief that came from vindication.

Pixie reached into her Louis Vuitton bag, opened a delicate ring box, and took out the Cartier – the one Spencer had given her one romantic evening in Palm Beach. Now, as she held it, the diamond sparkling in the sunlight, she realized it represented nothing but false charm and lies. She glanced at Caleb, her heart surging, and with a small flick, tossed the ring into the sea. He turned and asked, "Everything good?"

Pixie broke into a Texas-size smile and blew him a kiss.

Author's Note

Lobster Trap is a work of entertainment and should be read as nothing more. The names, characters, places, and incidents portrayed in the story are the product of the author's imagination or have been used fictitiously. Any resemblance to actual persons, living or dead, businesses, companies, events, locales is entirely coincidental.

As an author, I have the good fortune of living on the island where I grew up, with my writing desk overlooking the broad expanse of the Atlantic. On this frigid January morning, I hear the steady chug of a lobster boat and see its LED lights cutting through the darkness as it heads for open water. But the industry that has sustained generations is facing mounting challenges. Regulatory threats, environmental concerns, and the effects of climate change are making the future of lobstering increasingly uncertain. The fishing communities that depend on the lobster trade – both for their livelihoods and the tourism it attracts – may have to adapt in ways they never expected. These issues are real and pose an existential threat to Maine's fragile economy and to the men and women who make their living from the sea.

Acknowledgements

I'm deeply grateful for the following people who have championed my writing and provided valuable insight: Annie, Jen, Jennifer, Kevin, Brian, Tom, Arnie, Jon, and Cindy. Special thanks go to Eddie, whose attention to detail and suggestions helped spark several ideas for the novel.

As always, I am indebted to my friend and superb editor, Wright Abbot, who has devoted untold hours to *Lobster Trap* and supported and guided me through the ups and downs of writing four novels. Wright's insights are invaluable.

I am fortunate to have a loving family who supports my writing obsession: thanks to Trevor, Annie, Kyle, and Jen, whose love and encouragement have been amazing.

About the Author

C.W. Wells began his professional life as an award-winning newspaper reporter before turning to a career in education. He grew up in a small town in Maine. *Lobster Trap* is his fourth novel. He is the author of *Eight-Man Cowboy*, *LONESTAR*, and *No Heart to Kill*.

Learn more by visiting Wells' website at:

https://cwwellswriter.wordpress.com/

About The Publisher

Creative Texts is a boutique independent publishing house devoted to high quality content that readers enjoy. We publish best-selling authors such as Jerry D. Young, N.C. Reed, Sean Liscom, Jared McVay, Laurence Dahners, and many more. Our audiobook performers are among the best in the business including Hollywood legends like Barry Corbin and top talent like Christopher Lane, Alyssa Bresnaham, Erin Moon and Graham Hallstead.

Whether its post-apocalyptic or dystopian fiction, biography, history, true crime science fiction, thrillers, or even classic westerns, our goal is to produce highly rated customer preferred content. If there is anything we can do to enhance your reader experience, please contact us directly at info@creativetexts.com. As always, we do appreciate your reviews on your book seller's website.

Finally, if you would like to find more great books like this one, please search for us by name in your favorite search engine or on your bookseller's website to see books by all Creative Texts authors. Thank you for reading.

Made in the USA
Middletown, DE
09 August 2025

11994893R00146